Blood In the Chapel Royal

Royal

The Whispers: Book Two

Tasha Sheipline

Tasha L Sheipline

To my daughters:

May the sound of the shards of that glass ceiling crunching below your feet be the song of your people. Keep that air of discontent, always knowing you can do more.

To my husband:

I have some curtain rods for you to hang when you get a chance.

Dear Reader,

As a writer, music has always played a vital role in providing inspiration for the stories I tell. Songs not only stir the soul, but capture the spirit of the characters as they grow. Below, you will find a list of songs that helped to spark my creativity and bring this book to life:

"Too Much to Ask" *Niall Horan*

"All These Things That I've Done" *The Killers*

"Heart Don't Break Even" *The Script*

"Immortality" *Celine Dion*

"Superwoman" *Alicia Keys*

Chapter One

England 1961

Change is an inevitable part of growth, no matter how much we hate the idea. Adelia Grey was no stranger to either one these days. Since she made the abrupt decision to abandon her life in Boston and pursue her education in England, change had been at the center of her life.

Just a few short years ago, she was a naive young woman, finishing her first year of college at Boston University. It had drudged by, not helped by her severe social anxiety, which she'd been plagued with for as long as she could remember, with some of her experiences bordering on paranoia. When her father presented her with the opportunity to spend a summer with her grandma at Hampton Court Palace, she had jumped at it, knowing it was something she could not pass up. However, the idea of living so far away from everything predictable caused her a great deal of distress, to say the least.

Yet, she took the risk, and with it her entire life changed. Once at Hampton Court, the world as she knew it seemed to shift on its axis. Lost in the majesty of the palace, she had felt its raw tension on a daily basis, and voices, with their demanding presence, came to her through the silence. Her world felt crowded, with an inexplicable sense that an invisible veil cloaked the unseen that filled those empty spaces.

When she was close to breaking point, her Grandma Marjorie came out with the startling revelation that made perfect sense of everything. Marjorie belonged to a unique line of descendants who could read and interpret events of the past. Only present in the female line, the inherent ability to hear *the whispers* allowed them to have a close-up view of events that took place in a specific location far before their own time, along with the emotions experienced by the people involved. The veil of time was thinner for those who heard the whispers, and while some considered it a gift, others saw it as a burden.

Over time, Adelia learned so much about her ability, becoming aware of how the whispers could inhabit her being in a way that made the present nearly disappear. While she could not impact events of the past—without proper control, the whispers could change the present. With the guidance of her grandma, she learned to hone her abilities, almost to a point that they surpassed the strength of the woman who had passed them onto her. She learned to use her gifts to her advantage and, with the subsequent added confidence, changed her major to historical studies and set about conducting research on various aspects of England's rich history. With the help of Daniel Brown, an Oxford professor she'd befriended at Hampton Court, her endeavors proved quite successful.

Perhaps the term *befriended* was too inaccurate a word to describe her relationship with Daniel. In truth, he'd swept her off her feet in the palace where Henry VIII had courted all six of his queens at one time or another. Adelia found the romantic ambiance of the old Tudor palace far too powerful to resist. Daniel's intelligent and charming demeanor captured her heart from the moment she set eyes on him. She had stayed in England partly for herself, but mostly for him, and did not regret any part of that decision. Now, more than four years into their relationship, he was ready to move things to another level—something she had not agreed to yet, and his impatience was starting to surface.

The past four years had flown by with such intensity, and she was no longer the shy, insecure woman of before. She had completed her undergraduate degree, working through every summer to ensure she finished early. Likewise, her Masters had been achieved in record time. Everything was going better than planned, until the day she received the shocking call that her grandma had passed away. At that moment, her entire world stopped. With the exception of Daniel, her grandma was the only other person who knew about the whispers. Together they were keepers of the family secret, and Marjorie had warned her how sharing it, other than with a loved and trusted one, would only bring trouble. If she wanted to be respected in the academic world, such a revelation would potentially subject her to ridicule. No, if she had any hopes of achieving greatness on her own, she could never tell a soul what she knew.

Now, with her grandma gone, she was left as the only remaining *keeper*. While Marjorie had held many secrets in her life, Adelia soon discovered there were more to be revealed after her death. While at the funeral, she became acquainted with a distant relative who hailed from the Babington line of the family. It seems that, before her death, Marjorie had arranged for one of her long-departed sister's granddaughters to pay a visit to Adelia. Cassandra was also a history major. Knowing that Adelia would be starting her research for her doctorate, Marjorie thought the two could work together, with Cassandra playing the role of assistant. Though she never mentioned it to Adelia, her grandma had worked to plan out an entire summer for the two.

Now, in the midst of her grieving, Adelia found herself in a difficult position. She was not at all excited about taking on Cassandra as a protégé. The thought stirred up memories of her grandma, which were almost too painful to bear. Yet a sense of duty hung heavy in her heart. If this was something Marjorie wanted, and, judging by the great deal of planning, it clearly was, then who was she to dishonor her grandma's wishes by refusing?

Oh, but the timing could not be worse, with everything in her life in significant turmoil. She had just lost her grandma and, with her parents in America, now felt so alone in the world. Things with Daniel were on shaky ground, which, to be honest, was her own fault. Also, she had been offered a probationary position as professor of historical studies at Leeds University, which she had yet to decide upon. By and large, this was the most inopportune time to even think about mentoring Cassandra. Not only that, despite all she had achieved thus far, she found herself wondering if she might be a disappointment for her cousin. She was not convinced that her research would be something anyone outside of herself would find interesting. However, while she wanted to say no, her sense of duty would not let her do so.

Also, a curiosity kept her open to the idea. If Cassandra hailed from the Babington line, a slight possibility existed that she was a keeper of the whispers too. It wasn't something Adelia could just come right out and ask. In fact, Cassandra was not much older than she had been when she discovered the ability herself. Maybe, just maybe, there was another person who shared the gift. She had long suspected the existence of others, and remembered meeting a widowed innkeeper who mentioned his wife hearing the whispers. Digging further, her grandma revealed they were distant relations. Perhaps Marjorie had known it about Cassandra, too, which is why she'd arranged for the two to meet. If she was the only keeper of the family secret left, she wanted to know. If she wasn't, well, she wanted to know that too.

Chapter Two

Adelia sat in the lecture hall listening to the echoing voice of Dr. Daniel Brown. As she shifted on the hard wooden chair, she tucked her walnut-colored hair behind her ear. Despite the hall being filled with the fall semester of Oxford's new blood, the large interior still sounded hollow. Daniel's masculine voice reverberated off the walls, like distant thunder on a moonless night.

With just a few weeks left in the semester, the students would soon be leaving for the holiday break. She couldn't help but notice the small number of female students—so few compared to their male counterparts. Universities always touted the equity extended to women, but the numbers did not lie. It was just as difficult for a woman to become a student here as it was to become a member of the faculty. While the numbers were increasing, it was still far too slow to be considered equitable.

A tinge of jealousy bubbled in her stomach. There always had been and always would be what could only be described as a "good old boys'" system at work here. Even as the old prestigious universities had to evolve into modern times, name and money would always be a factor in who was admitted. Despite her own father graduating from the university, she had been rejected when she'd applied.

"I am just as happy attending any of the other quality universities England has to offer," she'd said with fraudulent assurance.

Even if she acted as though it didn't faze her, a well of resentment existed deep inside. She was as qualified as any of the new blood who sat in this room, but it didn't matter with the many barriers her hard work and ambition could not overcome. It was a bitter pill to swallow.

The positive side to such rejection was that it lit a fire within her. She had finished both of her degrees with haste and set her sights on doing everything to prove that she could still be successful, even if her transcripts may not have had a prestigious school listed.

As she set out to find a teaching position, the realities of life became even clearer. She would interview time and again, only to be passed up by a man with less knowledge. On more than one occasion, she had been flat-out told by potential employers her gender was something of concern. There seemed to be a widespread fear that she would be hired and, then, out of the blue, decide to marry and start a family. Many employers just did not want to take the chance. She had assured them, while that prospect was far off, she intended to continue working as a mother. That did little to help her cause, as they seemed even more appalled by such a revelation. The only school that gave her hope had been the University of Leeds; it helped that the department chair was female, giving her a fair shot at the job. When she left the interview, she'd felt confident, which was more than she could say for any of the others. It was so frustrating to think that her education and abilities would not hold as much weight as her sex when it came to finding employment.

When she received the call from the university, she was overjoyed, but kept it to herself, wanting time to think about it. The university was situated about a four-hour drive from Oxford, where she had moved to be close to Daniel. They'd settled into a comfortable relationship, doing their best to spend their free time together, even when such time was short to come by. Daniel had been one of her main reasons for staying in England, yet something beyond her comprehension had held her back from fully committing to their relationship. She was twenty-four years old now, with Daniel almost thirty-two, and far more established in his education and career than her. While he had time to grow from his youthful inexperience, she was still trying to work through these things herself. Even though he was always willing to lend a hand or even put in a good word for her, she'd insisted on being able to make her own way. She did not want his influence to play a part in where she went to school or who hired her. Not only that, she also rejected attempts by her esteemed father to help her get ahead. When she decided to pursue her future as a professional historian, she wanted it to be her accomplishment. Anything else would diminish the personal triumph.

By her own choice, she decided to do things the hard way, and with that came all the challenges one would expect. The world was always presenting itself as contemporary, while still holding to old ideologies in the shadows. One could feel the imbalance of opportunities for males and females in this line of work, yet know it would never be acknowledged in any way that mattered. As time progressed, bitterness crept through Adelia, and anger, concerning the many obstacles in her way. All she wanted was to go out and do good work, but the weight of bureaucracy and blatant inequality hindered her attempts. Some days she was emboldened and willing to fight for herself, while on others she felt exhausted—tired of every step being a battle.

Now, the prospect of her first academic job lay at her feet. She'd fought hard for this opportunity but should not have found herself feeling so torn. The university had asked her to begin teaching in the spring session, little more than six weeks away. It was impossible for her to take this position, and stay in Oxford, with the commute being too long to make it work. Expecting Daniel to relocate to accommodate her was unrealistic when he only lived a few blocks from his own job. But taking this position was a great opportunity. After the spring semester, she would be able to begin her doctoral work, with the prospect of funding to help support her research. Although presented as a probationary position, this was the job she had worked so hard to secure. She wanted this, but how could she hold things together with Daniel in the process?

She surveyed the mass of students as they hung on his every word—no surprise considering how captivating he was as a speaker. He had a way of conveying anything with a comfortable simplicity that made it easy to understand. Despite being highly intelligent, he never conducted himself in a way that said he knew. He didn't flaunt it in the face of others, in stark contrast to many of his Oxford colleagues. There was so much she admired about him.

However, for all she felt for him, she had never been able to take those last few steps. Together for more than four years now, he had never made a secret of wanting to marry her. But she just wasn't ready. There was so much she wanted to accomplish, and the idea of settling down into married life threatened to put a halt to all of her plans. Of course, Daniel didn't understand. The man was ready, and the fact she wasn't frustrated him even more. He had a habit of forgetting that he'd been afforded the chance to go out and pursue his dreams, on his terms. Everything about their relationship felt right, except the timing. She knew she could happily spend forever with this man—she just wasn't sure when she wanted that forever to start.

It was times like these she wished she could meet up with Kate, her old high school friend back in Boston. Even if she didn't want her brutal honesty, Kate would have given it anyway, knowing exactly what she should do. They hadn't talked in over a year, which was a shame, but moving overseas exacerbated the reality that the casualty of growing up saw you growing apart. Life for both women had taken unexpected turns, with the fading of their friendship an unintended consequence.

As Daniel finished his lecture on the social and political changes that occurred during the marriage of Elizabeth of York and Henry

VII, she thought back to the days when she had first met him, and how he'd referenced the merging of the red rose of Lancaster and the white rose of York. The Tudor rose—the symbol of the union of a house divided against itself. Now, more than ever, she felt a connection to that rose. Inside, she was but two halves trying to find the pathway that would unite her life in peace.

While the last students left the hall, Daniel gathered his papers at the podium before stuffing them into his worn leather satchel. He pulled on his brown tweed dress coat and buttoned it with precise movements. Adelia did not budge from her spot, all too aware of the heat creeping along her neck and settling at the back of her ears. The next hour would take a kind of immeasurable courage she thought she possessed, yet wasn't so sure about. She had replayed this conversation over in her mind a thousand times, and now the time had come.

Daniel smiled as he walked up the steps to her. "Hello, Doll." He bent to kiss her cheek. "I am starving, how about you?"

His eyes were so loving and gentle. She groaned inside. There was nothing about this day that was meant to be easy.

"Daniel…" Her voice cracked, dripping with hesitancy. "I have some news to share."

"I can't wait to hear it, but can it wait until we grab some lunch? I skipped breakfast and I really am ravenous."

His playful plea gave her little choice. She smiled back in agreement, although she really did not want to wait. Her stomach was churning, and the thought of choking down lunch was less than appealing. She wanted to have a serious talk with him, and feared the longer it was prolonged, the more her resolve might lessen. Still, she could not expect him to take this news well on an empty stomach, so she grabbed up her coat and handbag and followed him out of the lecture hall.

They went to one of his favorite spots across the street to grab a sandwich. Alice's had long been an institution for the university's breakfast and lunch crowd. The small café was bursting with patrons, so Daniel decided they would take their lunch to a nearby park. On any other day she would have thought it a little cool for a comfortable lunch outside, with it being December, but by now she felt as though she was sweating bullets.

After they ordered, Daniel chatted away, filling her in about his activities over the past few days since they'd last seen each other; being unmarried, they had maintained separate flats out of propriety. With quiet patience, she listened, sighing with relief when the conversation was interrupted by the clerk at the counter shoving two paper-wrapped sandwiches into Daniel's hands.

She took hers, and they crossed the busy street, making their way to a small metal bench, one of several set along a tree-lined pathway overlooking one of the many buildings that made up Oxford University. The university did not have a main campus like other colleges, consisting instead of individual buildings sprinkled throughout the city.

Daniel unwrapped his sandwich and dove into it. Still not feeling up to eating, Adelia nibbled on a corner of hers, staring off into the distance. As Daniel polished off the last few crumbs of his lunch, he turned to her.

"I am so sorry, Doll. You had something that you wanted to tell me?" His voice was softer than before, maybe with a hint of guilt at the edges.

"Yes." She looked down at her uneaten sandwich. "Something wonderful has come up."

"Well, don't delay," he said. "Tell me all about it."

"W-well," she stammered, trying to recall all the words she had rehearsed with such care, "I received a call the other day. I have been offered a position teaching at a university."

"This is great," he said, his excitement clear. "This is exactly what you wanted. We have to celebrate."

"It is wonderful news, to be sure." Her voice felt muffled to her own ears. "I can start in January, for the spring semester. They are even offering to fund some of the research I want to do for my doctorate."

"Are you still planning on basing your research on Richard III?"

"Yes, that is the plan. I haven't narrowed down exactly what I will concentrate my research on in regards to him, but I have a few ideas." She was a little grateful for the detour in the conversation.

"There are plenty of directions you could go with your studies." He looked off into the distance, as though sifting through some unspoken list.

"I know, that is what makes it so difficult to decide upon. I still feel that his character is so completely misunderstood. I would just like to have some time to sift through the Tudor propaganda and get to the heart of him as a man." She coughed into her hand.

"Being so close to Middleham where he spent so much time will be a start."

"Middleham?" he said, one brow arched. "That is up North."

"Yes, it is," she replied, trying not to fumble her words. "I have been offered a position in Leeds. It will place me much closer to the castles he held there—the old Neville holdings."

"Leeds, you say." His voice took on a somber tone. "That is several hours from here."

"I know." She took a moment to muster her courage. "This is the opportunity I have been waiting for, and I don't want to turn it down. I have tried to get something closer, you know that, but it just has not panned out. I really believe that this is a chance to get some traction in my career."

"I am so happy for you—really, I am." But his tone did not match his words. "I just don't understand where that puts us in the equation. I guess we could see each other on weekends, and holiday breaks."

She pressed her feet into the ground to stop him seeing her legs tremble. "I want us to stay connected. I really do. I just know in my heart that it's not fair to expect you to wait for me. I want you to know that...it is okay for you to move on." She placed her hand on his, as though the gesture might soothe his dismay.

His gaze fixed on her hand. In one swift motion, he pulled his own back, as if her touch was like being branded by a hot iron.

"So, this is not just a move a couple of hours away? You are leaving me altogether. You want your freedom from me too."

His voice held a bitter ring, and it hit hard, making her feel as though she had been punched in the stomach. She wanted to disagree and tell him that was not the case—reassure him that she was not breaking off their relationship—but she knew it wasn't true. Daniel had been her biggest supporter through the past few years, and he deserved the truth. She was leaving him, though now she wasn't sure why anymore. For sure, they could work to maintain some form of relationship. She could travel to him on weekends, and he could visit her too. It would be a lot of work but could be done if she really wanted. Or could it? As much as she struggled to deny it, she was vain and selfish, putting his feelings on the back burner to pursue her own dreams. She could try to justify it in a million ways to make it sound better but the truth was she had goals and aspirations that just did not leave time for him. In order to concentrate all of her time on what *she* wanted to do, she needed to distance herself from their relationship. The prospect of dividing her time between Daniel and her research felt overwhelming. There was no nice way to put it—she had to accept that she was being cruel to him to satisfy her own ambitions.

"I care about you more than you can ever understand, Daniel. I could not have made it this far without you. I just need to make it the rest of the way on my own. This is not forever. I just need more time." She groaned inside again, well aware of her miserable attempts to pacify him. "Just a little more time."

"Adelia, if you want me to tell you that you have not shattered my heart into a million pieces, I won't. I will not lie to you to spare your feelings."

His face held a mix of hurt and anger. They'd had disagreements before, and she'd hurt him before, but not at this level. An odd sensation rushed through her, as though she could feel his pain herself.

"Just think of it like that time you traveled to Scotland after graduation," she said, trying to sound cheery. "When you told your parents that you wanted to find some meaning to your life."

"That was meant to be a cautionary tale, though I see you did not perceive it that way."

"No, I rather thought it was an inspiration." She shrugged one shoulder.

"I guess what I am failing to understand is why we can't stay together while you try this thing out."

Try this thing out? His words offended her, though she knew him well enough to know that wasn't his intention. Even so, she couldn't rid her mind of the barrage of interviews she had gone through before her successful one for the Leeds' job. Those smug and condescending expressions of each interviewer staring back across the table. That look of "Aw, isn't that cute, she has big dreams," written across their faces. This was something Daniel could never come close to understanding. He had interviewed one time in his life and gotten the job on the spot. Yes, he had worked hard for his position—that she could not deny—but he'd never been subjected to half of what she had to be taken seriously.

"This is something I want to do, Daniel. I don't want to put you on the backburner while I pursue my dreams."

He pursed his lips and nodded once to himself, then looked at her. "I have never expected you to give up any of your dreams for me. I want for you to have accomplishments to call your own, and I have always felt that we could coexist with our own ambitions. Indeed, I have never sought to have a partner who is dependent on me. Your success makes me happy." He shifted on the bench and changed the crumpled sandwich wrap to his other hand. "Look, if this is what you want, then I won't be the one who stands in your way. I don't ever want to be in your way."

"You are not in my way, Daniel. You are not being fair. You are making this more difficult." She knew arguing was futile. His emotions were taking over his reasoning, and it wasn't going to be easy to turn the conversation around.

"That is not my intention," he said. "I am sorry you expected that you would be able to leave me easily. You underestimate my feelings for you."

"No, Dan—"

"Please, Adelia, allow me to speak."

"Yes, but—"

"I love you, Adelia, but what is fair about you not wanting to be with me?"

The pleading in his eyes made it hard for her to look at him. She focused on the ground, trying to regain the confidence that had all but abandoned her.

"It isn't that I don't want to be with you. I just need this time. This is not goodbye forever."

As each word left her lips, she wanted to stop the entire thing and start over. The whole conversation felt like a runaway train, out of control. She tensed as her frustration built. Each time she responded, she was becoming more insensitive—something she had never intended to do. He did not deserve to be treated this way.

"Not everything can be on your terms," he said, his defensiveness sharpening his tone. "Throughout our relationship, I have done everything on your terms. You can say it's over between us but you don't get to decide if I am hurt or not. You don't get to decide to bounce in and out of my life at will."

"I...just need more time to get my life figured out." Her explanation was far clearer in her head. She realized she was more frustrated with herself than with Daniel. Nothing she could say would sound remotely sensible. Most would think that leaving him was not a rational choice, by any means, yet she had come to rationalize it in her own mind. Right or wrong, she knew that this was something she was going to do.

"It has been four years," he snapped, almost snarling the words, like a tiger with a thorn in its paw. "You have not decided in four years. You can believe that some revelation is going to come to you in a couple of months but I do not." He scrunched up the wrapper even tighter, his knuckles white with tension. "I wish you all the happiness in the world, and I want nothing more than to see you content in whatever you pursue. I want you to do things in your own time, Adelia, but for now I just want my heart back. I need my own time to heal."

"I understand." The bitter salt of tears stung her eyes.

"I will always be your friend, Adelia. Sometimes, the collateral damage of change is that relationships end. The injustice is that you take with you a bigger part of my heart than I do yours. I can accept that, if it means that you finally find the answers you seek."

"Can we please keep in touch while I am gone? I still need you, even if this is something I have to do for myself. I don't want our friendship to end."

He gave her a cold roll of the eyes, as if the suggestion was out of the question.

"Just do me a favor and walk away now. Don't look back. I will reach out to you when I am ready." He picked up his satchel from the ground.

She hesitated. So much felt...finished. This was never the way she'd intended the conversation to go. He was right, everything in their relationship had been on her terms. For once, he deserved to have her do something he asked. With reluctance, she picked up her handbag and rose from the bench. As she walked away, it was so much harder than she'd imagined, with each step telling her she had made the worst mistake of her life. But while she regretted what she had done, or how it had turned out, there was no going back now. Anyway, she couldn't turn around and say she had been a fool and beg for his forgiveness. Throughout, Daniel acted as a loyal and supportive companion, and she had thrown it all away. She'd fractured the bond between them, perhaps irreparably. Some idiotic notion in her had hoped he would understand, but she'd known all along that he wouldn't. She had repaid his devotion and love with rejection. Not an easy pill to swallow for any man, even one so patient as Daniel.

In her life, she had muddled up a great many things but none so much as this moment. Just like Daniel, she needed time for her heart to heal. But time was not a luxury she had on her side. In just a few weeks, she would start her new life up north, and there were a great many things to prepare for. So much was riding on her now, and with much to prove, there wasn't time to dwell on a broken heart.

Chapter Three

I t took a few weeks before Adelia secured an apartment at
a place called Middleham Manor, finding it to be the most
charming one of those she had visited. Though it lacked many of
the modern conveniences of the newer flats in the actual city of
Leeds, she was happy to trade comfort for the history of the old
house. In the countryside, about fifteen minutes' drive north of
the city, the location was perfect for her.

Middleham Manor was a moderate-sized country estate,
thought to have been constructed somewhere in the mid-sixteenth
century. Upon entering the property, you had to pass through the
original gatehouse, which was attached to a low stone wall that
surrounded the house and grounds. Invasive ivy covered much
of the wall's crumbling façade, giving it something of a fairy tale
appearance.

The house itself was situated further along a stone path that
curved around a small pond before heading uphill. Its stone ex-

terior and moss-covered slate roof gave it an altogether gloomy appearance. From the moment she saw it, her first impression was *Wuthering Heights* meets *The Hound of the Baskervilles*. Its haunting presence drew her right in—the perfect place to nurse a broken heart, as though it held a certain melancholy that could only be appreciated by someone immersed in the same condition.

She loved how it was broken up into different sections. While it served as the main residence of its owners, Laura and Ross Bickel, who had lived there for more than thirty years, the rest of the house held a few apartments for rent, a wing of bed & breakfast rooms for tourists, along with some shared areas. As with most homes in England, it had undergone many renovations throughout the years. One could say the manor was the Frankenstein monster of houses, with each room showing the design marks of its previous owners. Every generation was lovingly represented in some area of the house. Oh, if the walls could talk. Well...to Adelia Grey, they did; the whispers were ever-present. Yet, with diligence, and having learnt to hone her skills over the years, she could filter the mass of voices down to a singular one. It was a milestone she was grateful to achieve because it had been her saving grace in not driving herself utterly mad at times.

As enchanting as Middleham Manor was, its owners brought an added level of color that made it almost irresistible. Laura and Ross had been married for forty years. He'd worked as a teacher, specializing in classical literature, evidenced by his constant quoting of his favorite works.

Like many other families, the Bickel's had lost their only son in the war, which, Adelia assumed, had led to a dramatic turning point in their marriage. By all accounts, their grief was deflected by a form of mutual loathing. It was rare to engage with them where some sort of quarrel did not occur.

Their constant squabbling brought a welcome comic relief to all the manor's residents. It only took a day or two around the couple for one to realize that whatever hardship you were experiencing in your own life, it was probably not as bad as theirs. Over time, most of the residents had become numb to the constant bantering between the two. Laura often made reference to Ross's untimely death, which she was plotting daily. Most amusing was the way he said her name, drawing out each consonant and vowel until it sounded like he was expelling demons. Adelia once counted it out, and it took ten seconds for him to say "Laura."

Deep down, she suspected a miniscule form of affection still existed between them, but it could be hard to pinpoint. The only joy they derived from each other came in the form of hurling insults, and they seemed to enjoy that pastime immensely.

She thought back to her arrival at the manor to negotiate her lease. Her anxiety levels were high, excited about her new job but nursing a wounded heart over Daniel. When she'd knocked at the old arched, wooden door, she was struck by an overwhelming sense of belonging. After a few well-spaced raps, the door swung open with a force that nearly knocked her off the stone stoop.

"I have it, Ross. For heaven's sake, will you go take a walk in a snake-infested swamp or something."

Laura Bickel stood before her clad in earth-streaked pants and a floral-print apron. Muddy gardening boots left tiny clods of dirt on the floor at her feet. Her fiery red hair was covered in a haphazard manner by a green handkerchief that matched her dazzling emerald eyes. For a woman of nearly sixty, her skin looked taut beyond belief. To Adelia, she was a dead ringer for Greer Garson.

"Miss Grey, I presume? Aren't you a pretty girl." She reached out to shake hands, only to pull back with apologies on realizing that she was wearing gardening gloves.

Adelia hardly noticed, still blushing at the reference to her being pretty. She had never been good at accepting compliments.

"Goodness me, what a mess I must look," Laura said, brushing dirt and dust from her apron onto the floor. "Follow me into the kitchen here, and I will get washed up."

"Sure," Adelia said, stepping in after her.

All the familiar markings of Tudor construction existed inside the foyer, like dark, exposed oak beams and pale-white plaster walls. They passed a steep narrow wooden staircase that had a beautifully carved newel post at its base. Laura made a sharp turn and they came to a narrow timber-framed doorway. The clearance was so low, as the woman stepped down, she ducked to keep from hitting the top. Adelia followed her movements, entering a large kitchen with neat plastering on three of its walls. The fourth held an enormous fireplace made of gray stone. Not far above, the ceiling was constructed of large oak beams that intersected with smaller ones to create an intricate pattern, and hanging bunches of dried herbs and old copper pots and pans gave the room a rustic charm. An older gentleman sat eating breakfast at a long wooden table lined with benches.

"This is Miss Grey, Ross. She's the girl looking to rent one of the rooms." Laura motioned for Adelia to have a seat opposite the man, then moved over to the sink, pulled off her dirt-covered gloves, and began to wash her hands.

"Oh, very nice to meet you, Miss Grey." He stared at her with eyes amplified by the lenses of black heavy-rimmed glasses. Without another word, he returned to slurping from his bowl of white goo. His pale-silver hair—sparse and a little untidy, giving him a disheveled look—took on a hint of blue in the natural light filtering through the large windows. He looked like a cross between a mad scientist and someone having just suffered an apoplexy.

"Do you mind not slurping that mess while we are in here?" Laura glared at her husband. Adelia flinched, caught off guard by her curt tone.

He waved his hand back and forth, mumbling something through a mouthful of whatever substance he was consuming. Then he gave Adelia a satisfied look, as though she should know what he was saying.

She returned his stare with utter bewilderment. "I'm sorry?"

"Oh, pay no attention to him," Laura barked. "He gets a little lucid with that rat poison I sprinkled in his porridge." She dried her hands on a tea towel as she crossed to the table and seated herself by Ross.

He pushed the porcelain bowl away, giving her a scowl that should have made her skin burn. It was fast becoming apparent that constant animosity existed between this couple.

"Oh, you know I did no such thing, Ross," she said with an eye roll. She turned to Adelia. "I strongly considered it, though. Strongly considered it."

Ross pulled back the bowl and continued eating as the two women discussed details of the room to be leased. It was small, but so was the rent. Given her tight budget, until she started work, she was more than pleased. Each floor had a single shared bathroom, while the kitchen, library, den, and sitting room were all considered common areas. Laura expected tidiness, and wasn't shy about saying so. Aside from Adelia, there were currently only two other tenants in residence. The main source of revenue came from the bed & breakfast on the other side of the house.

"Well, I will get back to you within a day or so, once I've had a chance to talk it over with Ross. Mind you, he won't have anything useful to contribute to the conversation, but we need to discuss it just the same." She got up, either not noticing or caring about the side-eyed glare from her husband.

"Better your habitation be with lion wild or dragon foul, than with a woman who will nag and chide," he mocked in a deep baritone.

"Canterbury Tales, The Wife of Bath, correct?" Adelia asked, tapping her finger on her chin, sure she was right.

Peering through his thick lenses, his eyes seemed to grow two times their normal size.

"She stays," he announced to Laura, his stern tone giving no room for dispute.

"Maybe she wants a day or two to think about it, too, Ross. Lord knows, if I had a choice, I would not live with you." Her nose crinkled up as if she had just eaten something sour. "That reminds me, there is a loose tile on the roof. There are supposed to be high winds today. Perfect time for you to get up there to fix it, if you ask me." She gave Adelia a triumphant wink.

"Laura..." he said, drawing out the pronunciation to its extreme, "I desire that we were better strangers."

Ah...Shakespeare. *As you Like it.* Adelia decided against blurting it out this time. Best not to add fuel to the fire.

"Well," Laura said, her eyes narrowing with displeasure at her husband, "the room is yours if you are keen to have it, Miss Grey?"

"I would love to stay, as long as I don't have to be an accessory to murder as a contingency of the lease." She couldn't hold back a chuckle, though she was half serious.

"Oh, goodness no, dear girl," Laura said, her smile oozing with warmth. "I have it all worked out. Airtight alibi, you see. When the time comes, I will not need your assistance. I suppose you would like to see the room before you fully commit."

Given the reasonable price and the fact that her other options were slim, she doubted she would have refused the room even if it turned out to be an old canning chamber in a dark dank cellar. Not wanting to reek of desperation, she answered with a polite nod.

Laura led her potential renter back out into the hall and up the staircase. The house was particularly still, but not for Adelia, her head filled with the whispers of years upon years. Far from surprising, in a house this old, and, for someone with the gift of channeling the past, expected—a run-of-the-mill Tuesday.

By the time they reached the last step, the voices were so strong, she could barely hear Laura's words as she rattled on about the establishment's history. The high-pitched laughter of children, mingled with the chatter of servants, reverberated off the walls, to the extent that she had to make a conscious effort to block it out, thankful for her grandmother's assistance over the previous years in learning to filter out unwanted whispers.

Laura stopped at a door midway down the hall, turned the knob and swung it open, motioning for Adelia to follow her inside. The bright sunlight that streamed through the tall windows was so intense, it took a moment for her eyes to adjust. The room was larger than expected, a tad bigger than the one she had back in her flat at Oxford. A large wood-framed bed and side table took up the greater part of the space, with a writing desk and chair placed in the corner. It was small but perfect for grading the stacks of term papers she would be dragging home. A quaint little fireplace was set into the far wall, though it looked as if it hadn't been used for a while.

As she scanned the modest furnishings, she could not help but fix her gaze on the wisp of a woman who sat in the window inset, staring out at the garden below. Laura moved about the room, explaining more about the shared spaces available to tenants, unaware of the vision that had Adelia hooked. The reality for those with a gift such as hers, saw her own world far more populated than everyone else's. She simply had to accept that she would be sharing this space with a long-dead roommate, who would not be contributing to the rent.

"You will find it is nice and quiet at this end of the house," Laura said, her tone ever so sweet. "Our room is just down the hall, around the corner."

"Any sounds of a murder taking place should just be ignored, then?" Adelia gave a half- hearted chuckle. For a moment, she was unsure if she should have made yet another joke about Ross's unfortunate end so early in their meeting, but Laura smiled in response.

"Oh, I have a nice heavy goose down pillow reserved for the occasion. You won't hear a sound, dear."

The sardonic arch of her brow made Adelia question whether they were, indeed, still joking, and if she might be moving in with a homicidal maniac moonlighting as a landlady.

As a keeper of the whispers, one of the most important lessons Adelia learned was never to assume history to be accurate. One of the things that made the past so intriguing was that facts were only surface level. History had a way of giving us a prescribed glimpse, selecting what character traits were exposed and which remained unseen. The past inhabitants of Middleham Manor were no exception to this rule. It was human nature to want to make historical facts three dimensional, adding context and emotion to any given event to better understand it in a way that provides comfort. People interpret the actions of others as either having good or bad intentions, rarely ascribing much thought to the space between. Ironically, if we examine our own lives, we find that we often exist in that gray area ourselves.

While her landlords knew a great deal about the manor's past, little did they know that Adelia had the ability to see it in vivid technicolor. Middleham Manor was alive around her. The whispers allowed her to see, hear, and feel intricate details that historical documents could never provide. Just sitting in a room, she could watch as her surroundings melted away, revealing the past as it would have played out in that place. The images were so vivid, it felt as if she were the only person sitting in a movie theater. From the inflection of someone's voice, to the intricate patterns of clothing—even the pinkish hue in someone's cheeks—generations of souls vied for her attention, with each one playing out their lives, caught in the fabric of time. However, to them, she did not exist. She was a mere voyeur, unable to change anything that had already come to pass. Over the previous four years, she had come to understand that every glimpse into the past had significance even if she could not fathom its meaning. There was something in those moments, some residual effect of the soul, that needed to come through. To possess the gift of this sight, and still try to maintain a normal functional life, required a level of acceptance that things were rarely clear. The why was not always easy to decipher, and she had learned to accept things as they were.

The manor held numerous secrets, like many of the great houses in England. Each room spoke to her, and some days it was almost impossible to concentrate on her work for the volume of whispers that came through. While she could block them out, her curiosity usually got the better of her. If she was humble enough to admit that she was selfish by nature, then she had better tack *nosey* to the list as well. Like many, she was not excluded from enjoying a good story with a dramatic twist, and the old house had such a colorful past: a scheming landowner, an adulterous wife, and a matchmaking housekeeper, all conspiring against fate. Middleham Manor was as alive today as the day its first stone was laid.

Soon after moving in, she sent a letter to Daniel with her phone number and address, though she had yet to hear from him since departing Oxford. She spent Christmas alone, deciding not to tell her parents about her breakup for fear their holiday would be spoiled with worry. Since starting her new position, she'd established a day-to-day routine. While leaving Daniel may have been a mistake, she couldn't dwell on it. Life had to go on.

After two months of nothing, one weekend, without notice, he phoned. By then, she had convinced herself she would never hear from him again, and his voice melted her at her core.

At first, his calls were infrequent. After how she had treated him, she knew she wasn't entitled to anything more. He was correct that things were always on her terms, and he had every right to set boundaries for himself now. As the spring approached, their talks became more regular, and each made a point to talk to the other at least once a week. Daniel did not make any attempt to discuss their relationship, seeming to go out of his way to avoid the topic. Their conversations focused on their work, and her upcoming summer plans to conduct research for her doctoral degree. She intended to take a deep dive into the real life of Richard III, hoping to capture something to help dispel the long-held belief that he'd been an evil monarch. This topic had always held her interest, and she appreciated how excited Daniel was about it.

"I think there is a wealth of information out there," he said. "The biggest problem is that Richard lived in just about every corner of this country. You will have a great deal of traveling to do to connect the dots, but I know you can do it."

"Naturally, I will start here in Middleham, but I want to see many other places too." Her excitement often led to her rambling. "There is Pontefract, Fotheringay, and Ludlow too. I would love to see them all this summer, but it is such a distance to cover."

"Haven't you gone to Middleham yet? You're only a stone's throw away." He seemed surprised.

"I visited just a few weeks ago. It was a rather busy day, though, and I had a lot on my mind. Nothing really happened—" She stopped short, peering out of the hall nook to make sure no one was around. Although Daniel was well aware of her ability to hear the whispers, it wasn't something she dared share with anyone else. Now that her grandma had passed on, she felt more and more alone in her gift. While the whispers were passed through the female descendants of the Babington line, whether or not each and every one of them inherited the gift was unclear. Regardless, she was cognizant of the dangers of disclosing her abilities to those outside that circle.

"You should try again then," he said, his encouragement welcomed. "You always do much better when you're not surrounded by people. Something will come through. It just has to be the right time."

He had always been so supportive. She missed him, in truth, more than she thought she would, but starting her research in the summer, and how busy that would keep her, was some consolation.

"Have you given any thought to your cousin coming to help you?" he asked, interrupting her thoughts.

"Actually, I spoke to her father just the other day. While I'm still a little shaky about the whole situation, I agreed that she could come assist me. I guess I feel obligated, knowing it was something my grandma wanted."

"I understand completely. I can see why you would want to honor her wishes, even if she was working behind the scenes on getting it arranged." He laughed. "That is so like Marjorie."

"Absolutely something she would do." Even as she laughed, the pain of missing her grandma didn't ease.

"You know I took on an assistant once. It worked out really well, actually. It is a great opportunity for you to get some help with your work and for her to learn too. What do you know about this long-lost cousin of yours?"

"Well, she is finishing her first year of college. She is a Londoner. As—"

"A Londoner!" he interrupted. "Oh my, Adelia Grey and the city girl. This ought to be a fine match."

"What do you mean?" She looked at the phone for a moment, as if to see his expression. "I was born and raised in Boston. I am a city girl, Daniel."

"Don't take this the wrong way but you are the most un-city city girl I have ever met."

"Hmm. I guess you're not wrong about that. But then Cassandra is a history major so maybe she will be good and boring like me."

"You are anything but boring. I am just anxious to see how you and she will get along."

She sensed a smile in his voice, his tone doing nothing to camouflage the clear message that he still found the whole situation comical.

"I am anxious, too," she confessed. "Just not the excited kind."

"You will be fine," he said, sounding a bit like her father. "You just may have to learn to be patient at first. I think you both will get some growth out of this whole thing."

Cassandra would be staying the summer at the manor. As luck had it, there were still rooms for rent, so Laura and Ross were more than willing to allow her to stay a few months. They would spend a great deal of time traveling to different locations, staying at the manor in between. And Cassandra's parents were funding her expenses, so there was no reason why her presence would be a hindrance.

Chapter Four

Each morning Adelia rode into town with Paul, one of the other residents at the manor, who had retired after a long career as an army pilot. He'd sold his home and moved to Middleham, working part-time in an antique store his brother owned in Leeds. With him being about the same age as her father, she had taken to him from the first day, and even though he was the polar opposite to John Grey, she looked up to him as a daughter would. After years of adhering to the rigid protocol of life in the service, in retirement he adopted what could only be regarded as a rebellious nature. Vibrant streaks of silver drizzled through the shoulder-length waves that hung around his full face, and he always wore an untucked dress shirt, the buttons at its collar left undone. He loved to end his evenings with a slow-burning cigar, a glass of Kilbeggan, and a classical record playing in the library—things her father would never do.

In all of their varied conversations, he never mentioned a wife or children. Adelia never asked about them either, content not to pry into the matter. It seemed a topic he would have brought up if he wanted to discuss it.

For as much as she didn't know about him, she allowed him to be privy to much about her life. She told him how she'd ended up in Leeds, her uncertainty with Daniel, and her upcoming summer with Cassandra. He served to fill the void created by an absence of close friends. Of course, she stopped short of telling him about the whispers, having taken to heart her grandma's warning of the ridicule that was sure to follow such a revelation. She didn't want him thinking she was some sort of loon. As much as she trusted him, it was a risk she couldn't take.

"You are sure you won't need a lift after work?" he asked during their morning commute.

"I'm meeting Cassandra today. She will be dropping by the university this afternoon, and she has a car so I will be riding back with her."

"Good enough." He gave her a thumbs up. "I am sure it will be nice for you to get acquainted with her this summer."

"I think so too." It would be nice to have someone her own age to converse with now and then. "Up until now, I have communicated with her parents while she has been off at school. They seem eager to have her spend some time with me, believing it will be beneficial, giving her the direction she needs."

"Direction, you say?" His thick brows furrowed for a moment. "That's never good."

She stared at him. "How so?"

"From my experience, that's a delicate phrase parents use to tell you that a challenge awaits."

"Oh, I hadn't thought of that." She gripped her handbag with both hands. "You know, between you and Daniel, I am starting to have second thoughts about this whole Cassandra business."

"Well, pay no mind to what I just said. I am an old man, tending to read things negatively by nature. I'm sure they just meant she will need your guidance. You are wise beyond your years, my friend, and I'm sure your cousin will learn quite a bit just from being your shadow."

"I hope I didn't sign on for something terrible," she said, her mind racing with worry.

He tapped the steering wheel. "Forget I said anything."

Too late, her stomach was already knotting. "Well...maybe it's a good thing she will be staying at the manor. It will allow me to keep a close eye on her while she's here."

"Indeed, I'm sure she will benefit from your experience."

She smiled, appreciating his support. "We will be traveling quite a bit together this summer, so I won't be around as much. I will miss our morning chats."

"Same here, kid," he replied, his smile lighting his eyes. "It will be good for you to have a traveling companion your own age, though. Let's just hope she is a better driver than I am." He swerved to avoid a pothole but his attempt failed, the jarring effect doing little to help Adelia's already tense stomach.

"Sorry, kid," he said with a mischievous laugh.

She barely heard him, though, trying to digest the predicament she had gotten herself into by taking on Cassandra for the summer. A picture emerged of some wayward twenty-year-old, whose parents were trying to reel her back in before she went off the deep end. Maybe she was one of those party girls, more concerned with her overfilled social calendar than her term papers. Had she decided on being a history major, thinking it was the easiest subject she could pass without having to do much work? Just a semester into teaching, Adelia could already pick those students out of the crowd almost straight away.

It didn't matter what type of person Cassandra was, nothing could be allowed to hinder this project. She had moved heaven and earth to get to this point in her life, having worked her ass off day and night to earn both her degrees in quick time, and even wrecked her relationship to secure this job. Now she was on the cusp of completing the work that would be her most crowning academic accomplishment yet, she would not permit someone to create a pothole in the road to achieving that. No, she would send Cassandra packing back to her parents if she so much as tried to derail this project. If the young woman thought this summer would be all play, she was in for a surprise. When it came to her career, Adelia Grey was not the sporting type.

When Paul dropped her off at the entrance to her building, she turned back and waved goodbye. He gave a toothy grin and sped off in the direction of the antique shop.

With today being the end of her first semester, she would have her last full classes before examinations. She faced a marathon of a day, with her lectures stretching late into the afternoon.

As she made her way to the tiny lecture hall on the second floor, her mind swirled with all the information she planned to cover today to accommodate the classes wrapping up.

The campus would soon be empty for the summer, and as far as she knew, she would be asked to return in the fall. Nancy Charles, the historical-studies' department chair, was pleased with her performance so far, even going as far as securing a small grant to cover some of her expenses for her summer research. The woman had served as a wonderful mentor for her during the semester, and everything seemed to be falling into place.

Just as she entered the lecture hall, her name was called from behind. When she turned, Nancy was walking toward her.

"Good morning, Ms. Charles." She held a certain admiration for her, liking how she was always polished and well put together.

"I hoped to catch you. With examinations coming up next week, I figured it might be hard for us to connect."

"Yes, it will be hectic, I am sure."

"I just wanted to wish you luck on your summer project, and give you this list of allowable expenditures for the grant." She handed over an olive-green folder, with a small stack of papers tucked inside.

"That's great," Adelia said. "Thank you again for getting this for me. I don't know how to thank you enough."

"Hey, I am excited to see you get what you need for your dissertation. The world needs more great leaders. Women leaders." She winked. "Are you still taking your cousin along with you?"

"Yes, she is actually coming here today. I suggested she attend my last class. I will be meeting her for the first time."

"That's exciting. For her, too, I bet. The two of you can get a lot done together. I am sure she will enjoy being part of your success."

"Is it really my success if I have help?" she asked. "I am nervous about what I should have her contribute to this whole project."

Nancy leaned closer. "Great women are not simply born. They are honed by the challenges they face and the grit it takes to achieve results. None of those things can occur in pure isolation. You must learn to draw from the strengths of those around you. To glean the knowledge from others until it, too, becomes your own. That is the secret to true success."

"You are right. I'm sure Cassandra will bring something unique to the table." Her response, though pleasant, wasn't truthful. She had no idea what she could learn from her cousin. At this point, she wasn't sure her summer would be anything more than babysitting a self-indulgent brat.

"Nothing is as empowering as true collaboration," Nancy said, giving a subtle wink. "You will see what I mean this summer. Now, good luck, and reach out if you need anything."

Adelia nodded, then tucked the folder under her arm as she turned back to the lecture hall, filing her fears about Cassandra into the back of her mind.

Chapter Five

Several hours later, she leaned against the podium and glanced back over her notes before beginning her final lecture. The day had already been long, but the end was drawing near. One by one her students filed into the room, their muffled chatter filling the space as she waited for the clock to strike three. She always experienced apprehension as the last few seconds ticked away, something her colleagues had assured her would never fully go away.

When she first began teaching at the university, she had been a nervous wreck. However, with each passing day, her confidence started to build as the rapport with her students increased. No matter how much a person knew about a given topic, teaching it to others was an altogether different animal. A level of trust had to be established between herself and her students before real learning could begin. She had worked diligently on that bond, and now, after one semester, her efforts were bearing fruit.

"A horse! A horse! My kingdom for a horse!" she declaimed, addressing her students in her best attempt at a Shakespearean actor's voice. "Shakespeare did a marvelous job of pleasing the Tudor queen, Elizabeth I, with his portrayal of Richard III in the play by the same name. Yet, we cannot forget that he was writing his works to gain the favor of the very family who had usurped the crown from Richard III."

She'd nearly stopped mid-sentence on seeing a tall, lean woman enter the room, her blonde hair shining like silver moonbeams. *Not one of my students. Has to be Cassandra.* She was statuesque, bearing a strong resemblance to something da Vinci would have carved in marble. Her face was smooth and peppered with pale freckles, and her fair skin had just the perfect hint of pink resting on the tops of her cheeks. She radiated a carefree vibe, like a summer's day, as though, no matter what life threw at her, she would find a way to sweep through it.

Her black top was tucked into a skirt that just about hit her mid-thigh. *Way too short.* Adelia knew that fashions had started to change in London, yet she held tight to the more conservative tastes of the 50's over these new 60's trends. Indeed, her own sense of dress had been out of style for some time. If the room full of turned heads and gaping mouths gave a clue, it wasn't difficult to see that none of the male students seemed to take any issue with Cassandra's choice of attire.

She grimaced inside at the instinctive pang of jealousy rising through her. To be fair, every other female in the room probably felt it too. Cassandra was not just pretty, she radiated beauty. Girls like that didn't need to be smart. Some rich guy would come along and shower her with whatever she wanted. Amidst her envy, she felt a bit guilty for thinking so critically of another woman. As a rule, it was something she opposed doing. She had allowed herself to get caught up in the moment, and now had to refocus and rein her students' attention back in again.

"It is highly improbable that Richard ever uttered the words Shakespeare gives us," she continued, trying to act as though she was not distracted by the visitor's intrusion. "Once he was knocked to the ground at the Battle of Bosworth, I doubt he had time to waste looking for a horse. It is really utter pish-posh to think he did not understand that he was likely finished at that point."

She winced inside after saying "pish posh." That had been Daniel's favorite expression, used whenever he considered something to be historical rubbish. She walked over and pointed to the words written on the chalkboard.

"Richard III and Macbeth." Her voice echoed off the walls. "Who among you can tell me how these two men are similar?"

When she turned back to her class, she was met with a sea of blank stares and absolute silence. She scanned the expressionless faces. Nothing. Considering it was the last day, she should not have expected anything less. Her students were no doubt perplexed as to why she was bothering to teach a new subject today with final examinations looming ahead.

"Anyone at all?" she prodded, remaining patient.

Just as she was about to explain the words, a slender arm in the back rose up. It was none other than Cassandra, who once again commanded the attention of everyone present. Adelia supposed because she had said "anyone," it could have been perceived that it did not have to be an actual student in the class. She nodded for her cousin to share whatever knowledge she wished to impart, though she did not have high expectations.

"Both men were known as noble and loyal servants to their country," Cassandra offered. "Though neither originally anticipated it, both eventually became kings of those nations they served. Macbeth's ambitions for the crown began when he came upon the three witches in the forest. But Richard's ambitions came when his brother, Edward IV, unexpectedly passed away."

"Exactly," Adelia said, somewhat stunned, and scolding herself for assuming that just because Cassandra was so pretty, she would automatically lack intelligence. She deserved a heaping dose of karma for being so judgmental.

Another hand went up, and she gave the young man the nod.

"While Richard and Macbeth both seemed to be content with the success they achieved on their own, they were propelled onto a darker path by the external influences in their lives." The student looked at Cassandra to be sure she was impressed.

"Well done," Adelia said, still reeling. It was about the most participation she'd had all week in the class. Cassandra's easy confidence allowed her to command the room without trying. "Both Richard and Macbeth were successful in their own right," she continued, endeavoring to draw the attention of her students away from her cousin and back to the subject at hand. If she waited another second, every male in the room might melt into a puddle of goo. "They were both looked upon as men of the people. Once the seed of ambition was planted in their minds, it appears that neither were able to resist the temptation to seize power for themselves. From there, if the stories are to be believed, their paths took a more sinister turn."

Another young man raised his hand. "In Shakespeare's plays, both had to commit murder to become king. Richard III had to kill his nephews, the rightful heirs to the throne. Macbeth had to kill King Duncan." He glanced over at Cassandra, inciting frowns and glares from many of his male colleagues. She gave him a gracious smile, and Adelia thought he would turn to mush on the floor. The young woman had a serious effect on the opposite sex. Adelia took in the faces of all her students. Hmm, maybe the same sex too. It was safe to say Cassandra had effectively taken over the room, even though she was not part of the class.

"In today's lecture, we will continue to explore this theme," she announced, turning back to the chalkboard to scribble a few more words. "I believe there is much that is misunderstood about Richard III. Today, we might be appalled by the things he is accused of, but Richard was a man of his time—a time when being a good soldier and a good man could be accepted as mutually exclusive. For both men, the pursuit of the crown awoke a dark desire in them. Both had spent their lives being loyal to their sovereign. They showed unparalleled bravery on the battlefield, willing to lay down their lives for the king they served. Each was in such a position of trust that the king they served bestowed great honor in the form of titles and wealth upon them. Yet, when the fuse of ambition was lit, were both Richard III and Macbeth willing to kill those who trusted them most? It is up to us to sift through the fact and the fiction."

Another hand went up. "Professor, pardon me for asking, but why are we not doing a comparison between Shakespeare's Richard III and the real one? Why Macbeth?"

"That is a great question, but I think we already established that Shakespeare's portrayal would be considered biased based on his affiliation with Elizabeth I. Let us not forget that she was the granddaughter of Henry VII, the man who defeated, killed, and took the crown from Richard. I believe using Macbeth as a comparison might allow us to think more objectively, as I suspect Richard's story, as we know it, is just as fictionalized as the character of Macbeth."

Several of her students nodded their understanding, though many continued staring at Cassandra. Adelia smiled to herself and carried on with her lecture.

"The only thing we can say for Macbeth is that he was wracked with guilt for all he had done. I don't know if the same could be said about Richard. We don't even know if he was guilty of any crime. Unfortunately, history doesn't give us any credible insight into his true inner thoughts on the matter of the accusations. This is where we must dig deeper. Was Richard really a bad guy, as history portrays him? He lived in a time where if you lose, you die. Tell me when have any of us ever had such a burden on our shoulders? This was a time when you might be executed for simply being inconvenient. When who your parents happened to be might render you a threat, and therefore open to being eliminated. These were very high gain and high-risk times."

At the conclusion of class, all the students departed, leaving Cassandra still sitting in her seat. It was past five o'clock now and the campus would be emptying. Adelia shoved the few papers on her desk into her bag and slung it over her shoulder. She exhaled a deep breath, readying herself to at last meet her cousin for the first time.

"You must be Cassandra," she said as she approached. She reached out her hand.

In a flash, Cassandra leaped up and pulled her into an unexpected embrace. It caught her off guard so much she dropped her bag. The loud thump on the floor caused both women to flinch and pull back.

"I'm sorry," Cassandra gasped. "I am just so happy to finally get the chance to meet you in person." She held out her arms. "I am a hugger, as you've seen."

"I am not, but it's okay," Adelia said, realizing her manner was way too stiff. "I am pleased to meet you too."

Cassandra gave a halfhearted smile, her shoulders lowering.

"I dare say I was impressed with your contribution to the class." She hoped this would ease the awkwardness. "It's the last day of classes, before exams. None of the students are particularly motivated at this point to approach a new topic."

"I never met a college student excited about a full day of learning the day before exams," Cassandra said, the sting of brutal honesty dripping from her voice.

"Good, then we can at least admit my students are normal." She just about held back an eyeroll. "What do you say we take our leave of this place?" She turned to go. "I'm sure you are anxious to get settled in at Middleham Manor."

"Great idea." Cassandra grabbed up her belongings and rushed to catch up with Adelia.

The two women walked in an uneasy silence on their way to the car. Adelia had no idea what the girl was thinking, and wasn't sure she cared. Were her fears about spending the summer with her cousin coming to fruition? Was it too late to back out now? If so, she could come up with ways to shake her loose before the summer's end. She was good at that—driving people out of her life, even the ones who mattered most. Daniel. If I can do such a horrible thing to him, Cassandra will not be much of a challenge. However, as they walked, her guilty conscience made its presence known. I owe this to Grandma, after all the things she did for me. I owe her this little token of commitment.

Not only did Cassandra own a car, it was a fairly new model. The exterior still held the gleam of one that had just rolled off the showroom floor. Adelia could only guess that her parents had provided her with such a lavish gift, as it wasn't something the average college student could afford.

The interior was almost packed to the brim with boxes and bags. Will there be enough room for me to even fit into the passenger seat? Her stomach flipped at the thought of riding in what felt like a tuna can rather than a car. What Cassandra had packed for a mere summer, looked to be far more than all the possessions she owned herself. When she'd moved to Middleham Manor, her belongings filled only a couple of boxes. Money was not something she had at her disposal, and paying her tuition had taken every last dime she was able to afford. She flicked a look as Cassandra opened the driver's door and slid into her seat. If ever there were two completely different people in the world, they had just found one another.

Chapter Six

The drive back to the manor did not take long, but the confining conditions in the car made it feel as though it stretched on for years. Despite all of her other nervous tendencies, Adelia had never known herself to be claustrophobic but being closed in by so many boxes and suitcases made those feelings emerge. It didn't help that she sat in the passenger seat with her chest almost touching her knees, a result of the overflow of stuff from the backseat. She sucked in a deep breath, the faint wisp of Cassandra's perfume evoking a jolt of familiarity. It was Chanel No.5, the scent Grandma Marjorie once wore. A sharp pinch emanated from the hollow of her empty stomach. Stifled, she cracked the window open, relieved when the warm May breeze helped to ease the nausea bubbling in her belly.

"I think you will find Middleham Manor humble yet pleasing," she said, attempting small talk to distract her mind from her uncomfortable position, and to ease the cold shoulder she'd offered earlier. "There is a delightful cast of characters who reside there."

Cassandra nodded as she focused on the road. "Father told me I will have my own room there. It's a pity we won't get to share. It would be nice to have a sister for a while." This came with a hint of disappointment.

"I am an only child too," Adelia said, thinking of growing up back in Boston. "I never really had to share much of anything, though there were many times I thought it would have been nice."

"Tell me about the people at the manor. I would like to know what I am getting myself into, if they are as colorful as you say."

"Well..."—excitement fizzed through her at the thought of describing her unusual housemates—"you will find the owners Laura and Ross to be most entertaining of all. They scarcely can manage to be in the same room without bickering. It might be a little annoying at times, but I promise you will get used to it after a while. Then there is old Mrs. Chambers. She is a widow, friendly, but keeps to herself most of the time, and rarely comes out of her room. Oh, she has two of the most beautiful Pembroke Welsh Corgi's, named Lord and Lady. You will find they are not much of a bother, although they lounge in the hallways quite often. They are both fairly old, and have lost the energy you would expect from a younger dog. They don't make any effort to move for you, so you have to step over them to get wherever you are going."

"I never had a dog growing up. I think I will like them very much." This came out with such glee, it was almost sung.

"Lastly, there is Paul. He is a retired military pilot who works during the day at his brother's antique shop. Until you came today, he has been my main mode of transportation back and forth to the university. I don't know much else about him. He is a docile creature. Reserved, knowledgeable, but, above all, a wonderful listener. He has become a good friend since I came to the northern country. In many ways, I think of him as a father figure. He helps counsel me with his good sense when I lose my way." She thought it best not to add that she had lost her way quite a lot in the last few months. Her ambitions were always clear but the path to get there was as murky as the Thames River.

"I think I will fit in at Middleham quite nicely. Try as I might, I come across as quirky to most people. Maybe I will fit in somewhere for once." She shrugged, then glanced at Adelia. "I guess quirky is not really your style."

"On the contrary, I seem to be a magnet for the quirky." She wondered just what Cassandra thought of her. Probably finds me rather dull and uptight—a book nerd paired up with a free spirit. It was difficult to imagine her cousin excited about the match. Perhaps she was feeling just as nervous about their summer pairing. It was understandable that the girl might have apprehensions. Still, she seemed to camouflage it well.

"Well, I try to be normal, but it just doesn't come naturally."

"I'm not so different," Adelia assured. "Not in the least. I always find myself in a series of unfortunate events."

"So, crazy things happen to you?" Cassandra asked, straight out. Adelia stared at her. "Huh?"

"Why say it so formally? 'A series of unfortunate events.' Just say crazy things happen to you. Sounds less wordy." Her voice held a tone that reminded Adelia of a teenager with a bad attitude.

"I would not consider myself wordy," she said.

"Of course not," Cassandra droned, arching her blonde eyebrows. "Dull people don't consider themselves to be dull. Annoying people don't consider themselves to be annoying. All I am saying is you don't have to be so formal with me. I am pretty easy to impress, even without all the words."

"Noted." Adelia huffed, close to gritting her teeth.

"So, tell me something about this research you are doing this summer," Cassandra said after another awkward silence—maybe an attempt at thawing the chill that had developed between them.

Adelia welcomed the change of subject with open arms. "All my life I have had theories about Richard III. I wanted to know who he was as a man. Who he was long before being crowned King of England. There is a certain following of Richard, you see. The Ricardians. They believe that history has painted a false picture. Like them, I believe that this man was not nearly as two dimensional as the narrative he has been assigned. Anyway, Cassandra, you seem to know a lot about Richard yourself, so this is all probably old news to you."

"Actually, I don't." She batted her eyelids, as if she'd been caught doing something bold. "I just read up on it a little before I came. I...tried reading Shakespeare's play but I couldn't finish." She gripped the steering wheel with both hands and shrugged. "I actually hate Shakespeare. I much prefer Agatha Christie."

She hates Shakespeare?

"Okay," she said, nodding, though she wanted to shake her head with exasperation, "Agatha Christie is perfect. Let's start there. Think of Richard's story like *Murder on the Orient Express*, but in real life."

"That sounds like something I can follow," Cassandra said, giving her hope that she had managed to pique the girl's interest.

"So, Edward IV is the king of England. Our Richard, Duke of Gloucester, is his brother. Edward is riding along one day on a road when he finds a beautiful widow waiting for him. Enter Elizabeth Woodville. She implores him to help her restore her husband's lands for her son's inheritance, saying they have been unjustly taken from her. Edward becomes so captivated by her beauty that he secretly marries her. Elizabeth is a commoner, considered low born among the aristocracy at the time. This causes an international scandal."

Cassandra's eyes widened. "Ooh, I do love a good scandal."

"This story is rife with them." She flashed a devious smile. "Anyway, Elizabeth and Edward go on to produce a brood of children, including two boys. Those boys are Edward, Prince of Wales, and Richard, Duke of York. Stick with me, there are lots of Edwards and Richards here. Years later in his turbulent reign, Edward IV dies. He is our murder victim on the train—"

"I thought Edward died of natural causes," Cassandra interjected. "Wasn't he morbidly obese and lived a promiscuous lifestyle?"

"Yes," Adelia said, groaning inside, though somewhat impressed that her cousin knew that much. "He did die of natural causes, but it was quite unexpected. Do you see me trying to connect this to Agatha Christie's novels here? I am doing this for you, Cassandra."

"Yes, I see." She shrugged again. "Go on then."

"Well now, let's get to the other passengers on the train. Everyone hates Elizabeth Woodville. Even though she was a commoner before becoming queen, she is highly intelligent and extremely cunning. She does everything to promote her low born family into positions of prestige. So much so, it makes everyone all the more jealous of her. She is completely aware that they distrust her, but, ultimately, her two sons are heirs to the throne. She holds all the cards. Enter Richard, Duke of Gloucester. Edward IV, on his deathbed, declares Richard, his brother, as Lord Protector over his oldest son, as he is only twelve."

"So, Prince Edward is too young to be king yet?"

Adelia cast the back of her hand to her forehead. "Woe to thee, oh land, when thy king is a child."

"Huh?" Cassandra wrinkled her nose up.

"It's a quote from the Bible. It just means a country with a child at its head is in trouble."

"I thought we were talking about Agatha Christie. Now we are talking about the Bible. My head is starting to spin."

Goodness, I need to remember just who I'm talking to here. "I'm sorry. Let me continue." She bit hard on her rising exasperation. Perhaps schooling Cassandra will be harder than I thought. "Immediately, a chain of events starts to happen. The Woodvilles, distrusting of Richard, don't even tell him his brother has died. He gets the news days later. The Woodvilles start to stockpile weapons and money, preparing for some inevitable clash. Sir Anthony Rivers—Elizabeth's brother, who, like many of her other family members, had been elevated when she became queen—raised young Edward for several years at Ludlow Castle in Wales. Now he secretly leaves Wales and tries to get Prince Edward to London to be crowned king, before Richard can take over. Richard hears of this attempted coup and leaves his lands up north, intercepting them at Stony Stratford. The next day, he has Rivers and one of Elizabeth's sons arrested and taken to Pontefract. They are executed shortly after."

"Sounds like the Woodvilles are not exactly playing by the rules here?"

Adelia nodded, relieved her cousin seemed to be getting it. "No, they are not. There is so much happening in the background, it's hard to know who is the antagonist and who is the protagonist in the story."

"But we are still on the train, right?"

The train? "Yes, Cassandra, still on the train. So...Richard takes Prince Edward to the Tower of London to prepare for the coronation."

Cassandra looked almost horrified. "Why is he putting his own nephew in prison?"

"In fourteen eighty-three, the Tower was not just a prison, it was a luxurious palace, and the official residence of every monarch before their coronation at Westminster Cathedral. Prince Edward would have been held in very fine accommodations."

"Okay, that makes more sense." Cassandra nodded away, both hands on the steering wheel.

"Elizabeth Woodville, hearing of her brother and son's execution, and that Richard has Prince Edward, immediately takes sanctuary at Westminster. She has with her all of her other children, including her other son, Richard, Duke of York. Before long she is convinced, many think forced, to allow Prince Richard to join his older brother for the coronation. Now Richard III has both heirs."

"That is not good," Cassandra chimed in with a solemn voice, shaking her head to herself.

"No, it is not good if you are thinking from Elizabeth's perspective. I think it's important to remember that she rarely made any move in her life without an ulterior motive lurking in the background. It's not unthinkable to imagine she assumed Richard to be doing the same. So now that all of the players are on the train, the stage is set for the ultimate showdown."

Cassandra opened both hands, her thumbs hooked on the steering wheel. "So, this is where Richard kills his nephews and takes the throne."

"Not exactly," Adelia said. "This is the part where it really gets good. A bishop comes forward to say that he actually married Edward IV to another woman before he was married to Elizabeth Woodville. If that is true, then the children between Edward and Elizabeth would be considered illegitimate and therefore not entitled to take the throne. As Richard, Duke of Gloucester, is the next surviving brother of Edward IV, he becomes king. King Richard III. There is some other stuff wedged in between there but we can get to those details later. In the end, the two princes just vanished, and no one knows what happened."

Cassandra pursed her lips beneath a frown. "Couldn't Richard III just have paid the bishop to say that about the other marriage? Maybe he had some grand master plan all along."

Adelia almost smiled. For someone who didn't know much about the story, Cassandra was catching on fast.

"It's completely possible, but the fact is we have no evidence. Just like there is absolutely no evidence that Richard killed either of his nephews. There are only contemporary accounts from authors who had no firsthand knowledge of any of the events. Those authors were also under the patronage of Henry VII, who defeated Richard and took the crown for himself. That is why we are going to do some digging this summer."

"So, we are setting out to find documents that prove Richard was innocent?" Cassandra said, more than asked.

"Well, we know that Henry VII had many documents pertaining to Richard destroyed. There is no real explanation why, because we don't know what they contained. It's unlikely we can uncover much physical evidence, but I am still hopeful."

"Now, what of the Woodvilles? Did they go into exile? Were they all killed?"

Adelia had to laugh at her cousin's rapid-fire questions. "No," she said, ready to add another layer of suspense to the story. She had been set on putting it to rest right there but, on Cassandra's insistence, was happy to continue. "As I said, Elizabeth had gone into sanctuary, with her other children. Yet, quite mysteriously, she emerged one day, even going as far as bringing her daughters to the court of their uncle, Richard the king. Nothing was ever spoken of the princes after that, and that is the one thing that has baffled historians ever since."

"So let me get this straight..." Cassandra tapped away at the steering wheel with her forefinger. "Two royal princes, who were heir to the throne, just disappear, and nobody says anything? How is that even possible? Weren't there rumors about what happened to them? It's nineteen sixty-one, and this is a great story. You can't tell me tongues were not wagging in fourteen eighty-three."

"Yes," Adelia agreed, excited. "There were a great many rumors, most of which were spread by Richard's opposition. What was odd is that Richard himself, who was always quick to dispel mistruth, never uttered a word. More perplexing was Elizabeth Woodville herself. Can we really believe that her two sons, heirs to the throne, would just simply disappear and she would be completely silent on the matter? Elizabeth Woodville was not the silent type. She was not the type to just retire into seclusion and allow fate to have its own designs. This woman spent her entire life intervening in situations to ensure the best outcome for herself."

"Adelia, I rather think this story might be better than an Agatha Christie novel," Cassandra said with a devilish smile, looking as though she had just heard the most delicious gossip. Her comment made Adelia laugh, and both women smirked at one another as though they were knee-deep in some conspiracy.

"Personally, I love that history is littered with complexity such as this particular case. It never allows my brain a moment's peace, though. My thoughts are never completely shut off."

Cassandra nodded, arching her brows again. Adelia smiled, though more to herself. Despite her cousin's aversion to Shakespeare, this was one thing they could agree on.

Chapter Seven

Cassandra pulled into the front approach to the house and parked the car. When she stepped out, she took in all the surroundings that made up Middleham Manor. Adelia expected the rustic charm she adored would have the opposite effect on her cousin, who was used to the modern pace of London. Cassandra spun around, her eyes closed, breathing in the fragrant country air.

"It's just as you described it, Adelia. I am in love, even as I stand outside. I have grown up in London all my life, and it feels so good to get away from the confines of that city." She shuddered with excitement.

"Confines of the city? It is one of the biggest in the world." Adelia closed her car door. "I find it hard to think you felt confined in London."

"Oh, but I did. There are just so many people. So many buildings. There was hardly room to breathe at times. This place is so different. I just love it already."

Adelia couldn't hold in a grin. "Well, I am glad you like it so much. Why don't we grab a few of your things and get you settled?"

Having grabbed every loose item they could carry, Adelia led Cassandra through the front entrance of the old house. She giggled to herself when her cousin gasped behind her on viewing the ancient decor.

Sounds filtered out from the sitting room, just off the foyer, of light music and laughter—someone enjoying much-needed winding down after a busy day. Adelia poked her head into the room. Laura and Ross were conversing with a few guests who were staying in the bed & breakfast suites.

"Oh, hello," she said, keeping her voice down. "I didn't mean to intrude." She shuffled the bundle of items, trying not to let anything fall. "I just wanted to introduce you to my cousin Cassandra. She has arrived from London today." She glanced back at her new research assistant. "This is Laura and Ross."

Perhaps it was the pale lighting of the many table lamps scattered about, but as Cassandra stepped in behind her, a glittering aura stretched to every corner of the room. The music had changed to something that sounded like an angelic choir, and her porcelain skin, the pale-pink flush to her cheeks, and her long golden locks took on an ethereal glow. Each man's gaze swept up and down her shapely form, their mouths hanging open. This did not go down well, met by the scowls of their wives as they took in their men's lustful reaction. Tonight, the silent treatment would be in full force at the manor.

Laura punched Ross's shoulder. "Welcome, dear. We are so excited to have you at Middleham Manor."

"She walks in beauty like the night..." Ross recited to himself, his theatrical voice filling the room.

"...of cloudless climes and starry skies," Cassandra added in a soulful tone, finishing his sentence. Her voice could have been mistaken for Venus herself. "Oh, I do love Lord Byron," she said, with an innocent flutter of her long lashes.

Adelia almost smacked her hand square on her own forehead. Oh, Cassandra, you shall never be free of that man now.

Ross stared at her as though poetry had come to life, looking like the existence of his worldly soul could be saved if only she would recite one more verse. Thankfully, she did not. She just stood there beaming, happy to be at Middleham at last and oblivious to the marital discord she had caused in the room.

"Well, then!" Adelia exclaimed, breaching the strained silence beneath the music. "I will show Cassandra to her room. We have to unload her things from the car, so don't mind us if we make a few trips in and out."

Like the thunderous startup of a marching band, voices called out over one another.

"No, allow me. I will help," the men bellowed, yelling over one another.

They seemed to rise in unison, with a clatter of movement, like a stampede of wildebeest across the African savanna, pushing and shoving, each determined to exit the room first.

The two women stepped out of the way to avoid the mad dash to the doorway, with each man trying to get out faster than the next. Ross and another gent collided in the narrow doorway, nearly sending the contents of a table spilling to the floor. Adelia rolled her eyes. Never had she witnessed such a display of masculine ignorance, or been on the receiving end of one. For a moment, she felt both jealous and appalled.

Still stunned, she motioned for Cassandra to follow her up the stairs to the second floor. Cassandra's room faced hers, across the hallway. As they heaved their load, she nodded for her to mind a fluffy white mass of fawn and white on the floor, and they took care to step over Lord, one of Mrs. Chamber's cherished Corgis. The dog never so much as moved a hair, content as he was in his slumber. At least one male in the house was unaffected by Cassandra's charms.

If Adelia had been told that the entire contents of Cassandra's car could be unloaded in less than five minutes, she would have declared the feat impossible. However, the men of Middleham Manor proved her wrong tonight. They placed every last box into Cassandra's room, with great care, then stood, a sea of smiles, waiting to be graced with her words of appreciation. And as they departed, heads hung low knowing the fate they faced from their wives, Cassandra remained blissfully unaware.

"People are so nice here," she declared with her dazzling smile.

Adelia gave a polite nod. As her cousin busied herself unpacking her belongings, she slipped down to the kitchen and returned with two plates of food for dinner. They ate together, using Cassandra's own writing desk as a makeshift dining table. The conversation was light, centering on the visitor's life in London. While Adelia had been raised in Boston, and they were both accustomed to the hustle and bustle of city life, the similarities ended there. Cassandra had embraced her vibrant social life, while Adelia had done her best to shy far away from any hint of one. Yet, it eased her mind to know that they had at least one more thing in common.

She gathered up the empty plates and took them down to the kitchen to wash and put away. In the morning, they would meet for breakfast and start the planning stage of the summer. She hoped to plot out the sites they would visit, and in what order. While she was still unsure just what Cassandra could contribute to the project, she was confident it could all be sorted out later. For now, she needed her own downtime, her senses overloaded enough for one day.

After popping back in to say goodnight to Cassandra, she thought it would be nice to pay a quick visit to Paul, who might be wondering how their day had gone. It felt a little odd not to end her workday talking to him. In the coming months, she would see him less and less—a big shift considering he had become her only friend in a time when she needed someone to confide in. Besides, after the mayhem she had witnessed downstairs, Paul's wisdom would help restore her faith in the male of their species.

As she strolled down to the library at the rear of the house, faint music came to her, and she strained to make out the sounds. Cello. She closed her eyes as it reverberated through her, filling her with a deep melancholy. It was low and ominous, stirring her with such intensity that tears welled. Knowing full well it was Paul engaging in his nightly ritual, her heart lifted. She continued down the hall, the inviting tang of cigar smoke drawing her on.

She approached the door with hesitancy. The music was unlike the usual whimsical symphonies he listened to most nights. This was something one put on when you wanted to be alone. Yet, in her selfishness, she did not want to be alone. So, despite her better judgment, she entered. As she did, with the music filling the room, she found herself almost regretful for invading his personal space.

If Paul had reason to be downtrodden, it was out of character for him to share why. The man was a deeply guarded person. Gracious and approachable, sure, yet there had always been something about him that set him off from others. Some unspoken sadness.

Two small logs crackled in the fireplace, taking the crispness out of the night air.

"This is a beautiful piece," she said, lowering herself into one of the high-backed chairs. As she rested her head back, the weight of her day lifted, even in the somber atmosphere.

"It draws out emotion from the murky depths of the soul." He took a slow pull from his cigar, his loose hair hanging like silver thread upon his shoulders.

"If you have emotions that run that deep." Adelia trailed her fingers along the arm of the chair, reflecting for a moment on her own life.

"Everyone does," he assured, with surprising certainty. He jingled the ice in his empty bourbon glass. "It's just a matter of time before they surface. They always do."

She stared off in silence, unsure of what else to say, and unable to shake the feeling she had encroached on something seminal.

"By the way, you had a call tonight. Your gentleman friend, I believe."

"Oh, Daniel," she said, snapping out of it. She glanced up at the clock on the mantle. It was nearly eight o'clock. Daniel would be up but she still had papers to grade before turning in for the night. "It's late now. I will return his call in the morning."

"If I am prying, don't hesitate to tell me so, yet I wonder why you have chosen to leave your Daniel when your eyes light up as they do at the mention of his name. I think it's clear from the disappointment in his voice tonight, when I said you were not in, that he fancies you too."

"Daniel loves me. He wants to marry me, or at least he did once." She looked at her hands in her lap. "Yet I am selfish, Paul. Somehow, I have convinced myself that I can't be his wife and still do the things I want to do in my life. I am not unashamed to admit my fault. I am just a selfish person." She was always guarded in admitting her faults aloud, but things were different with Paul. He seemed to understand that faults lie in us all, yet he cast no stones.

"There are a great many people who would not be so honest to admit such a character flaw. You should at least be content that you can be genuine to yourself. You know, I was in love once."

"You were in love?" His revelation struck her with an astonishment that was nearly impossible to hide. He had never been inclined to reveal much about his past. Perhaps the haunting tones of the cello, and the bourbon, were drawing out long-hidden feelings.

"I am not so different from you, Adelia, and not so different from Daniel either. I can see your struggles from both sides of the coin."

"You were in love?" she repeated, almost drawing the words out. Her disbelief brought instant shame, and she scolded herself for daring to repeat the question. Paul just laughed, taking another draw from his half-smoked cigar. He paused for a moment, then blew out a thick stream of smoke.

"It was a long time ago. I loved a woman who was entirely out of my reach, but I loved her just the same. I wanted her to go away with me but she could not, and then I broke her heart out of sheer selfishness. In the end, far more people suffered heartbreak because of my wrongdoing. I am not a good man. I am actually quite terrible. I was very selfish in my desires, and then I lost the only thing that mattered to me. My punishment has been to live with that knowledge my entire life." He tapped the cigar over the ashtray. "Think wisely about the things you sacrifice, Adelia Grey. Think wisely. Karma blows in like a Tempestarius' storm. If you make the wrong decision, you must be willing to live a lifetime of regrets."

She blinked away salty tears gathering in her lashes. "I think I have already started that lifetime."

"Hold your tears, dear," he said, empathy oozing from his words. "You have what I do not have anymore. A chance to make it right."

Chapter Eight

In the morning, Adelia's thoughts had cleared. Cassandra was a free spirit but no less her flesh and blood. She thought of the long journey she had made to this place herself, coming through those years of indecision about who she was and what she would become, including the anxiety that had once plagued her life, twisting and turning every step she took into something to dread.

She remembered the beautiful face of her grandmother as they sat together, hands clasped, as Marjorie shared the Babington secret with her. Her life had changed that day. While she knew it was for the better, sometimes she doubted her fortune. That day burned in her mind like a hot coal, filling her with longing for the grandma who was gone. Though Marjorie had departed from this earth, the bond they shared defied mortality. She could feel it even stronger now. It was as if all the power of the whispers—the gift—had multiplied within her the day the woman died.

There were a million different things a person could seek to do with such a gift. Adelia sought to use it to propel her career. She wanted to experience the past as more than a voyeur—to be a presence in the room, encased in the dynamism of the energy as it happened.

Whatever the coming days held for her and Cassandra, she knew the whispers never happened by chance. There was always a message to be sent, a mystery to be deciphered. Their paths had been drawn together for a reason, and the only way to derive its meaning was to live in the moment and embrace whatever came. Cassandra's personality was a stark contrast to hers, the woman's mannerisms grating her nerves. They were different in every conceivable way, but that was the point, wasn't it? She was supposed to be put in this situation. This cringeworthy, uncomfortable predicament was all part of the plan.

After breakfast, they loaded into the car and set off in the direction of the small village of Middleham. The village was not much to speak of, being a market town built to serve the needs of the locals. For lovers of bygone eras, it was picturesque, holding a quaintness straight out of a book. But anyone seeking the modern hustle and bustle of the city would see Middleham as little more than a dot on the map. Its only real tourist draw was the well-known castle that sat at its edge. The castle, like many others, was a shell of its former glory, far removed from the age when the great Earl of Warwick held it in his keep, or when Richard III stalked its grounds.

As they passed through the village, Adelia could not hide her surprise that it was Cassandra who looked in awe at the waltz of locals up and down the street filled with sleepy little shops. Considering she had been raised in London, it was surprising just how much she seemed to find the quiet life appealing.

"I don't know that I could live in a place like this every day," she said with certainty. "I only know that I would holiday in a town like Middleham if I could." She changed gear before turning a corner. "All of Yorkshire is known for its textile trade. You can find some very fine silks and wool up here."

Adelia laughed. "Holiday? There wouldn't be much to do here, and you would certainly be devoid of the nightlife of London."

"That's the point of a holiday, isn't it?" Cassandra said, as though the answer was already clear in her mind. "To get away from all the things that you're surrounded with every day."

"You are asking the wrong person." Adelia shook her head. "I make a point of staying away from as many people as humanly possible every day. I can't say that my holiday destination would be any different, though." She nodded at the castle ahead. "I certainly would want these views no matter where I go."

Middleham Castle was a majestic ruin, seated high upon a hill overlooking the village. It was massive, even with it being just a shadow of its former glory. For all that had been lost over time, much of the structure remained, allowing one to imagine what it had looked like in its heyday.

The north country was well known for its rugged weather, with soaking rains and blustery winds ravaging the old fortress over time. It had been established as the central stronghold of the powerful Neville family for hundreds of years. Like all of the many imposing castles in the north, it served as a source of protection from the continued conflict with Scottish forces. Now the once-grand stone fortification was lovingly cared for by the country's historical preservation society, though, like many of the other historical sites in the country, there had been no attempt to restore the grounds. The focus was to keep the castle in its present state so visitors could appreciate it for what it had been through the ages. Middleham stood stoic, like a veteran of war, scarred by battle wounds but ever a survivor.

They entered the site together but it wasn't long before they separated, with each exploring on their own. The topic of the whispers had yet to come up between them. Cassandra had given no indication of having the gift herself, and Adelia was not inclined to start off their summer with a revelation of such magnitude. Things were already on shaky ground as it was.

Adelia walked in silence. After Cassandra's incessant chatter in the car, the solitude felt good. The grounds were sparsely littered with tourists so far this morning. As a child, she had seen Middleham in pictures—old black and white sketches in her father's books. To explore its fabled grounds offered something of a magnificent experience. She found herself walking in the footsteps of the castle's former servants, winding her way up narrow corridors which led to beautiful archways to nowhere.

Without warning, she let out a hefty sneeze. Dust—unavoidable, and a serious downside of being a historian. But it never stopped her. And treading the same earth as Richard III held a majestic charm she could barely put into words. She could feel him here, his presence strong within the castle's walls.

Middleham had served as the home of Richard Neville, the Earl of Warwick. While known as 'The King Maker' for his powerful influence restoring the House of York to the throne, Warwick had also served as caregiver to a number of young charges of noble lineage. It was here that young Richard had come as a teen, to be trained as a fierce and honorable knight under the guardianship of Warwick. Richard formed a strong bond to his guardian, who treated him like a son in return.

This was the place where Richard first met Anne, the Earl's youngest daughter, and his future wife. They would have been raised together for some years. How close they became during that time was not clear, yet it was a fair assumption that being so far from his childhood home at Fotheringhay must have been hard on the young man. Despite knowing that his time here was a fulfillment of duty, he was still a child, and inclined to miss his family. Children like Richard were raised differently in those days. They would have spent most of their time under the care of governesses and tutors, rarely seeing their parents. In his early years, Richard had been raised by his mother but his interactions were probably still limited. Even if their time with their parents was sparse, children were still taught to view them with deep love and reverence. Coming under the care of Warwick would have been a bittersweet time for the boy. He would long for the familiarity of home, while being excited at the prospect of undergoing the training to turn him into a great man and warrior.

While human nature tells us the Neville family would have become dear to Richard, there is no record of such sentiments. Notions such as duty and honor don't always give us a true glimpse into someone's personal attachments. There was so little to speak of his emotional state throughout the many challenges he faced in his life. He was a deeply guarded man in many ways, and there is evidence that he was highly respected by the people of the north, being looked upon as a man who sought to bring justice and rights to the common man. Yet, as fortune's wheel turned and he saw himself rise to power, those who opposed him tried, with some success, to tarnish his reputation. No one person could go through the things he experienced in his life and not have been flooded with emotion. History gives us a Richard who was a dark and foreboding sea, lying placid just before the storm. Adelia would have to use her gift to truly see all the colors of the storm. If it worked, it could be her window to understanding his unspoken thoughts.

She felt compelled to run her fingers across the weathered stone of the castle walls, knowing that some surface she touched may have been grazed by Richard III himself. As she did so, she filled her mind with nothing but thoughts of him. Somewhere in the great palace, Richard's essence existed, his energy caught in the fibers of time. She was determined to search every square inch until she found him.

It took a while—close to an hour. Though she could now hone her ability to channel certain energies, it still wasn't an exact science. Sometimes channeling a specific person came easy. Other times not at all. The whispers came at their own will, most times without prompting. Just what conducted the energy or blocked it still remained a bit of a mystery.

She moved through the maze of stone with deliberate steps. The further she progressed into the ruin, the more energy swirled around her. Carefree innocence came to the fore—childhood at its prime. Her spirit felt untroubled, as though these were the best days of her life. No danger. Peace and sanctuary coexisted here at Middleham—a refuge from all the evils of the world.

Walking through a fragmented archway, she came upon a space of magnificent proportions. The great hall. She closed her eyes and filled her lungs, the breeze caressing her face, as if history was inviting her in. The family would have taken their meals here, as well as entertaining guests. It was now reduced to four exposed walls stretching up several stories, yet, in the remnants, a hint of its former opulence existed through a patchwork of crumbling grand fireplaces and stonework. She sat on a loose stone that had once been part of a stairway leading into the hall from the kitchens. A fluttering above caught her attention, in time to see birds swooping in and out of the old gothic arched windows. A potpourri of sunlight and shadows streamed through the hollow frames that once contained leaded glass.

Over and over, she repeated Richard's name in a quiet whisper. This had been his home, as a child and a man. His energy pulsed through her. He was here, his soul trapped within the stones, his essence lingering in the air. She knew every recorded aspect of this man's life. Some were well-documented facts, others mere fiction, and she had waited many years to walk in his shadow. At last, she was ready to allow this gift she possessed to show her the Richard no one else could know. She wanted to feel his innermost thoughts as though they were her own.

"Richard," she whispered again, into the breeze.

As the quiet peace enveloped her, the familiar tingle of fire and ice coursed through her fingertips. Conflicting temperatures raced through her as she breathed in the powerful force, producing such a magnetic charge that the hairs on her arms stood erect.

It was a sunny day, yet the imposing walls of the great hall cast a dark shadow. In an instant, their monochromatic grayness melted into a stream of color, like molten lava, encasing them in brilliance. She caught the musky scent of wood in the large fireplace along one of the walls. Dishes clanked as they were moved around tables, accompanied by the hushed sound of taking. Lavish tapestries came to life above bright-painted tables and wooden chairs. It was stunning in its opulence, and almost impossible to connect with the hollow ruin she'd entered.

In the blink of an eye, people appeared—fifteen or more—seated at two long tables. Servants darted in and out of the hall, delivering and removing dishes with haste. Several adults sat at a high table at the head of the room. The children, varying in age, the oldest no more than fifteen years, were all clad in the most lavish of fifteenth-century attire.

Adelia's judgment told her this was not a special occasion. The room was far too empty for some grand event. It looked like they were partaking in an ordinary afternoon meal, though the vision outrivaled any simple lunch she had ever had, her senses sparked by a sweet and smoky aroma permeating the air, the smell of roasted meats triggered a muffled growl from her own stomach.

The children dined under the watchful eye of the adults. What was then considered a carefree childhood would no doubt be seen as controlled and formal by today's youth. Each detail was clear and distinct in her mind's eye: the slightest bend of a boy's tousled hair; the gleam in a girl's eyes; the sunlight as it played upon the curve of their cheeks. Their features were as lifelike as her own, and she could almost feel the warmth radiating off their bodies. Just a few steps across the room and she could touch them, though she dared not. They all ate in silence, each consumed by their own thoughts.

Her focus was drawn to a dark-haired boy, and she didn't need the whispers to tell her it was Richard; she could feel it down to her toes. She had waited years for this moment, and her heart thundered. It was like getting a university acceptance letter and being too terrified to open it. She scanned the room again, taking in each person one by one, savoring the self-induced torture of saving Richard for last. It reminded her of her childhood days, filled with anticipation at the prospect of tasting her mother's beautiful strawberry tart, that could only be experienced after she'd devoured a plate of brussel sprouts.

She watched the older girl, her eyes as dark as her hair. A beautiful young woman, even by today's standards, with smooth porcelain skin and dark inky lashes. And she was well aware of her beauty—something she had been praised for often. She was exquisite in all things, having the natural ability to be pleasing to all who were so fortunate to make her acquaintance. Her manners, by any measure, were impeccable, honed by years of etiquette befitting a girl of such a high-born station. Drawing from her research, Adelia recognized her as Isabel Neville, the oldest daughter to the Earl of Warwick and his wife Countess Anne de Beauchamp.

The resemblance to the woman seated in the prominent position at the head table was remarkable. This had to be the countess herself, eyeing her children and her other young charges with a disciplined glare. She was a beacon of model upbringing and a refined bloodline, raised to view her family's lineage as superior to most others, and her children would have been brought up in that mindset. These were the most notable people in the land. As was the custom, those such as the Nevilles would marry comparable nobility and continue to reign in wealth and standing.

Isabel, the daughter of the most powerful man, second only to the king, could not have been more than fifteen. She had been raised understanding her importance in the game of political prominence, and treated to the same reverence as a royal princess. This knowledge no doubt made her sure of herself, and certain that she was above everyone else. From an early age she would have been groomed to expect an advantageous marital match, one far more beneficial to her family and heirs than herself. Her happiness was inconsequential. Being the natural order of things, this would not have troubled the young Isabel.

Adelia read into the girl's thoughts as though she was curled up with a good book on a Sunday afternoon. Isabel's anticipation was palpable, wanting to know who would be her betrothed. To marry well and produce an heir was not only her duty but the central point of her existence. It would provide her with a life of wealth beyond measure.

While her life had revolved around her desire for a worthy marital match, she was still too young to understand the weight of such an expectation. Her happiness was not guaranteed—a loving and loyal husband not promised. She would be like every other bride in the upper echelon of society, a bargaining chip for others' gain—nothing more. It was a cruel reality that a young girl on the cusp of womanhood could never fully comprehend. Isabel's head was still filled with whimsical notions of love—tales of King Arthur and Guinevere—a sentiment she would soon find almost nonexistent in the world she was about to enter. Marriage would not be so far off for her, maybe a year or two at most.

Seated at her side was a young man with silken locks that glimmered like spun cloth of gold. The boy was handsome and, like Isabel, cognizant of this fact. He had a haughty countenance and an overconfidence that, even in a teenage boy, could be viewed as arrogance. As Adelia studied him, she had the gut feeling he was best taken in small doses. The boy was ambitious for himself, with the happiness of others of no concern. This could be none other than the king's own brother, George, Duke of Clarence.

Just then, her breath caught as a black form dipped out from behind his chair. A large black hound, its coat shimmering with the deep onyx depth of cooled lava. Its hollow-eyed gaze sent an uncomfortable ripple of cold through her frame, like an impending storm cloud that promised to break the calm with its turbulent fury.

As a man, George would betray just about everyone in his attempts to seize the crown from his brother, Edward IV. He was next in line to the throne until his brother had sons of his own, and would never be content with his position, always wanting more, going so far as to accuse his mother of adultery in order to declare his brother a bastard. Both he and the Earl of Warwick would stage a rebellion against Edward, and lose. Despite repeated forgiveness from his brother, he would go on to betray him one too many times, be branded a traitor and sentenced to death, meeting his end in the Tower of London, drowned in a barrel of Malmsey Wine.

Little did Isabel know that her dreams of securing a husband of importance would meet great misfortune, with George being that man. He ran his fingers through his locks, eyeing the young Isabel with affection. Despite his selfish ambitions, he did harbor strong affection for her, though he saw her as a prospect he was determined to win, both for her beauty and her inevitable inheritance. Even in matters of the heart, he always had an ulterior motive.

Adelia scanned the other figures at the table, her focus settling on a pencil-thin child. Not more than ten years old, the girl was sallow in complexion, her bronze-colored hair neatly arranged beneath a netted headpiece. She had an unassuming beauty about her and a gentleness of spirit, and she sat with her gaze lowered, barely allowing her fair lashes to reveal the mystery of her hazel eyes.

Movement beneath the table revealed the nervous tapping of her foot against the chair leg. Adelia sat up, sensing the child's natural propensity for anxiousness, a feeling she related to. The girl glanced through her lashes at the countess, somehow expecting to be scolded. Adelia was overcome with the notion that this child had spent more time being told what she was doing wrong than being praised. She was accustomed to being overlooked. Not only as she was the youngest but because of the unlucky fortune of her gender.

Adelia smiled in sheer delight at the realization that this was none other than Anne Neville, a historical figure who had captivated her for years. Her story had brought so many questions, and so few answers. As was the case with many female figures of this time, their stories were always shallow, with far less effort to chronicle their lives than males, unless she was someone who'd caused a great stir. Only then did the annals of history give her attention, and oftentimes the accounts of events were of a dim view.

As the youngest daughter of the Earl of Warwick, she would be heir to half of the family's fortune. In reality, whoever she married would control this vast fortune, as a woman's property was not her own in Anne's time. As her father would fall out of favor with Edward IV after a staged rebellion, she would find herself married off to the former Prince of Wales, the son of the usurped

Lancastrian king Henry VI and Margaret of Anjou, both former enemies of the Neville family.

As Warwick had switched sides, fighting against Edward now, the Lancastrian queen would barter the betrothal to her son as a promise of an alliance between the two houses. Being married to a former family enemy, there would be much distrust, and Anne would find no happiness in her short marriage. Yet fate would intervene. Her father would be killed at the Battle of Barnet, followed by her husband, killed by Edward IV's army at the Battle of Tewksbury. Anne would be taken prisoner, and later released to the care of her brother-in-law George and sister Isabel. More dark days would lie ahead for her, though. The ever-scheming George was determined to retain her inheritance for himself, keeping her hidden from anyone who would see her as a marital prize. Historical sources claim that she was made to dress as a servant to keep her presence secret. These had to be the darkest days of her young life but, once again, fate would deal her another unexpected turn.

It would be Richard, the Duke of Gloucester, youngest brother to Edward IV and George, who would discover her whereabouts and rescue her from her predicament. They would be married a short time later. As her husband's fortunes changed, Anne would find herself Queen of England.

Thinking of all the familial strife in the House of York, Adelia couldn't help but think that being an only child was not such a bad lot after all.

Do not despair, little girl, you shall be Queen of England someday.

In unbridled anticipation, she turned her attention to the raven-haired boy, blinking back a hint of tears. The black hound that had stood by George, now rested on the floor by his chair. It was as though it had declared him his master, bound to follow him wherever he would go. Indeed, he would never find himself without the company of that black shadow.

Richard, the future king of England, though at this young age he would never have imagined such a thing possible. As the fourth son of Cecily Neville and Richard Plantagenet, it would have taken an act of divine intervention for him to secure the throne himself. Little did he know the fortunes had their eye on him, and one day he would rule England as king. Edmund, his older brother, would be killed in battle with Richard's father, changing the succession to Edward, George, then him. After dethroning Henry VI, Edward IV would rule as king, marrying Elizabeth Woodville, and producing heirs of his own. After George's execution, Richard would find himself far closer to the seat of power, and when Edward IV died aged only in his early forties, fate would lay its sights on him.

Named Lord Protector, Richard would be charged to see that his brother's son, Edward, aged just twelve, took his rightful place upon the throne—a responsibility that showed the great trust Edward IV felt for his brother. Richard had never failed him. Despite years of bloody battles and political turmoil, he remained a true and loyal servant to his brother the king. As he prepared for his role, he would soon be met with opposition from the queen's family, and events would spiral out of control.

When a well-respected bishop stepped forward with claims that Edward IV had married another woman in secret before he wed Elizabeth, everything was turned around again. This claim rendered all of Edward's male heirs illegitimate, and ineligible to rule as king. In the end Richard would find himself the only remaining son with rights to the throne. Thus, he would become Richard III, king of England. While the story seemed straightforward, rumors abound against Richard. And these would endure for centuries, branding him one of the most reviled kings in England's turbulent history.

As she sat watching the intense young man, she was struck by his seriousness. A little younger than his brother George, it was easy to observe the dramatic difference between the two. Richard had a chivalric air, having grown up in a time where tales of heroic knights were alive. There was also a strong sense of duty about him. No surprise considering duty would become his entire purpose on earth—a calling he held tight to. In years to come "Loyalty Binds Me" would be his personal motto. Even so, Adelia sensed his uncertainty about a great many things. At his young age, he was far from having aspirations of being king, seeing himself as nothing more than the younger brother of the king, titled Duke of Gloucester, who would eventually be paired in an advantageous marriage. He had a life of wealth and privilege to look forward to, yet he would always be last in line, left with the scraps of power his other brothers discarded. Like any child of his age, even like Anne Neville, his standing in the family would leave him with an element of inferiority that would plague him throughout his life.

He sat there at the table, cloaked in an intensity that felt misplaced on a boy just in his teens. As he stared down at his plate, his dark eyes reminded Adelia of the bottom of an ink well. A rush of near euphoria gripped her, knowing who this young man was—the true figure behind all of the lore. To gaze upon him, so near to flesh as he could be, was something she could only have imagined. She closed her eyes and listened. His mind was racing, and he was homesick, missing his mother and sisters back at Fotheringhay Castle. He had looked forward to the day he would receive training as a soldier, for he wanted to prove himself as a strong and resilient man. In comparison to his brothers, he had always been smaller and weaker in stature, and felt the need to prove his worth. Still, being a boy, he missed his home, his mother, but perhaps his sister Margret most of all. Being so close to each other, these years of separation had not been easy. Adelia relished being able to feel the ache of his loneliness in her heart.

"There you are," Cassandra shouted as she stumbled through one of the ancient archways. "I have been all over this place, twice, looking for you. What are you doing just sitting here all alone?"

Adelia let out a defeated groan as the vivid image faded to nothing, disappearing into the atmosphere like a fine mist. Having waited so long for this moment, and with so many questions left unanswered, she wanted nothing more than to call Richard back. She released a sigh of resignation. Maybe she could bring him back again, but there was no guarantee. She shot Cassandra a look of disdain, which evoked a nervous smile in response.

Still, she knew many of her curiosities could not be solved by this young boy. Surely Middleham had more to reveal about his later life. If so, the whispers would dictate when those images came through. And not only here. She would have to follow Richard along a great many paths that may lead her to every corner of the country. His thoughts and ambitions were confined to the space and time in which he lived them. He could not tell her what he didn't yet know, even with Middleham Castle later becoming his great stronghold in the North. The fact that he returned here many times throughout his life gave her hope. He had once lived here as a child, learning the skills of a noble knight. Later, he returned as a man, his devoted wife by his side, bearing witness to the birth of his first child. By then he was an experienced soldier and a seasoned politician. This was the Richard she must find among the centuries of ghostly shadows in this castle. It would take luck, and wishing for that could prove challenging with her bumbling cousin lurking about.

Chapter Nine

Nearly forgetting that her cousin had asked her a question, she let go of her disappointment and turned to her. "My apologies, Cassandra, what did you ask?"

"Why are you here sitting all alone? I thought we were supposed to be exploring. Looking for some clues. Or have you forgotten?"

"No, I had not forgotten. I just needed a rest. Middleham is such a large place to traverse—" She caught herself the moment the word left her lips. *I should not have used traverse. Cassandra will think it too wordy.* Her cousin looked fatigued. Perhaps she needed to sit and rest herself. "Are you tired too? Did you walk the entire grounds?"

"Well, I tried," she answered. "One of the guides insisted on following me around in case I had questions, which I did not." She frowned. "He didn't listen, though, and became a nuisance, until I was finally able to shake him off and scoot over to a large tower." Her shoulders dropped. "That was a big mistake. I didn't like that tower. It's a sad place, if you ask me. Finally, I just gave up and came looking for you."

Adelia wasn't sure whether to address the fact that Cassandra had once again managed to make a man swoon without even trying, or ask about the tower. She decided the tower was far more important.

"Which tower? That one there?" She pointed toward the looming gray structure. Part of its roofline had crumbled over time, giving it a tilted appearance.

"Yes, that's the one." Her smile said she was pleased to have piqued Adelia's interest instead of annoying her even more.

"That's the Prince's Tower. Richard's wife gave birth to their only child there. It held their son's nursery."

"Well, it's sad," Cassandra said with no uncertainty, putting her hands on her hips, as if taking a stance.

"Will you take me over to it?" Adelia stretched out a hand to be helped off the stone she had been perched on for too long. Her body ached more from sitting than from wandering the castle grounds.

"I don't really want to go back there." Cassandra stared at her for a long moment, until it became clear that her resolve was starting to crumble. "Okay, fine! But if we see that pesky tour guide, you give him the shake off this time."

Adelia laughed. "You would be surprised how good I am at repelling men."

Giggling amongst themselves, the two women climbed through one of the narrow staircases before connecting to another passageway. They snaked their way along what might once have been the great corridors traveled by the Neville family, emerging into the massive courtyard. After a quick look around, they crossed the never-ending plush lawns, coming into the shadow of the tower.

The structure lacked any indication of its former grandeur as the living quarters of the Nevilles, or Richard and Anne later in their marriage. Now it stood like a tower of pale stones linked together by deteriorating mortar. Its state had become a topic of much debate in recent years. For safety reasons, the heritage association in charge of the grounds only allowed access to a small part, which was more than enough for Adelia.

She led the way up the remnants of the curved stone staircase that wound along an outer wall. Cassandra followed close behind, treading at Adelia's heel as though they were entering a haunted house, so near she could almost feel her breath on her back. She wanted to laugh at the way she acted, like a frightened child waiting for something to jump out and take her into its clutches.

After stopping on a small landing, framed by a rudimentary guard rail, Adelia looked below. Large blackened squares in the stone walls were hallmarks of the massive oak beams that would have supported the floors at each level.

"It must really have been something to live in a castle," Cassandra declared. "I often wonder if they would look upon our homes as luxurious because of the modern conveniences, or consider us paupers."

"You know, I think living in one of these old palaces, or even the grand country estates that dot this country, would be something magical. Just the three months I spent with my grandma at Hampton Court was like nothing I ever experienced. Still, I agree, they would probably think we were paupers. I am pretty sure I couldn't fit one hundred servants into my rented room at the manor." She almost nodded to herself, impressed by the appreciation she and Cassandra shared for old places with a colorful past. They were different in so many ways, yet in some things they were quite the same.

As they turned to climb to the next landing, Cassandra hesitated, scrunching her angelic face in discomfort. "I don't like the sadness here. It's just such a dreary place. Don't you feel it?"

Adelia didn't feel anything. Had the conditions been right, as was the case in the great hall, she felt sure this tower would have something it wanted to whisper to her. She gave a half smile to Cassandra, conveying her understanding. Though she didn't dare ask so early in their acquaintance, it was clear that Cassandra had a gift of her own, but to what degree she couldn't be certain. Such a thing wasn't easy to decipher. One thing was definite, she could feel the emotions of this space, and given its past, the energy of this tower was strong.

"This is the tower where Edward of Middleham died," she said. "You are right, there is much sadness here."

"Another Edward." Cassandra's words came laden with a hint of frustration. "Which one was he?"

"Edward of Middleham was the son of Richard and Anne. He was their only child. It is said that they were at Nottingham Castle, stopping over before coming here to visit him. A messenger came and informed them of his death after a short illness. Chroniclers of the day say they were both half mad with grief over his loss. It is believed that neither visited Middleham afterwards."

"That makes sense," Cassandra said with a slow nod. "When I first entered the tower, I picked up a great deal of happiness here. It felt safe, almost like coming home after a long journey. That soon faded into a hollow sadness, like my heart was broken and could never be made whole again."

"You can feel the loss—a mother's loss." Adelia traced her hands along the rugged stone walls. Even as tiny grit shards dug into her skin, she did not wince. "I suppose you don't have to be a mother to truly understand devastation to an infinite degree. It is unmistakable, that pain."

"Can we please go?" Cassandra begged, the corners of her eyes glistening.

Adelia looked at her with a mix of surprise and guilt, realizing she should not have forced her back into the tower. In retrospect, it was cruel to make her relive the pain of a grieving mother.

"Yes. Yes. I am s-sorry..." she stammered. "Let's go now."

On the trip down the stairs, it was Cassandra who led the charge, her desire to get as far away from the tower as her feet could carry her clear as day.

Just as they reached the last step, Adelia jumped back at the sight of a gangly red-haired boy drenched in freckles stepping out from behind the exit. His black-rimmed glasses held heavy lenses that made his eyes appear to be three times their actual size. It reminded her of looking at a bug under a microscope in her old high school science class. He smiled a large toothy grin, nearly salivating at the sight of Cassandra, whose muffled sigh at seeing her unwanted admirer was audible enough to be heard.

Adelia hesitated, thinking this would be the perfect opportunity to pay Cassandra back for ruining her time with Richard earlier. She could leave her cousin to be devoured by this little troll. She almost cackled like one of the witches in Macbeth at the thought of watching her squirm as he followed her around like a herding dog. Since meeting, she'd run hot and cold with her opinion of the girl. Sometimes, she liked her quite well—a person could admire many aspects of her personality—but most of the time she was an irritating hindrance.

The only thing that saved her was being here at Middleham Castle. Surrounded by the energy of Richard III, the overarching weight of loyalty felt culpable. Like a downpour, that sense of duty washed all of her devilish thoughts away. She had promised her support should the guide return, and just as Richard would do, she would ride into battle for her cousin.

She turned to Cassandra, reaching up to smooth a loose tendril of her golden hair from her face. Almost in slow motion, she traced her fingers along the smoothness of her cheek, then, in one swift motion, grabbed her hand and brought it to her lips. "Darling, this castle is so romantic. I could stay here forever just wrapped in your arms."

Clasping her cousin's fingers through hers, she pulled her along, passing the freckle-faced tour guide, his lips parted in disbelief.

Much to her surprise, he did not seem to be disappointed—just stunned.

When they were out of earshot, Cassandra pulled up, laughing. "What the hell was that?"

"Now he will leave you alone. He thinks we are lovers, and will be turned off from you for sure."

Cassandra jacked her shoulders almost to her ears. "I don't know about boys in Boston, but the guys in England would be more than happy with that prospect." She shook her head. "Now we are going to have that kid chasing the two of us."

"Damn it." Once again she had proven her utter lack of knowledge of men. "I wanted to do a little more exploring but I don't want to have to deck some idiot of a tour guide to defend your honor." She looked back the way they'd come. "Let's just get out of here. We can return another time.

"Aw, Adelia, you would defend my honor." As she sang this in glee, her voice echoed off the walls. "Thank you, cousin."

Realizing she was still holding her hand, Adelia let go and brushed her palms off on her skirt. She gave Cassandra a narrow-eyed glare, and her cousin smiled back.

As they exited the main gate on their way to the parking area, she chuckled. "You have to admit, even with my shabby acting, I pulled that off pretty well. I think he bought it."

"Yes, you did. For a second, I wondered if you'd forgotten we are related."

"Oh, I did not think about that, sorry. I probably freaked you out for a moment, huh?"

"It's okay, we got away. That is all that matters." This was conveyed in her usual calm and carefree voice. The car was just ahead. "The tour guide's tongue is probably still hanging halfway out of his mouth as we speak."

"I know, but I'm still mad. I wanted to come away with more information today. I have waited for a while to get back here but didn't accomplish much of anything."

"As you said, we can come back again. Besides, what exactly did you hope to learn from an empty castle?"

Her look of confusion reminded Adelia that they had never spoken of the Babington gift. If she doesn't have it, it's understandable why she would not comprehend my disappointment. It's clear that she felt something powerful enough to make her uneasy in the tower. Her normally jovial spirit became somber and subdued because something affected her, even if she wasn't aware of its origins on a conscious level. She wanted to ask her straight out, but doubted the girl would get *it*. By all accounts, she had no real ability to filter many of the thoughts that ran through her head, just blurting out what came to her, whenever it happened to cross her mind. Still, it might be worth trying.

"Sometimes, when I am in a location like Middleham Castle, I find myself able to see what the average person does not see."

"Like Sherlock Holmes?" Cassandra opened her car door and slid into the driver's seat.

Adelia went around and got into the car. "What?"

Cassandra's mouth hung open, as if waiting for clarity to arrive. "You know, how he explains his revelations to Watson as elementary?"

Adelia decided not to allow the girl to distract her further. "Have you ever had an experience? One that is hard to explain?"

"Like what?" Cassandra frowned, the scowl remaining fixed as she backed out of the parking space. She put the car into first gear and headed out onto the main road.

"I don't know... Heard things or saw things. A feeling that no one else does?" Even asking left her out of sorts. It would never be an easy subject to approach with anyone.

"Oh, the Babington thing," Cassandra said, without hesitation. She stared back at Adelia, her clear blue eyes full of innocence, as if the entire topic was as inconsequential as discussing the weather.

Adelia waved a finger, directing her to pay attention to the road. "You know about the Babington whispers then? You are a keeper of the secret."

"Yeah, I have known since I was about seven."

Her response was so nonchalant, Adelia wondered if she fully understood the concept. It wasn't as if being able to channel the energy of people who died centuries ago was a small deal.

"Seven? You figured it out when you were that young?" She found herself almost ashamed that she had not known about the whispers until she was twenty. Had her grandma not told her, she might still be in the dark about her gift. For years, she just thought she was an emotional wreck, prone to hearing voices. Before being told of her abilities, she was concerned that she might be going crazy.

When she thought about it, and how different they were, it came as no surprise that Casandra had picked up on her ability at such a young age. As for herself, she was far more guarded, with her cousin being unfiltered in many ways—far more receptive to accepting the things around her as they were. Unlike Cassandra, she questioned everything around her, so much that the lines between imagination and reality were irrevocably blurred.

"Well, at first, everyone just assumed I was imaginative," Cassandra said with a slow and easy countenance. "They thought I had an imaginary friend or something. Then there was a spell when my father thought we might have a poltergeist. Like some ghost had attached itself to me. He even went as far as having a local chaplain come in and cleanse the house. In time, I just figured it out on my own."

"What about your mother? If she is from the Babington line, she should have the gift too."

"If you knew my mother, you would know that she has never concentrated on anything long enough to really understand it. She is a vain sort, always consumed with her own life. Not really the type to concern herself with much else. I had a great aunt who explained it to me." She shrugged as she checked her rear-view mirror. "I just asked her one day."

Adelia couldn't hold back her curiosity. "Tell me, what was it like knowing about the whispers from such a young age?"

"I don't know. It's like a health condition, I guess. You just know you have it and you move on. It's not exactly a conversation piece, though. I don't go around blurting it out."

"No," Adelia agreed. "It is not something you readily share with the world, that is for sure."

"My aunt did," Cassandra said with a laugh. "Everyone thought she was looney. I didn't want to be lumped into that category, for sure. I am odd enough to most—I didn't want to add to my reputation by revealing that I have visions of dead people."

"My grandma told a great many stories too," Adelia said. "People always dubbed her an eccentric type."

"What about you? When did you figure it out?" She tapped the steering wheel as if playing a piano.

"It was only four years ago, when I came to England to stay with my grandma."

Cassandra's expression did little to hide her disbelief. "Why did it take you so long?"

"I am a terrible listener, with a soft spot for self-sabotage. I spent most of my younger years thinking I was going crazy, believing the voices and visions were a progression into madness. To be honest, I couldn't find a reasonable explanation outside being nuts."

"Well, I suppose, without someone to explain it to you, it would be easy to just assume that was the case. You sure missed out on a lot of juicy stories, though. I have always loved knowing what gossip is really true and what was false. Keeps things interesting."

Adelia chuckled. "Boy, does it ever." She smoothed down her skirt. "I never thought I would be such a busybody as I am now.

I have learned so much over the past few years. My visions have become so much clearer. Once the initial shock of channeling the whispers wore off, I learnt to concentrate on the details with more precision."

"I don't let the visions come through anymore," Cassandra said, nodding once in defiance. "As a child, I found them frightening. I only allow myself to hear and feel the emotions. I block out the visions completely."

Adelia looked at her in amazement. "You have learned how to do that?"

"I had to," she declared. "There is no other way. Every day, I am bombarded with everyone's thoughts and emotions, from both the living and the dead. It makes concentrating on my own life cumbersome enough—I just don't want to deal with the visions too."

Adelia stared at her for a moment, recalling her grandma's words of wisdom. "But those who have the gift cannot read the energies of the living."

"I can," Cassandra said. "I can read them just as if they were speaking directly to me. I can feel when you're frustrated. I can feel when you're excited. I can feel your emotions as well as I can my own."

Adelia stared at her in wide wonder, and Cassandra returned her stare, her face scribbled with the reality that she knew far more about her inner turmoil than she would have liked. Oh Lord.

"Yes, Adelia, you are a mess. Yet I love you, cousin, for all your knowledge and stupidity alike."

The ride home was far quieter, with Adelia's mind reeling at Cassandra's revelation. She marveled at the thought of her being able to read the inner thoughts of the living. *Have I that ability, as yet undiscovered? Sure, I can feel some degree of emotions in other people but nothing I would describe as anything more than intuition.*

She was a little unnerved at the realization that her cousin was privy to her own thoughts, as most had not been particularly kind where the girl was concerned. In what little time they had been acquainted, Cassandra was proving to be far more complex than she could have fathomed. She was beautiful, though not vain. Not particularly knowledgeable about her subject of study, yet her keen insight allowed her to navigate through the content unscathed. Last but not least, she was endowed with a gift of sight, which she regarded with lukewarm reception. The woman hardly acknowledged her gift, let alone sought to use it to her advantage. This was the thing Adelia found most confusing of all.

The day's events flashed before her. *Just what is Cassandra's presence supposed to mean in my life? Is it to bring intentional complexity or poignant clarity?* At the end of their second day together, she still had no idea.

After returning from their visit to Middleham Castle, Cassandra wanted to lie down, complaining of a dull headache she could not shake. Adelia knew that feeling all too well; the whispers often left her with a feeling of utter depletion. After taking a rest herself, she spent the remainder of the afternoon grading the last of her students' term papers for the semester.

That evening, for once, the house was somewhat quiet. Daniel had promised he would phone later. She thought it best to wait downstairs to be closer to the only phone in the house, so entered the front parlor, intending to scribble a few notes from the day.

Ross was reclining on one of the small couches, his feet propped up on a round pale-blue ottoman with gaudy gold fringe. His reading glasses had slipped down to the tip of his nose as he held a book way too close to his face. He mumbled to himself as he read, so lost in thought he barely noticed as she sat in a high-backed chair in the corner.

Without warning, she sneezed. The dusty ruins of the castle had played havoc with her sinuses most of the day. Ross lowered his book, looking surprised that he was no longer the room's only occupant. He produced a broad grin, which, coupled with his wiry gray hair standing up on his head, made him look...odd. Since the day she had met him, she could not recall a time when he ever looked put together. His personal style was one of utter disarray, with his shirts often misbuttoned, and his hair never combed. He always seemed to have more important things to worry about than a presentable appearance. She wondered if he'd donned this look in his working days. Before his retirement, he had taught classic literature, so his employer must have expected some established standard of dress. Then again, considering what an obstinate man Ross was, they may well have given up trying to enforce any such policy with him.

"I'm sorry. I didn't mean to interrupt your reading," she whispered, as though her hushed voice would make a difference having already disturbed him.

He leaned forward, looking as if he were about to share a secret. "What do you know about witchcraft?"

That stopped her in her tracks. "I'm sorry? Did you say witchcraft?"

He closed his book, keeping his page marked with his forefinger. "You see, Miss Grey,"—he pointed to the book with his other hand—"what I have here is a rare find. A copy of a book published in fifteen eighty-four. It's *The Discouerie of Witchcraft*, written by Reginald Scot."

"Really!" She sat straighter. "I don't think I'm familiar with it but I am intrigued just the same. Tell me more."

At that prompt, his face lit up like fireworks against the twilight sky. From her experience, he was used to being ignored, seen as a bit kooky for most people's taste, his disheveled façade giving the impression he was just a batty old man rambling nonsense. He reminded her of a dilapidated old building; uninteresting to a passerby, yet beneath his weathered exterior lurked a man with a deep understanding of the world. In truth, he was remarkable.

"It is a rare find indeed," he said, his excitement clear. "The original still exists, believe it or not. It was quite controversial at the time, so most of the copies were burned."

"Well, witchcraft was not exactly a widely accepted practice in fifteen eighty-four. I doubt owning such a book at that time was a safe thing to do." She could not imagine a person who would dare own a book like that in the sixteenth century. The persecution of women accused of being witches was almost a global epidemic then.

"What makes this particular book so unique is that it refutes witchcraft as a dark art. It claims it is really just a healing practice, practiced only by women of skillful intelligence. That they are apothecaries of the highest capability rather than practitioners of evil."

Adelia leaned forward in her chair. "A book that condones the practice of witchcraft as a form of medicine *and* promotes the intelligence of women. No wonder all the copies were burned. That would have completely gone against every ideology of the time. Wherever did you find such a jewel?" She got up and crossed the floor to have a closer look.

Her interest had him glowing so bright he could have rivaled Cassandra. He flipped through the pages of the rugged copy, pointing out a myriad of concoctions and practices.

"Paul found this copy at the antique store just the other day. I have no doubt it was hidden away for a very long time. Even though it isn't an original, the pages are quite fragile. This book has spent a great many years tucked away in some attic or priest's hole."

"Indeed." Adelia nodded her agreement. "This book would have been a one-way ticket to being burned at the stake or hung. It really is remarkable it ever survived, and in such good condition."

"Superstitious old fools," Ross spat with contempt. "Most of these remedies have been around for centuries, anyhow. There really isn't much in here that wasn't widely practiced as medicinal healing, long before it was written. Cavorting with the devil? Utter nonsense. Burning women and children alive for using garden herbs? I cannot stomach such stupidity."

"Those were sad times to be sure. As much as I love to learn about the past, I am grateful I did not live in those days." Especially as a woman...who hears the whispers.

"Oh, but our time is not so different," he said, shaking his head with sadness. "We still do horrible things to people. We are reluctant to admit it but we've not changed entirely. People are still enslaved because of their bloodline. In our very lifetime, we have seen people persecuted for their faith. Just because we like to *think* we have evolved, it does not mean we can say we have. Every cruelty we name in the time of these buffoons still exists to this day, in some form. Perhaps the players are different but the injustice is still happening."

She nodded again. "We do like to think we would act differently if we had lived back then."

Ross's cheek dimpled above a crooked smile, then he let out a heavy sigh. "Yet the truth is we are here talking about these injustices—ones that still exist to this day—and not one of us is doing anything to change them. The only difference is that perhaps we have evolved in our thinking, but years from now we'll look back and think we were all idiots."

"I would like to think we haven't lost our humanity. I hope not." A wash of sadness almost overcame her, as though she had connected with something of great distress in the room.

Ross closed the book. "If we do lose our humanity, tell me which of our personal qualities is so good to replace it?" He looked across the room, as if waiting for some divine voice to provide an answer.

They sat in silence for a long moment, the conversation weighing heavy.

"I shall give you something for a spell. What is it you need?" he asked, lightening the mood as he shifted from somber to the giddy elation of a child. He was such an unpredictable man.

"A great many things," she answered, laughing to herself. "I would not even know where to start."

"Well, you don't need intelligence. You have that in abundance." He thrummed his finger against his stubbled chin. "Beauty? No, definitely not a problem. Oh, wait, I have it! Wait right here."

He hopped up and dashed out of the room. Adelia listened to the trample of his feet as he ran down the hallway toward the back of the house. In no time, he returned with a palm full of leaves, varied in color and shape.

"You need love. That is the only thing you are missing. Don't worry, I have the remedy for such a conundrum right here."

"Love?" She couldn't hold in a nervous laugh. The fact that her shambled love life was clear to him, having never formally spoken on the matter, concerned her.

"Lavender, used by the Victorians," he said as he placed a fresh-cut sprig into her cupped hands. "Basil, a favorite of the Romans. Oh, and spearmint, the revenge of Persephone." He looked at her with hesitation. "I stopped short of saffron. The Egyptians used it as an aphrodisiac. I didn't think we needed to go quite that far."

"Yes,"—she squared her shoulders, aware of the heady scent emanating from Ross's gift—"I think we should take this in moderation."

With his pride at his herbal matchmaking attempt clear, he grabbed up the book and flipped through its pages before landing on one. "It says here you carry these on your person, or crush them up in food or drink." He looked at her, then at the pile of vegetation. "Perhaps you should do both."

Just as she was about to explain that her love life wasn't that bad—a complete lie—the phone in the hall rang. A welcome interruption. She sprang to her feet and rushed out to the gossip table, tucked into a private nook under the stairs.

Daniel's voice on the other end of the line set all the world to rights. She wanted to share about the day at Middleham Castle and about Cassandra having the Babington gift, but she had to be careful so spoke in hushed tones to keep the conversation as private as one could in a bustling house.

He listened as she recounted the day. It had been a long while since his last visit to Middleham Castle. He'd been there once with his father but never returned. As a professor, most of his work was focused on the Tudor eras. However, as a true scholar, he'd dabbled in just about all of England's history. Middleham did not hold a significant Tudor connection as many other palaces during their reigns, and Adelia took a certain delight that, for once, she was the one to educate him on a topic. Throughout their relationship, it seemed to always be the other way around.

Even if he knew more about the Plantagenets then he let on, he didn't say. He just let her babble on, knowing that it brought her joy. She had to make a concerted effort to curtail her rambling, aware that long-distance calls were not cheap. Even so, she had barely let him get a word in during the entire conversation. She took a breath, almost snuggled into the receiver, and asked him how his day had been.

"Now that the semester is over, I have a little time at my disposal," he said, sounding somewhat nervous. "I was thinking of coming up there to visit you. I know you have a lot going on with Cassandra and your research, and I will understand if you don't have time."

She hesitated for a moment, toying with the coiled phone cord. They had not seen each other in person since that day in Oxford. It was clear that her leaving had hurt him, and he hadn't called for quite a while. Things were starting to heal but it was slow and unsteady. The prospect of seeing him again made her nervous. There was no sense of where either of them stood in each other's lives, and she wondered if he might try to convince her to return to Oxford. No matter how much she missed him, she did not want to leave. Not yet. However, no matter how much conflict she felt at the idea of his visit, she did not have the heart to deny him. That would only add salt to the wound she had created.

"Oh, Daniel, I would love to see you," she said, trying to sound as cheerful as she could.

"Really?" His excitement was palpable. "When should I come up?"

The enthusiasm in his voice told her he had not known how she would react. Likely, he had prepared himself for rejection once again. It grieved her to know that every decision she had made for herself, always came at a greater cost to Daniel. Through no fault of his own, he was at times ill-positioned in her quest to find herself.

"As a matter of fact, we were thinking of visiting Pontefract Castle soon. Maybe you could come along. You are more familiar with its history than I. You could help fill in the blanks for me on a few things there." She adopted the strategy that had worked many times before: divert his attention. He was the type of person who loved a mystery to solve or a project to take on. If she played her cards right, she could keep him focused on the work at hand and buy herself more time before the topic of their relationship came up. Perfect.

"Pontefract," he said. "It is a favorite of mine. It is a pretty beat-up old ruin but I think you should be able to find something of interest just the same."

"I could probably arrange a room here at the manor for your stay."

"I think I would like that very much," he said after a moment's pause. "It certainly sounds like I won't be lacking in entertainment if I stay there. Just don't feel pressured, Adelia. I can easily find a place in town to stay if it would be more comfortable for you."

"Daniel, I honestly would love for you to stay here. I really would not want it any other way." The truth was there weren't a lot of options for him elsewhere, with only one inn in the nearby town, and though not far, it would only prove to be an inconvenience in the long run.

"Okay then," he agreed, much more cheerful. "I will make arrangements and come up in a few days' time."

"How long would you like to stay?"

"I have all summer, Adelia. I will stay as long as you like. When I become a distraction, you can send me packing back to Oxford."

She almost sighed with relief. In truth, she wanted to see him but there was a tremendous amount of work to be done in this short summer. To date, she had not made discernible progress, and Cassandra wasn't proving much of an assistant. Given the fact she had no knowledge of anything Richard III had ever done, having Daniel around for a short stay would be helpful. Yet, she wasn't convinced she could keep focused with him here. He always had a way of making her emotions go haywire, though he had at least given her a way out if things became too uncomfortable.

Chapter Ten

Adelia studied herself in the tarnished gold-framed mirror, tucking a lock of wayward hair back into her polished waves. She turned to her side and brushed a speck of dust from her dark-green dress, then straightened the black belt around her slender waist. Daniel was due to arrive any minute, and even though she had prepared all day, she was anxious.

Come on, Adelia, you knew you would have to do this someday.

A burst of excitement and apprehension flushed through her at the sound of a car pulling up the gravel drive. She had done everything she could to prepare herself in the days leading up to his arrival but the thought of seeing him for the first time was proving harder than expected. When the engine cut, she gripped the door's iron latch, drew in a deep breath, then pulled open the wooden mammoth before stepping out onto the old stone stoop.

He eased himself out of the car and leaned against its hood, shooting her his familiar brilliant smile as he surveyed the historic surroundings. His eyes gleamed as though he had just entered the gateway of another era. Even if she couldn't channel his thoughts, like Cassandra, she knew just what he was thinking. Middleham Manor had the same effect on her. It always felt suspended in time, unwilling to concede itself in any way to modern progress—a vessel of the past, rife with harbored memories.

She moved off the front step, smiling at his reaction, and leaned on the opposite side the warm hood. "Welcome, Doctor Brown, to the prestigious Middleham Manor. I trust your drive up was a pleasant one?"

"It was, thank you," he replied, with a smile as wide as the Thames River. "This place is magnificent. Where on earth did you find such a relic?"

"I'm glad you like it. I really do love it here." In the pale dusk of the evening, she could not help but notice the dazzling blue of his eyes. She loved how they took on a new level of brilliance every time she saw them. It reminded her of the first day she'd met him, back at Hampton Court. They had captivated her—drawn her into him—so much so the world faded to a blur. Daniel was still every bit as handsome as she remembered, and more so now after their time apart. None of the images of him that had played upon her mind in the last few months came close to the one of him standing before her now.

"Thank you for making all the arrangements for me to stay here," he said, returning her searching stare tenfold. "You could have arranged for me to stay elsewhere, and I would not have been offended. I would have respected your decision either way.

"Don't be silly. I would not have you stay in town. It wouldn't make sense. It is better all the way around if you just stay here with Cassandra and me."

"Just the same, I am grateful. I am as excited about staying here as I am to see you."

She smiled as a warm flush came to her cheeks. The conflict raging inside her was indescribable. On one hand she was overjoyed to be near him—his close proximity made her heart heavy with longing—yet, there was no clear name that could be placed on their relationship. It was like some form of purgatory of the heart, one she was to blame for creating. They existed in some nameless space, one most uncomfortable for two people who lived their lives by definitive plans. Were they friends? Were they lovers? Were they nothing? This time with him would be hard. Harder than she might have imagined, but it was far too late to turn back now.

He pushed himself up from the hood, opened the back side door, and slung a few heavy-looking brown traveling bags over his shoulder. Adelia offered to help but he politely declined.

She pulled away from the hood and walked toward the front door, with Daniel following a few steps behind. Inside the foyer, she paused, knowing he would want to take in the beautiful old entryway complete with its carved wooden staircase. He heaved the bags onto the floor, and she didn't miss his soft gasp as he stepped forward and turned in a circle, taking in the ancient splendor of the house. While Middleham wasn't as opulent as some of the grand treasure houses and vast country estates in England, what made it so interesting was its patchwork of changes over hundreds of years—like an antique shop, with no rhyme or reason to the contents, its unique finds jumbled together, waiting for the right person to discover gold among the straw.

The sound of bickering came trailing from one of the side rooms. Adelia let out a heavy sigh.

"It's Laura and Ross." She groaned through an exasperated grin. "Prepare yourself."

He had already been apprised well before his arrival of the cast of characters who dwelled at the manor.

"Here, Ross, let me bandage you up before you bleed to death," Laura said, grabbing his wounded arm. "Wait, on second thought, carry on."

"Get off me, woman. I would rather be nursed by Grendel's mother."

"Nice Beowulf reference," Daniel whispered as he leaned in.

Adelia did her best to contain her laugh, more caught up in the familiar scent of his cologne than the banter of the manor's owners. She looked down at her arms, savoring the sweet torture of goosebumps rippling along her skin. Even after four years together, he still had that effect on her. She had forgotten such unexpected sensations.

"Shut up, you old goat," Laura screeched as they passed Adelia and Daniel, barely noticing their existence. "I will clean it in the kitchen."

"Fine, Laura..." Ross called out with his usual extended pronunciation.

Daniel left brow arched. "Why does he say her name like that?"

"It's just a thing he does. You get used to it after a while." Even though she was used to it, she knew it had to be entertaining to Daniel.

"I see why you like it here," he said, looking around. "This place *does* hold a certain kind of charm."

"Actually, I'm not sure how much longer I can stay. Laura just told me today that she and Ross plan to put it on the market."

"We should buy it," he said, in a tone that was difficult to read.

"Buy it?" She laughed. "What on earth would you and I do with a medieval manor?"

She didn't want to state the obvious but, currently, Daniel and she were not even an official couple. Despite that minor detail, she barely had enough saved to buy a car. No, she was a long way from being able to buy a house, and even farther from purchasing a bed & breakfast.

"I am ready for something different in my life," he announced. "A new direction." He looked around the foyer again. "Perhaps trying my hand as an innkeeper-slash-landlord might be just what I need. I could always work on the writing I have been meaning to do for the past decade."

"Have you eaten today? You always get reckless and impulsive when you are hungry. Perhaps you are a bit woozy from the long drive up," she teased.

He shot her a cheeky grin, grabbed his bags, then stepped further down the hall and peered around the corner into the formal sitting room.

"Would you look at that fireplace," he said. "Now, you don't see that every day." He pushed his bags against the wall and entered the room, leaving Adelia trying to figure out how the conversation had taken such an odd turn. After a second or two, she followed him in.

As he walked around studying the array of antiques, she was reminded of just how much she'd missed him these past few months. They had talked on the phone on a frequent basis but nothing compared to him being here in the flesh. She missed his scent, his mild cologne and shaving soap, and the way the light played upon his burnished brown hair. His movements, also, so slow and sure. Now she thought about it, it was clear that she was still every bit in love with him today as when she fell for him during their time at Hampton Court.

She had given up so much when she'd left him. So much. He was an essential part of her being, his voice etched into the fine grains of her soul. She wanted him back but feared the damage was irreversible. Besides, she was building a life here in Middleham and he still had a promising future in Oxford. His joking about becoming an innkeeper aside, he would never want to give up the life he had worked so fiercely to build. She could not expect him to do that anyway.

There were so many reasons a relationship between them would not work. Most were her own doing. However, that did not numb the gnawing at her heart of wanting to be with him. In all the world, he was the only man she desired.

She had to look away, the hot swell of tears burning her eyes. What another mess you've gotten yourself into. He will never want you back anyway.

"Are you okay?" he asked, snapping her back to reality. He'd stopped his exploration and was staring at her. "You got a little quiet there."

"It's just good to see you, Daniel." She smiled, pushing her emotions back into place.

"I feel the same."

Her heart jumped a little, his sincere tone making her think he had read her thoughts, as though he knew just what she wanted— No...needed to hear.

Just as the words escaped his mouth, the delicate glow that was Cassandra entered the room. She flopped onto one of the small couches, draping a new copy of a fashion magazine across her silky knees, blissfully unaware she had interrupted a serious moment. Her ability to read the energy of the living must have been on hiatus for the night.

"Daniel," Adelia said, "this is my cousin Cassandra."

Now aware of his presence, Cassandra jumped to her feet, holding out her hand to him. "How wonderful it is to finally meet you after all that I have heard."

He gave Adelia a little wink, no doubt flattered at being a topic of conversation between the two women. Ever the gentleman, he extended his greetings back to Cassandra.

"Is this Donegal Tweed?" She plucked the collar of his jacket, inspecting the fabric with care."

"Actually, it is," he said, following up with a shocked laugh.

"That's a good herringbone. Handwoven too."

His brow rose at her acute observation.

Adelia could not help but notice how unmoved by Cassandra's physical appearance he was as he engaged in the polite exchange. In between each bit of conversation, his focus switched from the newcomer to her. It was like he couldn't take his eyes off her for more than a second or two. Each time she caught his gaze, the magnetic energy between them strengthened, catching her breath. She wanted to touch his skin, feel the warmth of his hand in hers, and experience the familiar feelings once so common between them.

She watched as Cassandra's abilities switched back on and the realization that she was intruding on a serious moment swept across her face. Next second, she whipped up her magazine, gave a little yawn, then declared that the hour was late and she would be off to bed. Adelia laughed to herself as her cousin fled the scene. If only I had her gift, I might spare myself a great amount of trouble.

"I can show you to the room Laura has reserved for you," she said, wanting to change the mood, all of a sudden overwhelmed by Daniel's presence.

"That would be great," he said, moving to the bags he'd left outside.

His room was located just down the hall from hers. Since he was only expected for a short while, and he said he was not particular, Laura had set him up in one of the rented rooms. It was a busy season for the Bed & Breakfast and she wanted to keep the suites open for couples.

Adelia opened the door and turned the light on but stepped back to allow him move into the room. He dropped his bags onto the wooden floor, the resounding thud filling the interior. She waited as he walked its length, examining his temporary quarters. It was similar to most of the other rented rooms, all with substantial open spaces, polished oak floors, and high ceilings. Like hers, it had a big old fireplace with a carved wooden mantle, though they no longer worked and had been closed off with beautiful hand-painted cast iron doors. Tall leaded windows, their trim painted over year after year, lined the far wall, and large old woven rugs dotted the center of the floor, the corners tattered like a war-torn banner Richard III would have displayed on his triumphant return from battle.

After a minute or two, Daniel stepped back out to where she waited in the hall. His wide smile told her he was pleased with his accommodation. "Thank you," he mouthed.

He took her hand, and she watched as their fingers entwined. No words were spoken between them as she allowed the heat of his touch ease its way up through her arm. She raised her gaze, looking at him through her heavy black lashes. Baby-blue brilliance stared back through the gold-wire frame of his glasses. His familiar scent permeated the air, filling her senses with all the sensations she had found herself pining for these last few months.

She remained still and silent as he leaned closer. He seemed unsure of himself, which was something she had not witnessed in a long time—not since the early days of their relationship, back when they were both naive and inexperienced. It was like they had been transported to that time. This unrelenting bond between them still existed, only now it was cloaked in some haze of insecurity, like a raging fire in a hearth, detained behind a protective grate.

Even in the midst of that, Daniel had always been the one willing to take a risk. With his lips no more than an inch from her cheek, the warm wisp of his breath caressed her skin. Then he hesitated, as if allowing her the chance to pull away, but she parted her lips, anticipating the sensation of his mouth on hers. The sweet pressure of his lips melted her down like chocolate in a warm pot—exquisite—like silk bedsheets against bare skin on a warm summer night.

His eyes stayed closed as he eased away, as though his dream might fade at any moment.

"Those are the lips I have kissed a million times in my dreams." He blinked, resuming eye contact. "I have missed you."

"And I you," she whispered. She cast a nervous glance down the hall to see if anyone had spotted them, then squeezed his hand a little tighter, not wanting to let go. All she could think about was how much she wished he would pull her into his room and shut the door.

She wanted nothing more than to feel every inch of his skin against hers. To awaken with the soft tickle of his breath on her neck and his loving body pressed close. Yet even in the modern world of nineteen sixty-one, mindsets were still old fashioned.

Even now, to be unwed meant that appearances must be considered. They may have broken conventional rules in the past but, here at Middleham Manor, it was disrespectful.

As she lay in bed that night, she found herself crushed under the weight of desire for Daniel. The electricity in his kiss told her that despite the months of doubting, deep down he still loved her. She didn't deserve to still have his affection, having done so much to warrant him walking away and never turning back. Why did he stay? He could so easily find some beautiful girl like Cassandra. One who would dazzle him with her radiant good looks and effortless charm. What do I have that makes him stay?

When she rolled to her side, she made out the dried pile of leaves resting on the bedside table—the ones Ross had given her a few days ago. She smiled, unsure why she had kept them. Maybe, subconsciously, they had given her hope.

"Witchcraft," she said into the darkness, giggling, then ducking her head under the covers in embarrassment at the thought of it.

Yes, that's it! Some sort of witchcraft resides in me. Some source of power I wielded, dangerously. In ignorance. I tossed Daniel's love away, without a care, only to summon him back at will, always with the promise of something, held just out of his reach. Something he had to give his soul to attain.

She smiled at herself, almost flabbergasted at her utter lack of rationale. Had she been born four hundred years ago, she would be burned at the stake. She could almost feel the hot embers billowing down on her like the heavy stones of a falling temple.

This time, she laughed out loud, hoping Cassandra did not hear her. She will think I have gone mad. Whatever made Daniel return so willingly, I am grateful for this second chance. Be it a pile of herbs from the kitchen or some mythical magician's wind, it is welcomed.

Chapter Eleven

A weary-eyed Adelia descended the steps, bound straight for the kitchen. All the excitement of Daniel's arrival had left her sleep deprived, and the after effects were apparent this morning. Had the loud rumble of her empty stomach been more cooperative, she might have allowed herself a little longer in bed. Her ravenous belly had no such mercy to offer when the smell of rashers came wafting up the stairs.

As she dipped through the kitchen doorframe, she gave a startled gasp at the sight of Daniel seated at the table. The sound caught his attention, drawing his absentminded stare away from the contents of his tea cup. When he looked up, she would have to be a fool not to notice the sudden glint in his eyes. The only other people who lit up like that when she entered the room were her parents. But that's what she was, an absolute fool for ever letting this man go. She hated her stupidity. While she had spent so much time trying to prove her intellect, she couldn't deny, where matters of the heart were concerned, that there was such a thing as being an intelligent idiot.

"Have you been up long?" she asked, mustering up a cheery tone that shielded the internal lashing she had just given herself.

"I helped Laura with breakfast. The guests had to get an early start. Very nice people. A shame they couldn't stay a few more days." He gave the platter on the counter a rueful smirk. "Mind the rashers—I may have overdone them."

"You always do," she said, approaching the counter and studying the mound of over-crisped meat. "Lucky for you, when I am famished, I am not picky."

She picked up one of the stacked plates, selected a few of the least-leathery strips, and moved over to seat herself opposite him.

"Have you seen Cassandra yet?"

"No," he said, taking a slow draw from his cup, swallowing, then placing it back onto the saucer. "Is she much of an early riser?"

"Not particularly, but she is somewhat punctual when I give her a departure time." She took a bite, or rather an attempt at one, from a strip of bacon that resembled a strop a barber might use to sharpen his razor. Saying these were overdone might be putting it mildly. She felt like a vulture pecking away at a carcass that had been sundried for a week.

"Tell me, what is your opinion so far of your new assistant?" He leaned in, as though he were a gossip columnist in a busy tearoom.

She placed the remainder of the rawhide back on her plate, and met his intense gaze. "For starters, she is not dumb. Flighty and completely uninterested in the work I am doing, yes, but she is a quick learner and absorbs things well. She could tell you anything you want to know about jewelry—Anglo-Saxon to the present day—and she knows fabrics as well as I know the Tudors."

"I gathered that much the other night when she examined my jacket." He chuckled. "Do you think she is getting any enjoyment out of this summer?"

"Honestly, I do, or at least I think she will. She looks at most of these excursions as a bit of a holiday. She isn't as enamored with castles and churches as I but she likes the exploration just the same." She glanced behind, just to be sure her cousin wasn't lurking at the entrance. "As much as she gets in my way, I can't deny that she has an endearing quality. She has a way of abruptly disconnecting me from my seriousness. Whether I care to admit it or not, I need that sometimes."

Daniel's expression showed pure satisfaction, and she wasn't sure if it was happiness that she had come to this revelation, or because Cassandra was the taste of her own medicine she deserved. Switching gears, they went on to discuss the day's plans, involving a return to Middleham. She was looking forward to the excursion—a lot more than the remains of the charred breakfast before her. After a halfhearted attempt to finish it, she headed back upstairs to get ready.

She sat on the edge of her bed with a wrapped parcel on her lap, smiling at the Boston return address label on the brown paper covering. Using her fingernails, she pried at the tape until one corner came loose, then pulled away the wrapping and slung it to the floor. When she lifted the box top off, her heart warmed on seeing the note of congratulations from her parents inside. Her mother's unmistakably neat handwriting brought another smile.

Best of luck on your work this summer. Here is a little something to remind you that you are always in our hearts.

Love,

Mom and Dad

She tugged a small piece of tape from the tissue paper, excited at the sight of a new dress. Her mother knew her size and she had no doubt it would fit. She pulled it from the box and held it out in front of her. It was a fashionable sleeveless shift, in a deep mustard shade trimmed in white. She pulled it tight to her frame and stepped over to the vanity mirror by the window. Much to her surprise, her mother had chosen something a few inches shorter than anything she had ever owned. Her cheeks burned at the sight of her knobby kneecaps peeping out below the hemline. Though the dress wasn't as short as the usual attire Cassandra wore, for her, this was a real departure from the norm.

With care, she drew the zipper down the back and slid the new dress over her silk slip. She contorted herself as she pulled the zipper back up, catching a stray lock of hair in the last effort. Once she'd managed to wrangle the tendrils free, she chuckled to herself about all the effort it had taken to put on the darn dress.

She checked herself in the mirror. Her arms looked long and sleek, making her feel a little bare in the sleeveless dress, so she chose an onyx-colored cardigan from her wardrobe to cover them, tossing it over her purse on the bed. She pulled at the ends of her hair, settling it along her shoulders, then stood back. The contrast of her mocha locks against the rich yellow was complimentary. Though this was a bold choice, her mother, like Cassandra, had an eye for current fashion. For a long moment, she stared at herself in the mirror, her confidence growing. Is this what Cassandra feels like every day? Something about this dress made her feel sophisticated—ready to take on the day with fervor. After one more glance in the mirror, she grabbed her things and headed downstairs.

The plan was set. She, Daniel, and Cassandra would return to Middleham to give it another lookover. As she descended the narrow wooden staircase, she was surprised to only see Daniel waiting in the foyer. She stopped at the last step, hand on the carved newel post, returning his smile.

"You look wonderful," he said, his eyes glinting with the reflection of the dress's deep-yellow hues.

"Hasn't Cassandra been down yet?" she asked, groaning inside. She should have known, there was no such thing as time in Cassandra's world. It was more of a suggestion than an obligation for her cousin.

"She was down a little bit ago but insisted that you and I go alone today, as she is hoping to catch up on some phone calls and letter writing. I got the sense that Middleham wasn't exactly her cup of tea, if you know what I mean?"

Adelia looked back up the stairs, finding it hard to believe Cassandra would opt to spend the day in a quiet old manor house writing letters. That would be the perfect day for herself, but Cassandra was much too restless to be cooped up inside for any length of time. No, she was up to something, and it didn't take a scientist to see it for what it was—a devious plot to give her and Daniel time together.

A nervous flutter took her by surprise. She and Daniel had been together for nearly four years as a couple before their break up. They had spent countless hours together exploring museums, going to art galleries, and visiting historical sites. A trip to Middleham was nothing out of the ordinary for them to do together. Still, she couldn't help but feel that things were different now. What if he wants to talk about our relationship? She wasn't sure she had an answer. She'd need a distraction, just in case the subject came up. Not a problem—Cassandra wasn't the only one good at diverting male attention.

She slid into the passenger seat, fumbling as she placed her things on the floor. Daniel eased down the gravel drive, beginning the short journey to the village of Middleham and the magnificent castle at its edge.

"It does seem a shame that your love for gloomy castles wasn't inherited by your cousin," he said as they approached the town.

Something in the way he'd led the conversation back to Cassandra caught her off guard. She supposed it was to be expected; her cousin had a way of dominating every other man's thinking.

She sighed, leaning her head back against the seat. "Cassandra doesn't know much about the time period I am studying, so I basically have to teach her as we go. As I said, she is a quick learner."

"I thought she was a history major. She doesn't know about the Wars of the Roses? It is probably one of the most important times in English history."

"Dates and events are not her forte. As you know, she has a soft spot for textiles and jewelry. She loves anything from the Georgian era on, but her knowledge extends well beyond that. She could tell you just about anything you want to know about Victorian fashion. If you want to see her eyes light up, ask her the difference between Bucks Point and English Midland lace."

His brow lifted above a crooked smile. "Boy, that certainly makes a lot more work for you, doesn't it?"

"Tell me about it." She smoothed her dress across her lap, all too aware of her naked knees. "On the bright side, if you want to venture anywhere off limits in a dark and gloomy castle, Cassandra is pretty good at distracting tour guides."

"What does that mean?" he asked, a corner of his mouth quivering with amusement.

"Oh, come on, Daniel!" she said, unable to hold back her frustration. "You can't act like you haven't noticed that my cousin is stunningly beautiful and entrances every man she comes upon." Deep down, she couldn't help but wonder just how much he had noticed.

His shoulders went up in defense. "Cassandra is an attractive girl, but I think you're overexaggerating her power to 'entrance men,' as you put it."

She glared at him. "She has been here just over a week and has managed to disrupt every attempt at work I have made. We go to the library, and all the beady little eyes peering at us through the shelves makes my skin crawl. We visit a town hall to search the archives, and I can barely concentrate enough to read because some pesky little clerk insists on ogling Cassandra and making small talk about the weather. Middleham Castle and Barnard Castle had us stalked mercilessly by tour guides. In all truth, I couldn't be more grateful for the girl deciding to stay back this morning."

Daniel shot her a bemused look, and she scowled back at him in return. If she were being truthful, Cassandra had done nothing to go out of her way to attract the attention of her endless admirers. In fact, she seemed so accustomed to this appalling behavior that she barely paid it any mind. It was difficult to imagine, almost as if the girl was some sort of glamorous movie star hounded by photographers everywhere she went. In her own world, she could not begin to fathom how irritating such an existence would be, yet Cassandra had become numb to the whole thing. Her presence was proving a distraction, to say the least. Even so, she couldn't help pity her cousin, so long as she wasn't distracting the man at her side.

"My, I haven't seen this place since I was a teenager," Daniel exclaimed as they passed through the center of the village and the castle came into view. Traffic was light, and in just a minute or two they were pulling into the heritage society's car park outside the castle gates.

It was nearly opening time, and a misty morning fog still hung low. Daniel exited the car and leaned against the hood as Adelia pulled her cardigan from the backseat. As she stepped out, the heavy blanket of damp air brought goosebumps to her skin. She ran her hands along her forearms to chase the chill away, then slid into the sleeves.

They passed through the old gateway and into the castle's inner bailey. The lush green grass in the courtyard sparkled with misty droplets as the sun burned through the dark clouds. Adelia surveyed the sky. Darker gray clouds hovered just off in the distance, telling her their time here might be interrupted by rain. At least Middleham still had a few nooks that could serve as sufficient shelter should the weather turn bad.

"My lady," Daniel said, with a smile in his voice as he looked over the small souvenir map he'd picked up at the admission desk. "This is where I leave you. I shall do some exploring on my own and we can catch up later."

Something in her fluttered at this gesture. He knew her so well.

As she surveyed her surroundings, she considered returning to the shell of the great hall. With any luck, she might be able to pick up where she had left off with Cassandra the other day. Just as she went to step in that direction, something pulled against her shoulders, as if she had been tethered by some invisible rope. Her instinct was to fight against the unseen force, and she leaned against the pull, but it proved too great and she had no choice but to go with it, finding herself propelled in the direction of the Prince's Tower. She moved at a steady pace until she rounded the corner of the tower and a sudden jerk brought her to an abrupt halt.

She stood for a moment, somewhat breathless and a little light-headed. A whirring sound came from all directions, and her ears perked up trying to make sense of it. Her vision blurred, and she leaned against the tower's cold stone wall for support, fearing she might black out. Engulfed in a cloudy haze, her body caught in a gentle sway, she watched as the gray gloom of the morning yielded to bright rays of sunlight. She blinked several times to adjust to the sudden change, then, without warning, she sensed that she was not alone. Taking care, she shifted her weight to rest her back against the wall. Then she saw him.

Richard leaned against the edge of the tower, part-hidden in the shadows, watching as his little boy ran laughing through the lush grass of the inner courtyard. His merry cackle echoed off the high walls as he ran square into the open arms of his mother, burying himself in her skirt folds. Anne knelt and showered little Edward with a flood of kisses. Richard could never remember such real affection from his own mother. In certain company, such a display of love, especially toward a male child, might be considered improper for a lady of Anne's station. Boys were supposed to be raised as warriors, not lovingly held by their mothers, lest they be made soft. Yet, Richard felt none of these old ideas in his heart as he watched his wife and son play. Every single problem he had, and right now he had plenty, disappeared with the ringing of his son's laughter on this sunny morning.

He could not help but watch his wife; she was so beautiful dressed in joy. A pale copper lock of her hair had escaped her headdress and waved free in the wind. Her gentle frame was like a delicate reed on the edge of a tranquil pond, and her inner beauty matched with her outer magnificence, making her flawless in every way.

His love for Anne knew no bounds, and he could fully under-stand the security his son felt in her arms. He felt the same way. The whole of England could be set ablaze outside but the sanctuary of her embrace could wash all the mayhem away. When the burden of his duties became overwhelming, her gentle touch reassured him that all in the world could be set to right. She always knew how to save him from himself. As the darkness crept into his soul, it was Anne's voice, light and clear as silver church bells at a midnight mass, that brought the warmth back into his heart.

He had been her savior. Indeed, he had been her rescuer more than once. At fifteen, she had mercilessly been married off to the Lancastrian enemy in her father's rebellion. It was he who had convinced Edward to take mercy on her. Her marriage to the Lan-castrian prince was her father's doing. Even if she had protested the match, she would have been forced into it. Thankfully, Edward had listened, but things once again turned bad for her. Placed in the guardianship of her sister and George, she found herself nothing more than a prisoner again. His greedy brother devised a plan to rob her inheritance for himself. It had been he who came to her aid, stealing her away in the night. Her safety and happiness had always been his duty. They knew each other as children, and though the world led them in different directions more than once, they always found their way back to each other. He could not imagine a life without her. She was his friend, his confidant, his lover.

The moment was priceless, yet he remained in the shadows, not wanting to step out just yet as he beheld a sight he knew would carry him through his darkest hour. Fate had thrust him high, and brought him down a time or two. Yet, for all the carnage his young eyes had seen, God provided him with this gift—a loving wife and a beautiful son. All he wanted was to take it in for a while longer. Nothing he possessed—not money, lands, or title—could match these blessings. He prayed to God that he should never lose them.

Adelia hadn't noticed the light rain drops clinging to her lashes until they grew heavier. Richard was swept away in the sudden downpour and she rushed back to the main gate, taking shelter under the thick archway where the old iron portcullis would have been long ago. She leaned against the edge of the wall, peering back out into the castle's inner bailey, smiling to herself at the sight of visitors and guides scrambling to find shelter of their own. As she dabbed at her forehead with her handkerchief, Daniel burst through the murky haze, holding the tiny map over his head. He darted into the doorway, and she had to laugh on seeing the soaked piece of paper acting as a poor excuse for an umbrella. Now in the safety of the archway, he gave himself a bit of a shake, as though his feeble attempt to dry himself might work.

Looking at one another, they could do nothing but laugh at their misfortune. Both soaked to the bone, there was little doubt their day's adventure was over.

"I'm sorry," he croaked through his laughter. "I guess I am not any more luck for you than Cassandra would have been, huh?"

"I don't think I can blame the rain on you," she said. "This is England after all. Rain is always in the cards."

"Yeah, I guess you have a point." He wiped his brow and flicked water from his fingertips. "Hopefully, you found something useful on this wasted day."

She peered back out into the muddy courtyard. "Just to walk in Richard's footsteps, here in the home he loved so dearly, is everything. Every step I take may have been a place where his feet once tread. Every stone I touch may have been one his fingers grazed." She looked around. "His heart is still very much in this place. I would say that's more than enough."

On nights when she needed to rebalance her thoughts, she would walk outside the old stone boundary wall surrounding Middleham Manor. This was one of those nights. As she chugged her way up to the crest of the neighboring hill, she savored the delightful burn in her legs. At the top, she flopped down on the grass, as though her body weighed ten stone, and breathed in the last remnants of sunlight. A wicked breeze buffeted the hillside, sounding like a distraught mother as it swirled about, emitting an ominous howl like a baying hound in a Sherlock Holmes' novel.

A sharp shiver went down her spine. The howl was the kind that prompted folklore and legends—dark tales of some night beast that haunted the land. Though she knew it was her imagination, she swore she could hear the depth of sadness in the sound. The north country was still a place that felt wild and untamed, enduring centuries of rebellion and strife, and the sad moans of the wind seemed to echo that.

In the distance, a shadowy figure appeared, and she recognized the gait straight away. It was Daniel, trudging through the thick grass with Mrs. Chambers' two Corgis in tow. She surveyed his every movement, realizing she had forgotten so much about him in these long months apart: the slow easy way he moved through life, never appearing phased by any obstacle in his path. He approached everything with patience, the model of self-control, confident things would work out if he stayed the course. And by all accounts he was right. She wished she could be more like him—always sure, always steady, never afraid to be vulnerable. He told people just what he felt—so attuned to his own emotions.

She suspected losing his mother at such a young age accounted for that. He had always regretted never having the chance to tell her how much he loved her. Never knowing the true circumstance surrounding her death, he had lived his life with many questions. Most of all, he always wondered if he held some responsibility for her demise, and if she had done something rash to escape him.

To Adelia, it was unthinkable that she had done such a thing. As she watched him, she could not imagine him ever being a troublesome child. He wasn't even a difficult man to contend with now. A pang of guilt for all she had put him through tightened her heart. Once again, he finds himself questioning why he is not enough.

"Fancy meeting you here," he called as he approached. The two dogs chased each other back and forth. She had never seen them with so much energy.

"I thought I would get some air tonight," she said. "I like it out here. I imagine it is my favorite place these days."

"You will have no shortage of air out here."

His gentle smile melted her right down to her core. As he sat on the grass, she couldn't help but notice the extra distance he kept between them. Even after the kiss the other night, he seemed to have reverted to being unsure about where things stood, not daring to insinuate himself. He remained as casual as ever, as though they were nothing more than two friends sharing the splendor of a June evening.

"It is really beautiful out here," she said, hoping to fill the silence that had settled upon them.

"I couldn't agree more. It feels so good to get out of the city. I can see why this spot suits you."

"I come out here when I need to think. I just wanted a little break from all the commotion in the house tonight."

"Same here." He chuckled. "Laura and Ross were in full force when I left. Apparently, he found a copy of One Thousand and One Nights in the laundry chute. He accused Laura of hiding it from him, to which she referred to it as Georgian-era smut. He then quoted something from what I think was Lady Chatterley's Lover. Anyway, there was talk of a meat cleaver and a mallet, so I thought it best to take a walk. On the way out, Mrs. Chambers said Lord and Lady needed a good run, so here I am."

She tilted her head and gave an understanding nod. Nothing he had just described came as a surprise, sounding like every other weeknight.

"Where was Cassandra in the midst of all this ruckus? I feel a little bad that I left her behind."

"Don't worry about her. When I left, she was being entertained by one of the short-term guests, busy telling her about his weightlifting record. She seemed intrigued, but I doubt you could have stomached that blatantly obvious fable."

"The one thing I do know is that I am not like Cassandra, thank God." She giggled. "I don't have to fight off droves of drooling men wherever I go. It's the first time in my life I have been grateful for not being blessed with beauty."

"Don't you think you are beautiful?" he asked, his tone close to demanding.

"I have never thought of myself as beautiful, Daniel." She brushed away some imaginary dust on her shoe. "I am an average girl at best. Not particularly ugly. Not particularly pretty. Just average."

He shifted on to his hip so he faced her. "Clearly you do not see yourself through my eyes."

"Let's change the subject. I shouldn't have brought it up. I am just frustrated with the direction the summer is going. That's all. It will pass."

"You are terrible at accepting compliments. You have never been good at accepting a sincere and honest compliment."

"It's true. I won't deny it. I do about as well accepting criticism as I do compliments, so let's change the subject."

"No," he snapped, "not this time. You cannot always have your way, Adelia Grey. I am going to tell you exactly what I see when I look at you, and for once you need to just listen."

She leaned back, somewhat shocked. Daniel was rarely prone to being the dominant one in the relationship. For a moment she thought to protest but reconsidered, accepting, this time, that he was right. Perhaps, just this once, she should let him have his way in the matter.

"Okay, Daniel, tell me, just what do you see when you look at me?"

Now it was his turn to be stunned. He looked at her for a long moment, as if trying to gauge if she was actually going to let him speak. A slow nod told her he had made his mind up. He sat straighter and made eye contact.

"When I look at Adelia Grey, I see a subtle beauty. The very first time I saw you, I found you attractive. It's true. Yet, as time went on, I realized that your beauty is one that draws you in like relenting waves crashing on a seashore. It pulls you in and spits you out, never giving you a moment to catch your breath. Your beauty encompasses me—my head is never clear when I am in your presence. It's not just your looks. You *are* breathtaking, but if it were only on the surface, I could easily resolve myself to break away. It's your unending wonder. It's your unstoppable drive. It is your headstrong determination. You, Adelia Grey, have burrowed yourself so deep in my soul, there can never be another."

"I don't deserve you, Daniel. No matter how hard I try, I just can't seem to give you everything in this life that you truly deserve.

You are patient and oh so kind. You have given everything to make me happy and yet I fall short of doing the same for you."

"Maybe I just want too much from you. For me, there is just no one else in the world. There is only you. I can't expect you to feel the same. I am asking so much of you. Too much. I understand that now."

"You are not asking too much of me, though." She avoided his eyes by watching the two dogs frolic in the grass. "You are asking me to love you, and I do. I just don't know how to juggle us and myself. I am failing at doing both. I don't want to fail. I just don't know how not to let you down."

"So you run," he said, his tone flat. "You always run when things get uncomfortable. And I don't blame you for following your natural instincts. Quite the contrary."

"I have always been a runner," she admitted with a heavy-hearted sigh. "I thought I had changed but, in the end, I always revert to my comfort zone. I wish I could understand myself as well as you understand me."

"I have studied you like a— W-what the hell was that?" he stammered as a burst of wind swept across the field, howling and moaning like a banshee in an old Irish myth.

"'Tis just the wind." She laughed, rubbing his arm to calm him. It did not seem to help, with him stiffening beneath her touch, flicking sharp looks in every direction. She couldn't help but be a little appreciative of the break in the seriousness of their conversation, yet she really wanted to achieve some closure between them after these long months of regret.

"Why don't we finish this conversation inside," he said, somewhat insistent.

"The wind always sounds like that up here on the hill. There is nothing to be frightened of, Daniel." She chuckled with disbelief. This was a man who had explored every dark and ominous dungeon of nearly every castle in the country. She could scarcely believe he would be unnerved by the simple howl of nature. Anyway, she wasn't ready to go back inside, loving the solitude of this place, and how it made her feel as if all her cares were a thousand miles away. The only thing that going inside brought was reality, and she wasn't prepared to accept it just yet.

As he fidgeted about, staring out into the dusky twilight of the surrounding fields, she remembered that not everything centered around her own desires. She relented, if only for his sake.

"Shall we?" she said, getting to her feet.

He called out for Lord and Lady, who bounded across the hill with short strides to catch up with them.

Chapter Twelve

Adelia sat at the long wooden table in the kitchen, the smell of fresh herbs drying on the line perfuming the air, like an apothecary's shop. She poured a splash of milk into her tea, then stirred it with absentminded strokes. Now that Daniel was here, everything in her world had been turned upside down. She had not gotten a proper night's sleep in days, mainly because she found herself waking in the darkness, her mind filled with thoughts of him.

It was clear his feelings for her had not subsided, nor hers for him, but nothing changed the fact that things could never be as they once were. She was moving in a new direction, her path leading her further away from the life she had once imagined for them. Daniel still harbored these dreams, and the state of things since he had come to Middleham only fueled his hope. While she did not want to hurt him, she could not continue to give him false promises. She would have to set some ground rules, to keep him at a distance. It was so easy to just fall back into his arms and let him love her. His touch was so warm, his affection inviting. Yet, with every kiss, every embrace, the reality of the inevitable made it harder. She could not bear to break his heart again, even though it was probably already too late.

Indecision had always been her greatest weakness. Human nature came easy, it was the repercussions that made things difficult. She thought of yesterday, back at Middleham Castle, and how Richard's devotion to Anne had almost made her feel giddy with the notion of love. How could he be so sure of his feelings, even among the sizable odds they faced? She wished she could possess his strength of mind, or that she and Daniel could write such a love story as theirs.

She blinked away the welling tears at the sound of someone coming down the stairs, and lifted her cup to her mouth, peering over its rim as Daniel ducked through the doorframe.

He smiled when he spotted her, then walked over to the cupboard and pulled a tea cup from the shelf. As she sat in silence, she watched him shuffle about, readying a few biscuits as he let his tea leaves steep. She looked out the window to the immaculate herb garden. Laura was a master gardener, her herbs and vegetables rivaling any in the county. She followed the phases of the moon in her planting and harvesting, swearing that the results spoke for themselves, happy to prove this with the meticulous log she kept of each plant row, always knowing the precise time when its growth would be at its peak. The woman spent hours each day toiling in the soil, and Adelia had not decided yet if it was her favorite pastime, or an excuse to avoid Ross for the better part of the day. She chuckled to herself, thinking of the contrasts between Richard and Anne and Ross and Laura.

Daniel looked over his shoulder at the sound of her laugh. "Have I done something to amuse you?"

"No," she said, her cheeks heating. "It isn't you. I was just thinking about Ross and Laura."

"Oh well, in that case, your laughter is entirely understandable." He placed his cup and plate on the table in front of her and slid onto the bench. When he nibbled a corner of a biscuit, he raised his brow and nodded. "Nice."

"Laura is quite an accomplished cook," Adelia said.

"This one is lavender. I have never tried a lavender biscuit before. I was not expecting it to be so...delightful."

"It has everything to do with the phases of the moon and when it's planted," she explained, tempted to brush crumbs from his bottom lip as he chewed away.

He gave her a puzzled look, and she waved it off, indicating he shouldn't bother to ask. Taking her lead, he shrugged and went back to eating his biscuit.

"I trust you slept well?" he said, making light conversation to break the silence.

"I did not, actually. I keep waking in the middle of the night lately. I don't know what's gotten into me." It was a lie. She knew what was robbing her of her much-needed sleep. Daniel had a way of making her feel every possible emotion, and all at once, which was not conducive to a good night's rest.

"I have the same problem. My mind and body are not in sync. My body wants to rest and my mind is determined to keep racing."

Adelia nodded in agreement. She could not have described it better, and now wondered about the thoughts that kept him up late. Are they about me? About his own work? Maybe things he has never shared. Secrets he has kept to himself.

As they exchanged pleasantries, she struggled to find the best way to lead the conversation. It was time to come clean about how things needed to be between them. It was only fair that he knew how she felt, and she needed to muster her courage to do so. Before she spoke, she chose her words with care, not wanting to come across as rude.

"I have to tell you that I am so very happy to have you here," she said, keeping her voice serious.

"As am I," he replied, straightening in his seat, and she knew he had picked up on her change of tone.

"I just worry, not wanting to lose sight of the work I have planned for the summer."

He nodded twice, his mouth pursing a fraction. "Are you implying that my presence here might be a distraction for you?"

"I know myself, but you know me far better. I know that things between us are complicated. There is so much left unsaid, things...we have yet to deal with in our...relationship." Heat flushed through her as she stumbled over the last few words. " I..." She looked down at her hands in her lap.

"Adelia, I think I know what you are trying to say. Let me make it easier on you." She looked up, meeting his gentle smile. "I am perfectly content just to be here with you. I don't want to take anything away from the work you're doing. If I can be of assistance, I would like you to let me do that."

She managed a half-hearted grin. "So, we can work together as we did at Hampton Court, side by side, but—"

"No strings attached," he interrupted. "Let's just be colleagues, while I am here. There is less pressure on us both if we approach it that way. You are my dearest friend, my ally, and I don't want anything to spoil this time with you. It is just a visit between two good friends. Nothing more."

She didn't know why but "nothing more" held a sharp sting. He was giving her what she wanted, promising no pressure, and offering his infinite wisdom as an assistant—there was nothing in anything he was giving her that she should not be eternally grateful to receive—yet "nothing more" felt too final, like he had decided that, after all her stringing him along for months, he would accept her wish. He was giving her all she wanted, and she did not like it.

Oh, she wanted to smack herself on the forehead. *Just what did I expect from this man? For all his intelligence, he is the stupid one. If he had a lick of sense, he would walk out the door and leave me for good. If he had any idea what I was thinking, he would probably get up and go.* She expected the most impossible things from him, and her selfishness knew no bounds. The man could never do everything to make her happy, because she wasn't sure she could ever be satisfied with anything. The day he walked out the door and left her for good, she would not have one ounce of blame to lay on him.

Chapter Thirteen

The next few days seemed to fly by as Daniel and Adelia visited a few more northern country sites, trying to access any archives that could assist in learning more about the life Richard lived in that wider area. The deeper Adelia dug, the more her frustration grew. Historical archives were complex, and it was remarkable to think that documents nearly five hundred years old could survive at all. In reality, for everything that did survive, there were ten more important papers that had not, and those always seemed to be the missing pieces to the puzzle. To further compound the situation, there were documents scattered all across the country, some of which had managed to make their way to the most unlikely of places.

Over the past four to five hundred years, the country had seen such great change that things could easily be shuffled from place to place. Every now and then, a miraculous find would surface, maybe in some long-forgotten box discovered in an attic and, just like that, historians realized that what they thought they knew had been turned on its head. Every shred of knowledge Adelia collected had to be from a documented source—her gift could serve no purpose in her work, at least not publicly.

Since Daniel's arrival, Cassandra had been more than happy to stay back, allowing he and Adelia to work on their own. On the rare occasion she tagged along, Adelia could not help but notice how Daniel's presence seemed to curb men's unwanted advances toward her. Something the younger woman was appreciative of.

Daniel brought a sense of balance to Adelia's life, eliminating the proverbial tug of war between her and Cassandra, allowing her to focus on her work. His energy was contagious, and she found herself remembering her reasons for taking on this project all along. Also, his experience as a historian meant that he always knew how to ask the right questions, including being skeptical if an answer came too easily. His help had become invaluable, and she wasn't ready to see him leave anytime soon.

At one time, he'd relied on her to help him find answers to his questions about Amy Robsart Dudley, but now she depended on him to help her unravel the life of Richard III. They were a team, each resolved to crack the hidden codes of history together. Be it as a couple or just colleagues, they were bonded to one another, and she was starting to see that the force pushing them apart was no match for the one pulling them together.

It was late in the evening and the three of them sat in the library, each sharing old stories of their youth. Given their fathers' occupations as history professors, Adelia and Daniel's childhoods had been somewhat similar, with both spending many of their younger days in old libraries and museums. Cassandra, on the other hand, had spent far less time with her parents. Her life had been one afforded to the child of a wealthy entrepreneur, traveling on luxurious excursions and always being treated to the finer things in life. The more Adelia learned of her cousin's upbringing, the clearer it became that, for all the differences between them, they had each shared a lonely existence. Like her, Cassandra had been an only child, with the lack of a sibling creating a void in her life. While she'd always had the comforts of loving parents to fill the gap, Cassandra was raised by a variety of nannies. Though afforded the luxury of traveling the world to exotic places, her parents had rarely spent much in the way of quality time with her. It was easy to see how isolated an existence that would have been for a child.

As Cassandra shared her stories, Adelia found her understanding of her cousin growing. Her untamed spirit was a little rebellious—the result of years spent being nearly invisible. While the girl was probably overindulged in the way of material possessions, none of that could ever take the place of the sense of love and affection that came from doting parents. Her life had been a double-edged sword, so to speak. On one hand, Adelia could see herself being a little jealous of Cassandra's fortune, yet, she also felt pity, knowing well that she would not have traded Elaine and John Grey's love for any material possession. It would be so easy to sit back and count the things you didn't have in childhood—to compare your life with those who seemed to have it better—yet the absence of love strikes a cold blow that lingers far longer than the memory of a toy you always wanted but never received.

They had chatted well into the evening hours when Paul strode into the room, a book tucked under one arm and a glass of bourbon in hand. He smiled as he took the only available chair, next to Cassandra, setting his glass upon one of Laura's freshly pressed doilies.

With an anxious smile, he placed the book, a rather large hardcover volume, across his knees.

"I was going through the old books at the antique shop and happened to stumble upon this one." He handed it to Cassandra, who opened it and thumbed through the pages. Adelia left Daniel's side on the couch and crossed the room.

"What is it?" she asked, craning her neck over Cassandra's shoulder to get a better look.

"It is a pretty extensive catalog of all the churches in Britain and notable burials in each one. I thought it might help you track down Richard III and whoever else you are covering in your research."

Adelia gazed down at the black and white photos of ancient churches and abbeys. The book seemed to contain hundreds of them. For each location, the author had included interior and exterior pictures as well as a brief history. Just as Paul had said, there was also a detailed listing of notable burials within the chapels or on adjoining grounds.

"This is a marvelous find, Paul," she said. "Unfortunately, Richard III's gravesite has never been found. It was thought to have been in Greyfriars Priory in Leicester, but after the reformation, the church was destroyed in the mid-fifteen hundreds, and no records survive as to where exactly it might have been. That aside, there certainly is plenty of other information in here that will help us. Thank you."

"When I was looking through it, I came across one thing I thought might interest you." He put his hand out for Cassandra to hand him the book back. Adelia pushed down her impatience as he sat back and flipped through the pages.

"Here it is. Saint Matthew's Church in Coldridge." His face lit with delight. "The picture is a bit grainy but I would like you to take a look at this window. It struck me as a little odd, and I'm intrigued to see what you make of it."

She lifted the heavy tome from his hands, and squinted, trying to make out the details. The image showed a tall rectangular window of leaded glass, with the figure of a young man at its center. He held the royal sepulcher, and wore a crown. However, a much larger crown hovered over this, more ornate in its construction and lined in ermine. The man wore what may have been a coronation robe, dark in color, possibly blue or purple—the colors reserved for royalty. A banner at the bottom of the window spelled out *Edward the Fifth*.

"Edward V," she whispered, more to herself than Paul. "Remarkable. I don't think I have ever seen an image of him portrayed."

"Edward V?" Daniel jumped up from the couch and strode over, his eyes wide as he peered down at the page. "There are one or two more images that I know of but they are all posthumous. I would love to know when this was constructed."

"Why would there be an image of Edward V in his coronation robes?" Cassandra asked. "Adelia, didn't you say he was never actually crowned king? If it is widely thought that he was murdered by his uncle Richard in the tower, why would someone have placed this image in a small country church?"

"Perhaps its location might tell you something," Paul said. "Coldridge is a rather remote spot in Devon, and even more so in the fourteenth and fifteenth centuries. The chapel would have been under the private ownership of the landowner. Maybe it wasn't meant to be seen by just anybody."

"Adelia," Daniel exclaimed, "you know who owned the lands in Devon?"

She thought for a moment, trying to fit the pieces of the puzzle together. "Thomas Grey," she answered, her voice trembling. "The Marquess of Dorset."

"Exactly," he said, his excitement telling her they were both thinking the same thing.

"Thomas Grey?" Cassandra looked from one to the other, her inability to connect the dots clear in her questioning look. "Are you two related somehow?"

"I can't recall ever hearing that we were, but I doubt it. Everyone likes to think they are related to some great historical figures. Half of the tourists who visited Hampton Court Palace swore they were descendants of Anne Boleyn. Most of the time our relatives were just regular people with regular lives."

Cassandra flashed her a knowing look. Had Paul not been in the room, she might have mentioned the Babington line. Perhaps they couldn't tout a well-known name, but the ability to hear the whispers most certainly did not put them in the same category as regular people.

"Thomas Grey was the son of Elizabeth Woodville from her first marriage," Adelia continued. "Elizabeth was also Edward V's mother, making Thomas his half-brother. Thomas Grey owned the lands in Devon."

The room fell silent as she worked through the potentials. Was it possible that Grey commissioned the window? Maybe the hovering coronation crown was meant to signify what should have been. Was he trying to honor his brother, who he considered the rightful king? Was he trying to right an injustice he could not prevent in his lifetime?

"Cassandra, we have to go to Coldridge in Devon," she said, buzzing with excitement. Her mind swirled with so many questions, she could barely decide where to start.

Her cousin's mouth dropped open. "Adelia, that's a whole day's drive away. It's all the way down by Exeter."

Adelia straightened. "We have to get there. I have to see this window."

"I will take you," Daniel said. "Just give me a day or two to see if I can dig up a little more information."

She smiled. As much as she liked her independence, she always needed Daniel more than she admitted. He was her rock. Granted, a rock she had flung out the window of a moving car once or twice.

She was not worthy of the loyalty he gave her, and had done so little to return it to him. That needed to be rectified.

Chapter Fourteen

A few days later, Adelia walked over to the massive bookshelves in the library. The faint smell of Paul's nightly cigar smoke lingered. Cassandra lounged in a bay window, peering out more than reading the glossy-colored magazine in her hands. Fending off the incessant chatter of thoughts in her head, she traced her fingers along the rows of brightly bound volumes. marveling at how immaculate the shelves were kept, with not one speck of dust to be seen. These books were Ross's treasures, and he treated them as though they were as priceless as Fabergé eggs. To her knowledge, he did not accomplish much in his day-to-day routine. The most familiar image she could conjure was that of his face buried in a book, with his shiny forehead and feral hair peeking out from behind its pages.

She moved along, scanning the titles. It was still early—too soon to lock herself away in her room for the night—but too late to do much else. She slid her finger across the back of each volume, until a bright-blue tome with gold lettering caught her eye. Careful to note the location, she eased the large and bulky book from its cataloged resting place. The last thing she wanted was to upset Ross by replacing it incorrectly.

The title brought a smile: *Le Morte D'Arthur.* She opened its front cover and hovered over an introduction page filled with vivid images of a young Arthur clutching the sword Excalibur in his boyish hands. She had owned a copy of it back home in Boston, though it was not nearly as old as the one she held, which had been published in 1485, the year of Richard's death. Its author, Thomas Mallory, composed all the Arthurian tales of old into a complex collection of honor, betrayal, and human nature at its purest, and it had always been one of her favorite versions of the stories. Though the book itself came after Richard's time, these ancient stories were ones he had grown up hearing. They would have inspired his sense of chivalric pride and governed his actions just as much as the religious texts he had studied.

Richard himself owned a great many books, some of which still survived. She thought back to photographs she had seen in the past, with some showing his scribbled notes on the page margins. Books in his day would have been expensive, and not as easy to afford as the countless books made today. Valuable as his tomes may have been, his notes proved that he not only read the volumes but took ownership of them with the same love and care Ross did. She liked the idea of Richard being a book lover, and how it was something they shared. A notion she had never considered before was the simplicity of him having such an object that brought him joy. She turned the heavy volume over, thinking of the memories it evoked. Perhaps, once upon a time, Richard had a book that did the same for him. What could that have been, that transported him far away from a land filled with woe? She would never know the answer, but it didn't matter—the idea brought him to life a little more in her mind.

Footsteps at the library's entrance caught her attention. Daniel stood there, as though he needed to ask permission to enter. She gave him a subtle wave and he came through the doorway, clutching a stack of papers and a folded map. After pushing a chessboard aside, he spread the map out onto a small table, then used a few of the chess pieces to prevent the tattered corners from rolling back up. He picked up a few more chess pieces and motioned for Adelia and Cassandra to come over.

"I think we should make a few stops on the way to Devon. It is quite a distance away so let's make the most of it. I estimate we will be gone for about a week at most."

"I like that idea. Being cooped up in a car the entire day doesn't sound too appealing." She stood by his side. "I'd like to have some time to really walk around these places. I'm sure we could find some local inns to stay overnight along the way."

"Me too," Cassandra said, coming across all eager, though Adelia imagined it was more to do with the prospect of a change of scenery and not about visiting more ancient sites. "Maybe we could make a stop in London. I have a few friends I would like to see."

Daniel looked up at her. "I'm sorry, Cassandra, but we aren't going anywhere near the city on this trip. We will stay strictly to the west."

"Wouldn't the Tower of London be an ideal place for us to visit?" she asked. "It's the last known residence of the two princes. It would just make sense that we go there too."

Adelia gave a cold shudder to the thought of the Tower of London. "Of all the places in England I desire to visit, I find myself most content to avoid the Tower. There is far too much history there, good and bad alike. To be truthful, it frightens me, and my grandma always warned against it. I fear the energies there would be too strong. I cannot be sure that I am ready for such an undertaking yet. I will be in time, just not yet."

Cassandra's tight smile conveyed her disappointment. Adelia could not blame her. She was a young and vivacious girl, and spending her time trampling through medieval market towns was probably not her idea of an exciting week. As long as the summer had seemed, the days were already speeding by and she was starting to feel as though she had made little progress in learning more about Richard. She really needed to dedicate her time to her research, so Cassandra's trip to London would have to wait.

Daniel placed one of the chess pieces down onto the map. "First, we will pay a visit to Ludlow Castle. The drive is about four hours, if traffic is good, and not accounting for stops. If we leave here early, we should be able to get to the castle with plenty of time to explore before they close. Besides that, this would have been a significant place for Richard as a child, so you might be able to find something there too."

"Definitely Ludlow," Adelia agreed, buzzing with anticipation. "Richard would have been about six years old when his father was driven into exile and forced to abandon him there along with his mother and two other siblings. I can't imagine the fear they must have experienced being barricaded up in that old castle with Lancastrian troops surrounding them. Yes, I know I can get something at Ludlow."

Daniel set another piece down. "Tewksbury is next. It's not too far—maybe an hour or so. This is another significant place for Richard. He would have been about eighteen here when he fought alongside Edward IV. This was the final battle against Margaret of Anjou before she was captured."

Adelia was almost giddy at the prospect of walking among the old streets of Tewksbury. "It is also the very place where Richard took Anne Neville into custody after the death of her husband. By then, he might have already had designs on making her his wife. After all that Anne had been through in her short life, she had to be overcome with joy at seeing him. They had been childhood friends, and though she technically was taken as a prisoner, she had to be relieved it was by someone she knew, and liked."

"I thought Richard rescued her a few years later, when she was being guarded by her sister and brother-in-law," Cassandra said, her brow furrowed. "Why was this poor girl's life such a tragedy?"

Adelia smiled inside. Though Cassandra's interest in history was rather limited, she was clearly still paying attention along the way. Her cousin was far more capable than she let on.

"The common misconception we have about women of this time is that they lived these grand lives full of wealth and splendor. If you look at the lives of Richard's mother Cecily, or Elizabeth Woodville—even Anne Neville for that matter—they may have grown up in comfortable surroundings but they were no less sheltered from all the turbulence of the time. Anne Neville would be bartered to the highest bidder her whole life, married off to an exiled prince, only to find herself far too close to the battlefield that would claim his life. This girl was a widow at fourteen."

Daniel tapped a chess piece on the map. "As a widow, Anne was heiress to one of the most wealthy and powerful men in England. When her father was killed, and her mother took sanctuary in Beaulieu Abbey, she became the most sought-after woman for every man in the country. I cannot say that Richard did not have true affection for her. Still, you cannot discount that marrying her was an attractive prospect for the wealth she would bring alone."

"I think he loved her," Adelia said with fervor, drawing from the experience she had at Middleham. She had shared everything she'd seen with Daniel but it was clear he remained skeptical. "After her death, when he was accused of wanting to poison his wife to marry his own niece, he went to parliament to convey his anger at such allegations. He said his heart was as heavy as a man could be at the loss of his wife. Indeed, he went through a great deal of trouble to save her from the clutches of her scheming family."

"He also went through a great deal of trouble to marry her without papal dispensation," Daniel argued. "Then he went through a great deal of trouble to ensure a parliamentary order that, if he divorced her, their marriage would be considered invalid because of the lack of dispensation, thus entitling him to keep her fortune for himself. He could have left her destitute at any time he so desired, and I am sure she was well aware of that fact. I know you have a soft spot for Richard, Adelia, but that doesn't sound like a guy who wasn't looking out for himself."

She rolled her eyes, scoffing at the fact that he was correct on that point. The subject of Richard's true intentions had always been a point of contention between them.

Cassandra sat there, remaining silent, no doubt unwilling to interject in an argument that was out of her knowledge base. Her gaze darted back and forth between the two of them, as if trying to gauge who would be the first to relent.

"All I am saying," Daniel said, his tone softening, probably sensing he had hit a nerve, "is that I know you want to clear his name, but I don't think Richard was a simple guy to puzzle out. He may have been loyal and noble as a soldier but he had a self-serving side too."

"I can see that side of him. Really, I can." She wasn't sure she'd convinced him but it wasn't worth fighting over. "Okay, anyway, what is after Tewksbury?"

"So, from Tewksbury, we make our way to Coldridge, to the church of Saint Matthew. If we plan on these three stops, we can just play it by ear and stop over for the night, as needed, along the way. I'd like to keep the stop in Ludlow brief, staying over just one night in Tewkesbury, and that way we can spend at least three or four nights in Coldridge."

He raised his gaze to meet Adelia's, mirroring her disappointment. Like him, she could easily spend weeks in each location, pouring through any archives she might get her hands on. He knew the way her mind worked, but getting her to these points of interest was the priority. It was a given that she could handle herself from there.

"I think you have it all figured out, Daniel," Cassandra said through her glowing smile. "I like the plan." No doubt she was glad to have him doing all the work.

Adelia nodded her agreement, her mind stirring as she visualized all the places they should visit at each of the stops.

Daniel lifted the chess pieces, and the mapped rolled into itself. "Let's get packed up tonight and we can leave first thing in the morning. Who is driving, Cassandra, you or I?"

"You drive, Daniel," Adelia blurted out, already having had a few near-death experiences with her cousin behind the wheel.

"Yeah, maybe you should do the driving on this one, Daniel," Cassandra agreed. She shot Adelia a look that, however brief, showed she wasn't impressed.

Chapter Fifteen

They set out at sunrise, bound for Ludlow Castle. The morning had already been rocky, with Adelia and Cassandra squabbling over the vast amount of luggage the younger woman planned to bring. Adelia snapped, telling her they would only be gone for less than a week. After a heavy standoff, Cassandra relented, condensing her belongings to four oversized bags. Daniel somehow managed to shove his one bag, Adelia's one bag, and Cassandra's mobile department store into the car's trunk.

After handing the folded map to Adelia, he eased the car out of Middleham Manor's gate and got them on the road. The plan was to keep to the main roads as much as they could, but some of the journey would take them along smaller country roads. Adelia didn't mind, happy to see some of the countryside along the way. They passed endless fields that reminded her of the old patchwork quilts her mother made. Beautiful squares of brilliant green and glistening gold dotted the landscape, broken by lush forests of deep emerald, with swathes of wildflowers bordering pastures of grazing sheep. The scent of flowers and grass perfumed the air with a delightful aroma.

With her window down, the warm summer breeze tore apart the smooth waves she had worked so diligently into place earlier. She didn't mind. Driving along these ancient thoroughfares, she had never felt quite so alive. Every village or town they passed through made her wish they had no itinerary to follow. She jotted down each location's name in the little notebook on her lap, determined to return someday. As beautiful as the landscape was by car, she expected it had been much more picturesque in Richard's day as he traveled by horseback, traversing lands that modernization had yet to spoil. She doubted he would have been quite as comfortable with his mode of travel but the beauty of the land had to be breathtaking.

"You know what I have always loved about Richard?" she said, out of the blue.

"Everything," Cassandra remarked from the backseat, the word dripping with sarcasm.

Adelia turned and responded with a wrinkled scowl, and her cousin retaliated by flashing her trademark dazzling smile. Daniel chuckled but then straightened, as if preparing to be scolded.

"Richard got the last word," she said. "I think that in itself proves his brilliance."

Daniel raised a brow. "Henry Tudor defeated Richard at Bosworth. Killed him, slung him naked over a horse, and took his crown. I guess I am struggling to see how he got the last word."

She stared at him for a moment. "I don't know if he knew what he was doing, but it was brilliant just the same. The fact that he never revealed what happened to the princes far surpassed any battlefield wound he could have given Henry Tudor." She nodded to herself, satisfied. "The mental war he waged on Tudor lasted for the rest of Henry's life. The man never knew what happened to the princes so he spent the rest of his days knee-deep in paranoia. So-called pretenders came out of the woodwork, and Henry spent a fortune trying to quell the rebellions that sprang up. He never had a moment's rest, and was never secure on the throne he stole."

"You do have a solid point," Daniel said. "It really was a vicious move on Richard's part. Tudor did his best to paint him in the worst light possible, but, deep down, Richard did have one up on him."

"He sure did." Adelia almost sang this. "Whether it was a calculated move or not, he made sure Henry Tudor never had the chance to forget him. No one knows where Richard is buried, but it is safe to say he spent part of his afterlife taking up residence in Tudor's head."

"If he was buried at Greyfriars, don't they at least have some idea where his grave is?" Cassandra looked astonished, as if it was unthinkable that a king could lie buried in an unknown location.

"No," Adelia said, her tone flat. "Henry Tudor wasn't inclined to give him a proper burial, and Henry VIII showed even less respect when the priory was dissolved. After the church was leveled, Richard's grave, wherever that may be, has been lost to time. I am not sure it will ever be found."

"That is terribly sad." Cassandra's somber tone made her words almost inaudible.

"Well," Daniel said after a moment, "stranger things have happened. Perhaps, someday, they will find him. The two of you could certainly make that your next project."

Cassandra pursed her lips and looked out her window, leaving Adelia to figure she would be on her own for that adventure. Her cousin was a perplexing soul—a history major, who did not seem to have a particular interest in the past. Up to this point, she had been almost no help at all, save for the occasional chiming in. Even so, she could not say she had not grown to like her presence. The girl took some of the seriousness out of life. As for herself, if left to her own devices, she would have shut herself up in a room studying for hours at a time—a self-imposed recluse—scorched by the sun's rays when she emerged from her dark lair. Her cousin brought out the lighter side of life. If she had to be honest, Cassandra had made the summer better, if only by giving her a much-needed break from her thoughts.

She was still undecided on what the future held for Cassandra, who probably knew her fate even less. No doubt there would be an endless stream of admirers, no matter where she went—the only thing about her life that was in any way pre-determined.

Passing by the sign for the town of Ludlow, with its bold lettering, Daniel suggested that they stop off at a filling station before exploring the town. His plans had not included a great length of time in Ludlow or Tewkesbury but Adelia was convinced she could spend days or weeks in both places. It anguished her to have to pass so many intriguing sites and buildings and not stop. Daniel had been to many of these places in the past, so their attraction was a little dulled compared to hers. Each significant location they passed, she pouted like a child whose birthday had been forgotten. However, she knew the stop-offs at Ludlow and Tewkesbury were meant to be short so the bulk of their time could be spent in their priority destination in Devon.

As Daniel worked on tending to the car, Adelia and Cassandra pulled a basket for lunch out of the backseat and headed for the bank of the nearby River Teme. The position of Ludlow along the river had not been a coincidence, with the water course being an important route for trade and development in the area, ensuring the town's survival even through the most turbulent of times.

Adelia spread out the wool blanket on the grass and she and Cassandra sat in the cool shade of a mature oak. She looked up along the river, to the soft curved arches of Ludlow Bridge. Before long, Daniel finished with the car and joined them. Cassandra filled three small cups from a flask of hot tea, and Adelia unwrapped her sandwich and took a large bite, trying to tame her ravenous appetite.

"I have been to Wales several times," Cassandra said, looking down at the steady moving water of the Teme. "I am sure I have passed by this town—I just don't remember it." She took a deep breath. "What about you, Daniel, have you ever been to Ludlow?"

"I have been here a couple of times, actually. My dad brought me along once with a few of his mates from the university when I was just a boy. I remember being bored out of my wits listening to them talk about Ludlow's history in the glove trade."

Adelia chuckled. "Glove trade? Sounds suspect." She took another bite of her sandwich.

"No, it means exactly as you would think," Cassandra said. "For a time, Ludlow was well known for the making of gloves. Some of the finest construction and high-quality fabrics."

Daniel and Adelia looked at her in surprise. Cassandra's vast knowledge of the fashion industry was impressive.

"Anyway," Daniel said, "I literally spent hours in the backseat of a car listening to a bunch of monotone chatter about gloves." He shivered, as though the memory had triggered some emotional flashback.

Adelia clutched at her chest. "How you survived that day is truly an act of God. Those scars will heal in time, my friend." She laughed, then sat up. "I think I may have one to top that torture, though. My father and I visited a medieval art exhibit. I was about sixteen, if I recall. Then, my father comes across some art expert, who he had never met, and they strike up a conversation. For two solid hours I stood in the gallery as my dad and his newfound friend discussed the depiction of cod pieces in art. I thought I would die. I never wanted to melt into the floorboards quite as much as I did that day."

Cassandra covered her mouth as she laughed, failing to prevent tea from dribbling through her fingers. Adelia couldn't hold back a cheeky grin.

"That is my new favorite story," Cassandra said with a giggle, wiping herself down with a napkin. "Honestly, I would have loved to see your face."

They finished lunch against the backdrop of the serene river. The blanket and basket were packed back up, and then it was time to enter the town. Its castle was no more than a minute or two up the road.

Passing by Ludlow bridge, Daniel maneuvered through one of the few remaining gateways to the town. Adelia could almost reach out and slide her hand along the massive archway's smooth stones. They proceeded up Broad Street, one of Ludlow's main thoroughfares.

The town dated back to the Norman Conquest. After his victorious win at the Battle of Hastings in 1066, William the Conqueror set about fortifying the border lands with the construction of great fortresses. Ludlow Castle was built to serve several purposes: to protect the Marches and defend the Welsh border. The town, renowned as being one of the most beautiful in England, lay just a few hundred feet from the castle walls, and boasted nearly 500 historically listed properties. Much like many medieval towns, Ludlow was a historical toy store, home to some of the most notable figures in British history, and equally notable events. Its streets were packed with hundreds of years of architecture, all sandwiched in side by side. Beautiful Georgian buildings of brick with alabaster white trimmings were butted against old Tudor-style houses of white plaster and oak beams that had been painted midnight black by the Victorians. Ludlow had survived for nearly a thousand years, and the residual effects of every century lined each street.

Daniel drove at a snail's pace up Broad Street, affording Adelia and Cassandra extra time to take in the beautiful buildings. Turning onto High Street, the road that led straight to the castle's gate, she could make out the silhouette of the expansive roofline glinting in the late morning sun. The air brewed with excitement, taking her anticipation to new heights. A place she had longed to visit, she could almost feel herself pulled toward the gate as Daniel eased into the carpark—a feeling similar to what she had felt back at Middleham Castle. There was something here, some unnamed force pulling her closer, but to what? All she knew was she couldn't wait another minute to find out.

Chapter Sixteen

She wasted no time, taking her leave of Cassandra and Daniel to wander off on her own. When she got to the top of the great keep, she turned to look upon the town. The streets, with their assortment of rooftops and chimneys, resembled a picturesque row of doll houses, with the River Teme snaking its way along the edge of the grounds, creating the perfect traveling route for centuries of traders. Further out, the Welsh Hills rose and dipped as they bordered the horizon, like faint images in a faded picture.

The Welsh Marches had been a frontier of sorts, on the border of Wales and England. Ludlow, built as a defense against the Welsh raiders, became a clear assertion of William the Conqueror's power after taking the English throne in 1066. Throughout its life, the castle would transform from a defensive structure to a grand palace, fit to serve as a place for the proper upbringing and education of whoever held the title of the Prince of Wales. Richard would have come here for a while as a child with his father, the

Duke of York. His brother Edward would send his own son, Edward Prince of Wales, to the castle under the guidance and training of his uncle Anthony Woodville. Prince Arthur, brother to the future Henry VIII, would call Ludlow his home for many years, dying here just a few months shy of his sixteenth birthday. Mary Tudor, daughter of Henry VIII, called it her home for much of her childhood. Its solid walls had seen triumph and turbulence alike, always finding a way to survive.

Ludlow held a mystical quality, but, then again, Adelia felt that way about every old castle she ever visited. When she closed her eyes, she could envision its once-opulent interior—a palace fit for the likes of royalty. Something about its mystery filled her with a profound sense of sadness. Of the three royal children who had called Ludlow home, two never made it to the throne. Only Mary Tudor did so, going on to become Mary I, but even her life was not an altogether happy one. Some might call Ludlow an omen of misfortune for its inhabitants, at least those of royal blood. Adelia was always drawn to such stories. Deep within her, she loved tales of ancient curses and things that go bump in the night.

With fond recollection, she thought back to a story her father once shared about the curse Howard Carter evoked when he opened King Tutankhamun's Tomb, and how several misfortunes befell the members of the expedition as a result.

"A plausible lie," her father had said. "You can make something out of nothing if you are so inclined."

Dark mysteries had always been something she found captivating. When she discovered her ability to hear the whispers, she realized quite soon that even a plausible lie could have some core truth. She hated to use the term *ghosts*, but some would say that was what she saw when she had her visions. However, she never considered those she saw to be apparitions. No, they were inhabitants of the same space, living as they had long ago. Even those who did not have her gift caught glimpses of the past from time to time, propelling the notion that ghosts really did exist.

Ludlow held a certain energy within its walls—more intense than average. As she descended the stairs of the keep, it grew stronger. This old shell's story had a great desire to tell itself, and she was ready to listen.

She stood in the inner courtyard, encircled by imposing walls and towers, and turned in each direction, soaking up the vibes of the monochromatic stone works whose shade cast a cool reprieve to the heat of the summer sun. Even so, the air was heavy and unmoving, scented with the hint of fresh-cut grass. She pulled her dark tresses from her neck, the day's increasing humidity taking no prisoners when it came to hair. A bead of sweat trickled down the trail of her spine, and the pale-yellow linen of her dress clung to her skin.

With the castle being so well preserved, there was much to explore, which made it all the more difficult to decide where to start. She inched herself out of the comfort of the shadows and strolled into the courtyard's center as she tried to decide which of the many doorways to enter. As she moved, a much-welcomed breeze caressed her face. It was light at first, cooling the sticky moisture on her skin, but with each step it picked up speed, though it didn't seem to move around her—rather against her. Its force became intentional, pushing against the small of her back and directing her forward. Taking its lead, she looked up to see a rounded structure not more than fifty feet ahead. A tower. Giving herself to the moment, she let the brisk wind push her forward. As she moved toward an open archway, the temperature began to drop, until the blazing heat of the summer faded into what resembled an autumn day. Just as she reached the entrance, the wind died, and she took a beat to see if it might push her in the rest of the way. Nothing. Even the chirp of the birds swooping in and out of the turrets had stopped. In such stillness, she imagined hearing the tiny patter of ants as they toiled in the soil below her feet.

Placing her hand against the carved stone doorway, she stepped into the tower's dim interior. The stone floor was unlevel, and her shoe caught on the corner of a large flagstone but she regained her balance enough to steady herself. It would not be good to trip in such an environment. As she walked into the center of the room, her breath caught when she looked up at the domed roof consisting of a fragmented fan-vaulted ceiling. She marveled at each of the identical arched coves recessed into the walls. A quick count told her there were thirteen. Though the coves were the only thing that remained, she visualized an image of thirteen carved chairs, each facing the center of the room. A small plaque on a wall read: 'The Chapel of St. Mary Magdalene.' It reminded her of the church of the Holy Sepulcher in Jerusalem, but on a miniature scale. She surveyed the coves again, getting a strong sense of a Templar connection, but whether it was symbolic or otherwise, she could not be sure. This space was important, and not only as a chapel royal for the princes it served.

In the silent stillness, conflicting flashes of hot and cold raced across her already icy skin. Dust glimmered within the dim rays of sunlight, and she gazed in awe at the particles as they sparkled before her like diamond shavings. She stepped back, watching the specks fall onto materializing furniture. The walls morphed from bare stone to pure white plaster, and a golden cross and chalice sat upon a strip of silk fabric draped over an altar in the center of the room.

Within seconds, the chapel was dressed in beauty, reminding her of Cinderella being visited by her fairy godmother. She continued to move back, until the hard stone wall jarred her to a stop. A silver stream of light pushed its way through the archway, illuminating the tiny altar where a young boy, raven haired, knelt in prayer. His lips moved as he recited his plea to a god he was sure heard him. He looked to be no older than five or six—far too young to have a face so marked with worry. Turmoil rose all around him, and he felt his safe and happy childhood taking an uncertain turn. Adelia watched as his heavy dark lashes flickered, his eyelids clenched shut.

"Richard," she whispered to herself.

The word had barely left her lips when the boy looked up. He stared at her, as if he'd heard her, though she knew it was impossible. She stood paralyzed, awaiting whatever was to come. He turned his head to the side as someone entered the room. Clothed in a black jerkin over a fine white cambric-linen shirt, the man moved to the altar. Richard stared up at the looming figure, his young face conveying awe, as though he had known more of this person through fables and myths than in flesh and blood.

"Have you completed all your studies?" the man asked, his deep voice stern.

"Yes, Father." The boy's words carried on a slight tremble.

His father pulled at the legs of his trousers as he bent to kneel beside the child. Adelia strained to get a good look at his face. So few pictures of Richard Plantagenet existed, and the ones that did were rudimentary depictions at best. His thick hair and beard had the sheen of varnished golden oak, and his hazel eyes took on the color of Ludlow's flat gray exterior. A life of difficult decisions framed his youthful face in harsh lines. The man was aging at an abnormal pace, and she sensed he had not slept a full night in a long time.

As they knelt side by side, young Richard shuffled, his unease at being alongside his father obvious. They were more strangers than family. Richard Plantagenet spent far more time traveling to do his duty for the crown than being a doting father. Although love existed between the two, it was distant and disconnected. Young Richard had an emotional attachment to his mother, who he saw in a limited capacity each day. To him, his father was larger than life. A man he had known in letters and stories of triumph. When he thought of his father, it was more as an adoring fan than a son.

Adelia recollected the way crowds reacted when celebrities arrived back in Boston. The fanfare, the chaotic swoon. In a way, it was the same here, with young Richard filled with adoration for the image of his father more than the man himself. He looked on him as a noble knight, sworn to duty for the good of the people, bound in every sense to the loyalty and dignity such a position demanded. Something a child might aspire to emulate as he grew up, that would take this young boy, trembling by the altar, and forge him into the anointed king he would become. For him, chivalry was like a second religion.

"This chapel is a sacred place," his father said. "It pays homage to the men who were defenders of the faith. They braved the most treacherous of lands, among the vilest of men, as protectors of the one true God. The knights of the crusades were a valiant breed indeed."

Young Richard looked up at his father and nodded as though he understood. Adelia smiled at the notion that a boy not more than six years could fully comprehend the perils faced by the Knights Templars in the Hold Land.

His father smiled down upon him, his harsh face softening at the innocence of his son.

"There are a great many challenges that we shall face in the future," he said, his voice tender, "but we must be willing to answer God's calling. Just as the knights were willing to shed blood to protect blood, we must be willing to do the same, Richard. Our country is in great peril, my son. Like the great knights of the past, we must be the defenders. You will be faced with many difficult decisions in your days to come. Fortune's wheel is a fickle thing—it brings us to the height of power just to thrust us down. It takes us from our darkest night and scorches us with the brilliance of the sun. No matter what fate may befall us, there is no greater treasure than our blood. Do you understand what I mean?"

"Our lives," the boy said, his voice soft.

"Our lives and the lives of our kin, my boy. You must protect your family at all costs. You and your brothers and sisters will go on to produce a great many sons. The family line depends on all of you. Above all, it is your duty, as a knight, to protect your family. Whatever is required, you must do. Loyalty must never falter when it comes to your kin."

"Yes, Father." The boy's heart swelled with the sense of duty his father had bestowed upon him. He was the fourth son, accustomed to scarcely having a role of significance. Just to be noticed filled him with profound joy.

"In the coming days, I will have to leave you. I am trusting you to keep your mother and your sisters safe. As a knight, Richard, it is your honor and your duty. Never forget your duty to your family."

He patted his son's shoulder but made no attempt to embrace him; it was not in his nature to be soft hearted with his children. Parental love, as Adelia knew it, was different in Richard's day. Within the high ranks of nobility, such as he had been born into, it wasn't uncommon to spend minimal time in the company of one's parents. Displays of tender affection would have been something of a foreign concept.

She felt a pang of empathy when she thought of Cassandra. To be born into great fortune and wealth was no more of a substitute for a father's love for Richard than it had been for her cousin. Richard wouldn't have been as forthcoming as Cassandra was

about the way it felt to be overlooked, but he was likely to have
suffered the sting just the same. Adelia was not a mother, yet her
maternal instinct had her wanting to pull the boy into her arms
and soothe away those fears—so intense, and so out of place in a
child so young. Like Cassandra, all Richard ever wanted was to be
noticed by the people he loved and admired most.

After the visions faded into oblivion, she exited the tower,
emerging into the courtyard, overlooked by the inner bailey. She
squinted, shielding her eyes from the afternoon sun, its beating
rays filling the space, making it look like it was suspended in a
golden haze. She had no idea where to go next, so determined to
allow the energies to decide.

As her vision came into focus, she saw a blurry figure crouched
low to the ground. It approached her with calculated slowness, its
image flickering like a skip in a movie reel. As it drew closer, it
became more defined. A dog—a hound of some kind—its short
coat, a deep shade of gray, with a glossy sheen like oil paint on a
palette. She stood motionless as it stopped just a few feet from her,
its black eyes dull, as if devoid of life. The hound stared at her,
and she stood transfixed but unafraid, which surprised her. It was
probably a minute, maybe longer, before the lean-bodied canine
turned and headed back toward the main gate. It had taken just
a few steps when it looked back over its shoulder, right at her. By
now, she was sure this dog was not part of the Ludlow landscape,
at least not in the present day.

The suspicion that these energies of the past could sense her
presence was new to her. It started after her grandma passed away,

and didn't occur often, thank heavens, for it sometimes unnerved her to the core. Now and again, when her connection to some person or place felt exceptionally strong, she couldn't help but notice the strange sensation that she had been, for lack of a better word, detected. It was as though when one keeper of the whispers left this sphere of existence, the strength of their gift was transferred. Maybe it was just wishful thinking—some deep desire to feel her grandma's connection—but she couldn't deny that something had changed.

She had the sense that the dog wanted her to follow, and like what had happened with the mysterious breeze earlier, she went with it. It was sleek and muscular, like a working dog, no doubt used for hunting in its day, and it walked along at a leisurely pace, as if time was of no consequence. Indeed, its work had ended long ago. Or had it? What was its intention now? The black hound had long been the omen of darkness to come. Her curiosity didn't allow her to dwell on those old legends long.

As she followed, her brain registered the presence of other tourists in her peripheral vision, their profiles distinguishable yet hazy around the edges. She kept a steady pace as she passed them, confident the dog was not visible to anyone but herself. Passing through the main gate, she glanced up to see the gap in the stonework where the original portcullis would have been, and wondered just how far the animal would take her. The gentle tap of its nails on the cobbled walkway drew her on, until it stopped at the edge of the main gate, looking out onto the countryside below.

Maybe it saw a different view, not the car park down the hill, or the main road that snaked its way up to the castle. She let her eyes adjust for a moment, taking in the idyllic landscape. Just as she was about to turn away, she caught sight of them, the vast army ahead. Her pulse quickened at the sheer number. Even from this great distance, she could make out the riders on horseback, their colorful banners waving in the wind. Every molecule in the air hung heavy with the essence of doom.

Just as she speculated what was to come next, a breeze came from nowhere and the black-eyed hound dissipated into ashes that floated up into the wind like charred paper. Its message had been delivered, its duty fulfilled.

She stood there in silence as another icy sensation came over her, and she shuddered, knowing she was not alone. When she turned, she jumped back, her hand over her heart. There, upon the stone steps of the gateway, stood a tall, lean woman, her blonde hair tucked under a high headdress. She looked polished and poised, as regal as a queen in her own right. Cecily Neville—a royal duchess, wife of the Duke of York and mother to two future kings—was a woman of great importance. She stood with confidence and grace, resembling a painted portrait hanging in a museum. Her skin was as smooth as a delicate piece of china, her eyes a deep sapphire blue. The woman's beauty was unmatched.

Her young children stood at her side, gripping each other's hands. As Richard clung to his sister's balmy palm, the tremble of fear rose within his little body. He looked up to his mother, staring out at the approaching troops with a stony expression. Her resolve was more unmovable than the high castle walls at their backs.

Having borne eleven children, she was not a frail being. She faced the uncertainty head on, her icy glare unwavering. Her husband had ridden off, doing the only thing he could on realizing the battle would not be in his favor. By now he was in Ireland, leaving his wife and children alone to stand against the army who would besiege Ludlow. The army would tear through the castle with reckless disregard, leaving its lavish contents in tattered disarray. Yet the duchess would stand her ground, as noble as the birthright she'd been given. She was a Neville, descended from one of the most powerful families in England.

Deep within her chest, Adelia was filled with the angst of both mother and children. Richard clutched his sister's hand with a panicked terror. They had lived a life shielded from all the discomforts of the world. The approaching army reflected in the tear-filled eyes of the children like a cavalry of ghost riders forged in hell. Every element of the safe and secure life they had was shattered.

Reaching out to pull her children into her skirt, the noble duchess had to steady her own trembling hand. These were uncertain times. Once, her safety and that of her children would have been assured by her lineage, but she could no longer rely on that. Her only protection was her unshakable faith in God.

Cecily was a woman of great piety, spending the majority of her days in prayer. Now, more than ever, faced with the lurching marauders approaching Ludlow Castle, she needed God's protection. Adelia felt the tug of faith and fear within the woman.

Even as she experienced the emotions of the terror-stricken mother and children, she took solace in knowing the outcome of this horrific day. Regardless of the Lancastrians' destruction of the castle, no harm would come to Cecily or her children. The risk of such an atrocity would do nothing for the Lancastrian cause, only leading to more opposition. The duchess was an object of value to the lords, born of great name and even greater fortune. Should the day come that she was left as a dowager duchess, her value would easily be transferred to the next man she married. She was far too much a treasure to be harmed.

In her husband's exile, the duchess and her younger children would be placed under the protection of her sister and brother-in-law. Once again, Richard would be shifted about the country, in the name of a war his father had started. The Wars of the Roses would spur division throughout England for more than thirty years. Little did the six-year-old boy know this division would be the way of things for the rest of his life. Today, the tranquility of his childhood was forever at an end. He would always be fighting someone else's war, with threats around every corner, and any promise of a peaceful existence short lived. Only his death, at thirty-two, would see the beginning of the long war's end.

Leaving Ludlow felt bittersweet. As they pulled the car back onto the road, bound for the town of Tewkesbury, Adelia closed her eyes as she lay her head on the cool glass of the window. With vivid imagination, she replayed the castle scenes in her mind, seeing details that had escaped her notice in the moment. With each new revelation, she added her own interpretation, trying to decipher what the whispers wanted her to see. A deeper meaning always existed—a hidden message buried beneath first impressions. Puzzling it out was the tricky part. She pulled out her notebook and jotted down a few more notes she could analyze later.

Chapter Seventeen

Tewkesbury Abbey was a monument of the ages, sitting high near the banks of the Severn River. Though the town was always prone to flooding, the cherished abbey had never been touched by the river's waters. For many, this was proof of it truly being a house of God, and a survivor of turbulence. Its body of gray stone had withstood the protestant reformation during the reign of Henry VIII. Under Thomas Cromwell, Henry's chief minister, the country's most beautiful abbeys were left as rubble. The soul of the country had been crushed by the whims of a tyrannical king and his advisors. During the English civil war, the abbey once again found itself in danger. The ever-determined citizens of Tewkesbury could not accept such a fate for their beloved house of worship that had withstood so many trials, and they stepped forward to save it once more. Pulling together every possible penny they could give, they purchased the abbey outright from the crown for the astounding amount of £450. Since that day, the abbey belonged to the people.

The compact town of Tewkesbury became the site of the final showdown between the Lancastrian Queen Margaret of Anjou and the Yorkist King Edward IV. This was a war waged between them for many years. The House of York were triumphant in removing the weak Henry VI from the throne, declaring Edward IV as the rightful king. Over the past nine years, Queen Margaret had fought tirelessly to find a way to restore her husband, now mentally incapacitated, to the throne. She led the army westward, hoping to cross the Severn and enter Wales, where they would join with Jasper Tudor's Lancastrian army and face off with the Yorkists once and for all. However, she would soon find that fortune had different plans. The Yorkist army had anticipated her arrival and moved to cut off their passage across the river.

Margaret would not see the bloodshed of the battlefield, seeking refuge in a local religious house, where she awaited the news. The battle of Tewkesbury did not bring her the victory she desired. Quite the opposite. Though details of his death are vague, the Prince of Wales was slain in the battle. In the wake of her husband's incapacity, Margaret hoped to rule as regent for her son. His death brought a mother's grief and the end of a fiery queen's dreams of restoring her family to the throne.

The death of the prince dealt a harsh blow to the Lancastrian army as well. Seeing the battle swaying in favor of the Yorkists, the Lancastrian lords abandoned their troops and fled for the sanctuary of the nearby abbey. Their troops were little more than peas-

ants or serfs—men and boys—given no choice but to be recruited
for the cause. The lords, in their selfish cowardice, left them at the
mercy of the opposing army in order to save their own skin. Yet
fortune's wheel and karma are blood sisters, hell-bent on justice.
As it turned out, Tewkesbury Abbey was not a house of sanctuary,
with no such rules of religious refuge applying there.

Adelia stood with her back against the cold wall, taking in all
before her. The nave of the great abbey was lit by the pale amber
glow of hundreds of candles. Smoke rolled off the charred wicks,
scenting the air with the earthy smell of melting wax. The light
only illuminated a fraction of the space, leaving the farthest reaches
of the walls cloaked in darkness, with the towering ceiling of vault-
ed stone nothing more than a black abyss to spur the imagination.

The energy felt heavy, almost ominous. Terror lurked somewhere, just beyond her vision. She could almost hear the thunder
of its approach, feel the sizzling heat of its breath on her skin.
Something was about to happen—something of earth-shattering
proportions. She snapped, as if to attention, as prickles climbed up
her back, the sensation so intense she was compelled to turn and
face the two massive arched oak doors at the back of the church.

As they swung open, a burst of wind blew her hair from her face.
A flash of vivid color emerged from a gray cloud of dust. Bloody
and battered men, their red and blue surcoats ripped and stained
with the markings of war, stormed the abbey with unrelenting
force. As the distant shrieks of the abbess reverberated off the stone
walls, Adelia stood as still as a saint carved in stone, unable to
muster any more movement than the rise and fall of her chest. Men

roared as they clamored up the aisle, the shove of their shoulders as they pushed their way through her, knocking her off her center of gravity.

A pungent stench of dirt, sweat, and blood permeated the nave as utter chaos took over. The knights of the House of York seized hold of the Lancastrian lords without a shred of humanity. Shouts and cries filled her ears as they were dragged from their false sanctuary to the impending darkness that lurked outside the looming doors. She closed her eyes to escape the horror but couldn't stop the barbarity ringing in her ears like the tolling of a church bell.

The energy hung thick in the air, emotions pelting her from every direction, one opposing the other: fear standing off to anger; victory facing defeat. Even with her eyes clenched shut, she watched as a river of deep red liquid flowed across the moonlit grass, dripping from the dull metal of an ax's honed blade and trickling across the cobblestone walkway that led to the church's steps. As she followed the red river, she gasped on seeing the lifeless bodies of the Lancastrian lords. She had known their fate all along but, here, as she witnessed the horror of severed flesh, it became so real.

She turned back to face the nave, struggling to shake the horrific images from her mind. The sound had ceased, the space now bathed in golden streams of sunlight as they danced through the massive windows. She stared ahead, past the rood screen to the altar draped in fine silk cloth, lit by streams of sunlight, each creating a hazy mist as they bounced off the air particles. The glow was almost blinding, and she squinted as she turned her head away, only to catch sight of a solitary figure kneeling in the front pew, oblivious to the bright light.

With his head bowed, the dirt-soaked strands of his blond hair cloaked his features. Even kneeling, she could tell he was tall in stature. Without thinking, she moved forward with silent steps, as if each action was not of her conscious bidding. Nearly halfway up the aisle, she sensed that someone was behind her, and just as she went to turn, a dark-haired figure passed inches from her right shoulder. She looked up into two ink-black eyes, the face streaked with dirt and sweat. He stared right at her, though her presence could not be known. His slight build was apparent beneath his layers of armor and, even by today's standards, he was handsome, his deep, dark stare giving him a mysterious quality that intoxicated her. She felt his strength, his self-possessed determination filling her heart.

He was just seventeen, young in her time, but, in his own, a full-grown man. It was clear he had already witnessed the ravages of war, watched as lives were taken, and taken them himself. She thought of the men returning from the second world war, little more than a decade ago. As a young girl, she had witnessed first-hand the unseen scars left from battle. The physical scars could be healed over time but the images remained long after the last of the artillery left the field. In all her time studying Richard, she had never really considered this. The weight of the bloodshed he had seen must have left an indelible mark on his life. Though considered a grown man by his peers, he had witnessed far too much brutality in his youth to escape the mental wounds that inevitably followed, going on to carry this with him throughout his life. He would always be fighting his inner demons, never free from the battlefield, even when the land was at peace.

The hold on her limbs eased, and she moved behind Richard as he approached his brother, the only sound being the shift of his padded vest and the soft tap of his riding boots on the stone floor. She kept a clear distance, not wanting to do anything to disturb this moment—to send it fading back into the past.

Richard eased his way onto the long wooden pew and sat beside Edward. For a moment, each stared at the high altar with the hazy eyes of exhaustion. This had been a great day, affording them immeasurable victory in their cause. The warrior queen had been captured, her Lancastrian alliance brought to its knees—her son, heir to the throne, slain on the battlefield, putting an end to her ambitions of ruling through him. Anne Neville, the prince's young widow, was in their custody—safe—her vast inheritance once again controlled by the House of York. The old king, the one Edward had deposed nearly a decade ago, was imprisoned in the Tower of London, too incapacitated to know a burning sun from a pale-lit moon. Now the stage was set for a final victory. Edward IV was closer than he had ever been in the last few months to retaking the throne he had stolen nine years ago.

Adelia witnessed this private moment from a safe distance but close enough to hear. The bitter scent of battle lingered heavy in the air, from sweat-soaked garments and skin caked with the dust kicked up as their war horses raced across the English landscape.

Edward raised his head and placed his hand on Richard's arm, as though he had just noticed his brother's presence. "It is time to put an end to this once and for all. We know what must be done."

Richard glanced around, ensuring that no one was within earshot, then bowed his head and steepled his hands at his mouth, as if praying. "The blood of an old king cannot be on the hands of the new king. Brother, I shall be the one to end this matter. You must be far away from any accusations."

"We must end this strife which has plagued our house for too long," Edward whispered, his heart heavy with the realization of how much had been given to see this victorious day.

"We must honor our father who gave his life to see this day for the House of York." Richard grimaced, having spoken of his fallen father. Edward was ten years older, and the leader of the family now. When the duke died, paving the way for his oldest son to seize the throne, the responsibility of looking after his younger siblings had fallen on him as well. From boyhood, Richard looked upon his older brother as a hero, and always would.

"You are a loyal brother, Richard. I shall never forget that you have fought by my side. Greatness is in your future. You shall be a man remembered through the ages for your valor."

Richard allowed a half smile. "It is you, my king, who shall be remembered. I will be of no significance to the world when I leave it."

Adelia smiled to herself as his words echoed through her. How little Richard had known that his story would live on through the ages, to be twisted and turned in a thousand ways, but never forgotten. He would be a hero and a villain alike; his colors changed any time it suited the storyteller.

The whispers had allowed her a glimpse into this intimate moment between Richard and his brother after the battle, but she struggled to understand why this particular interaction had come through. Was it to tell her that, despite this great victory, the tasks that lay ahead for Richard were less than pleasant? That even in the midst of great triumph, dark deeds still lay in his path? She understood full well what dark deeds those were.

It would not be long before the Lancastrian king, held safely in the Tower of London, would be dead. The official statement would be that the old king died of pure melancholy, stricken with grief over the death of his one and only son. Yet speculation that this was a false explanation would swirl like leaves on a windy day. Richard would be present in the tower on the day of the king's passing. As was the custom, the dead monarch's body would lie in state, allowing mourners to see for themselves that he was really dead. Historical accounts would tell of his hair matted with blood—hardly a sign of a man who had died of sadness. Even if she had never allowed herself to believe that his death was by Richard's hand, she could not deny that the evidence pointed squarely to foul play.

Now that the House of York had succeeded in reclaiming the crown, few would dare to accuse Richard, brother of King Edward IV, of such an atrocity—at least not in public. Yet, the rumors would linger like a boiling undercurrent, giving rise to the notion that he was capable of many kinds of evil. This would be the start of the persona that followed him for the rest of his life, and beyond.

Allowing the moment and their words to fully sink in, she felt a deep heaviness in her chest, which she strove to push aside. Though far removed from the research methodology she usually employed, she was here to find out the truth about Richard, and the whispers, while telling her the story, were under no obligation to make it the one she wanted to hear.

The flicker of candlelight gave Richard's war-weary face a warm glow. He sat still, even as Edward stood and walked away, his jaw clenched tight, his brow creased as a war waged inside him—insecurity and indecisiveness battling against his sense of duty. Just as his inner thoughts became audible enough for her to hear, another voice rang out, calling her name, its familiar chime echoing off the hollow walls of the enormous church.

"Did you see they have a gift shop," Cassandra said, full of glee as she held up a small bag, looking like a child with a handful of candy.

Dazed, Adelia's jaw tightening as the giddy Cassandra pulled some idiotic tourist knickknack from the brown bag. Whatever Richard was about to reveal had been dashed away by her absent-minded approach. For someone who claimed to be so aware of people's emotions, the woman did not seem to be the least bit fazed at her dark glare.

As Cassandra babbled on about the gift shop, Adelia was close to exploding. The only thing that kept her from doing so was the fact they were standing in a church. Every single time! She does this every single time.

With a swift inhalation, the heaviness of the scene revealed by the whispers dissolved, and Cassandra's exuberance at her bag of trinkets seeped into her heart. She was like a kid at a carnival, eager to show off a prize she had won at a game of chance. Chastising her now was unthinkable. As irritating as her constant interruptions were, they were also a saving grace for them both.

That evening, Adelia retired to her room at the inn right after dinner, leaving Cassandra and Daniel to entertain themselves. Had the day not been so exhausting, she would have gone out and explored the town. Also, after Cassandra's intrusion at the abbey, she found herself needing a bit of distance. She had too many thoughts to puzzle out, and was far too tired to go out sightseeing.

She leaned back against the headboard of her bed, journals and papers scattered around her, and thumbed through her black notebook as she began reviewing the mass of notes she had scribbled. Keeping focus was a struggle, her attention flitting away from her writing and coming to rest on the thick binding of the book Paul had given her. She pushed her body forward with a weary heave and pulled the heavy tome into her lap. Thankful that she'd marked the page with a scrap of paper, she opened it to the sketch of the little church in Coldridge. Her chest tingled with excitement as she skimmed over it with her fingertips.

Her thoughts of Richard couldn't be stilled, in particular how her own comfortable childhood was so opposite to the turmoil he had endured. How could the wide-eyed boy in the chapel at Ludlow even begin to fathom the life that awaited him? He had grown up on tales of chivalric knights in gleaming armor, who rescued fair maidens from impending doom. His poetic soul was filled with the bright colors of royal standards flapping in the wind. There, on the steps of Ludlow, as disaster approached, he saw those dreams shattered. And as the invading army ripped his family's home to pieces, he experienced his first real taste of what war was about: total destruction. The gleam of blood-soaked swords and battle axes was scorched into his heart like a branding iron. Loyalty and honor meant kill or be killed, concepts far too cruel for a child to understand, yet Richard comprehended them fully.

She could now understand the pure blackness in the eyes of the adolescent boy she saw at Middleham Castle. Richard had been sent there to begin his training as a knight under the tutelage of the Earl of Warwick. By then he would have seen enough death and destruction to understand that his training was about survival. Victory meant to live. Failure, to die.

As a man, at the start of his career at Tewkesbury Abbey, he no longer believed that being a knight was a fairytale existence. He held tight to the honor of his family, with everything existing outside that loyalty expendable. All that mattered was the protection of those he loved. He would prove time and again the lengths he would go to for those in his inner circle. No deed was too great or too dark when it came to the preservation of the House of York.

These were the parts of his story Adelia had always been drawn to. After his death, his legacy was long overshadowed by depictions of an evil man. Yet, again and again, historical accounts of the time showed that he was loved and respected by the people of the northern lands he ruled over before becoming king. He sought to bring real justice to the common man, and perpetuated the concept that a man was innocent until proven guilty. Indeed, he dared to go against the grain and challenge social norms of the time, with well-documented accounts of men of high rank being held accountable for their misdeeds, when they would have gotten away with such behavior before. Though being one of the most powerful men in the land, he had a way of making the common man feel as though he had a voice.

While he wasn't perfect, he was a man of his own time, when thoughts and practices were starkly different to those considered suitable today. As Adelia followed the story of a son, brother, husband, and king, she could not get past how much evidence existed to dispute the claims that he was a power-hungry monster. Each vision had provided new layers to the depth of his character, and none painted that established picture.

She stacked her papers and books on the bedside table, switched off the lamp, and slid under the cool linen of the bedcovers. When she closed her eyes, blocking out the silver shimmer of moonlight streaming through the windows, there, in the dim hollow of darkness, she saw the black eyes of Richard as he passed her in the old abbey's nave. She had spent years studying his life, but the whispers told her so many things about him that the filled pages of her notebooks could not reveal. As she stared into the inky abyss of his gaze, she sensed in the quickening of her heart that something was missing.

On the verge of slumber, she flinched at the uncanny sensation of a hand grasping hers. Richard? The serenity of its warmth was the only thing that kept her from bolting upright and fleeing the room. Is he trying to tell me something? With so much of his story yet to be unraveled, maybe he wants to be the one to guide me to the truth.

Chapter Eighteen

"Stop the car," Adelia shouted as they neared the edge of Tewkesbury, bound for Devon.

Without so much as a question, Daniel slammed on the brakes, the sudden jolt sending the contents of Adelia's purse spilling onto the floorboards like marbles tumbling from a jar. Before the handbrake had been pulled, she'd open the door, with Cassandra and Daniel looking at one another in a state of confusion.

She stepped out and stood at the edge of a field of tall grass. The low buzz of insects all but stopped as a strange quietness fell around her, as though she had just entered a desolate land. A car door opened behind as she waded through the heavy grass, heading for a small rise, where she found a mound shielded by overgrown shrubbery. Even through the dense foliage, the shattered remains of stone walls could be seen. It was difficult to make out what it had been, with most of its stones no doubt pillaged through the years to build other structures.

As she peered through the jumbled brambles, a faint whisper came to her on the wind. She released her tight grip on the fabric of her dress and raised her arms, not sure what she felt other than a certain denseness in the air. Clouds rolled in and blocked the burning rays of the morning sun, and though she was sure she was standing still, the earth gave a tiny shift, forcing her to sway to keep her balance.

Someone's approach from behind caught her attention, though they kept their distance. It was most likely Daniel, so she didn't turn around. A gust of wind blew past her and she watched, mesmerized, as the thick foliage among the rocks twittered away into a thousand emerald particles, rising to the sky. Stone by stone, the walls reformed until a modest little church stood before her. The earth around her gave out a low hum, barely audible but for its resonance within her.

The temperature around her changed from hot to cold in quick succession, and a gentle breeze brought soft whispers, their vibrations carrying two voices. Her senses pulled against her, drawing her to look away to her right. There on the edge of the clearing surrounding the church stood two shadowy figures. She moved toward them, inching along, every step cautious. The clouds parted just enough to bring the dusty-gray forms into focus. Out of the corner of her eye, she caught a rapid movement and flinched on seeing two tethered horses flicking their heads to avoid buzzing flies. The largest was broad, sturdy, and midnight black, while the other, a rich charcoal gray, was smaller, its flanks speckled white. She marveled at their sleek muscular forms, honed by countless hours of travel. Then the black horse lifted its head to stare right at her. Sensing the distraction, the gray followed suit, until both were scrutinizing her with the same intensity as she studied them.

This dumbfounded her. As with the hound back at Ludlow Castle, she was positive these magnificent creatures could sense her presence, even if they couldn't see her. They existed in another time, a world far removed from her own, yet they could feel her presence just as she felt theirs. In all the time she had possessed her gift, she had only ever focused on the people of the past. How the whispers worked with other creatures was something she had never thought to ask her grandma before she died. Right now, she stood in uncharted territory. Each time she channeled her gift, it seemed to change, as if the closer she got to understanding her power, the more it evolved, always keeping her at arm's length. It refused to allow her full control, not wanting to be harnessed to her will. For reasons she could not understand, it fought against her.

She shifted her gaze back to the two figures, a man and young woman in full color, standing just a few yards from the horses. Having been so caught up in her thoughts, their presence had slipped her mind.

Rogue streams of sunlight fought their way through the clouds, illuminating the lean features of Richard. He looked far more polished than the battle worn man she had observed back at the abbey, his dirt-stained livery replaced with a crisp black doublet, his raven locks washed and combed, and the stern masculine lines of his face much softer. Now he seemed well rested, though she could still hear the steady drum of his thoughts—restless and unrelenting. Standing tall, he looked down at a fair-skinned woman, her coppery hair spun and coiled under the netting of her headdress. She wore a black gown, the color of mourning.

It could only be one person: Anne Neville, recently widowed, her young husband lost in the skirmish at Tewkesbury. Her face held a solemn expression, but her sadness was not that of love lost. Surely there was anguish at the death of her husband? Adelia got no sense of a deep connection between them, though it was clear she grieved for his untimely passing. Her marriage had not been a love match—more a union of convenience between two people who had no voice to object—yet they had only been married for seventeen months. She and the young prince had little connection as friends, and he'd barely acknowledged her existence during their short marriage. She never felt fulfilled as a wife, always knowing she was a means to an end in her husband's quest to one day rule the kingdom. Her inheritance brought wealth and power; she was nothing more than that.

Even though she never felt secure as a wife, as a dowager princess her entire life was cast into more uncertainty than she had ever known. Once her period of mourning was through, she would be cast back onto the market like a prize calf. Her entire life had been controlled, always at the will of someone's political game. Now that her father was dead and her mother within the sanctuary of Beaulieu Abbey, she had no idea who would control her destiny. She grieved not only for the loss of her husband but, once again, for the absence of freedom she never really had in the first place.

Richard spoke in hushed tones, his head close to hers, as if hesitant to let others hear. The way he beheld the young widow, with a genuine fondness in his eyes, conveyed a real softness that touched Adelia. Even when they were children, back when he'd been under the guardianship of her father, he always felt a certain duty toward her. They were both the younger children, used to being overlooked and inconsequential, and to some degree, he could relate to her worry. He had never been entirely in control of his own future. Now that the prince was dead, the queen captured, and the incapable king imprisoned, the path was forged for Edward to reclaim the throne he'd lost a few months ago. Richard knew Anne was in a serious predicament, being a wealthy heiress and now a widow. He was also sure that, right now, in this moment, the fervent pounding in his chest was love.

As a child, he had been briefly betrothed to her. Though the negotiations for the match had fallen apart with her father's rebellion against Edward, he could never quell his hope to one day marry her. With their paths diverging along the way, many years had passed since they'd seen each other. Now, in the new light of morning, he looked upon her, so beautiful, her vulnerability plucking at his heart, the delicate frame he remembered replaced with an angelic presence. He had a need to possess her, not as a lord to rule over her but as a man driven by the desire to tend to her every need—to hold her in his arms and soothe all the worries of her mind—to kiss her rosebud mouth until her tears ceased.

He was not used to the softness he felt for her, having always controlled his emotions, knowing that any hint of fragility could be used against him. As much as he wanted to tell her how he felt, he could not be sure she would reciprocate. She had spent seventeen months as a wife to the Lancastrian prince, but what she felt for the man was unclear. Just days after learning that her husband had died, he could hardly confess his feelings and expect a receptive response. As lovers, they were as ill-fated as Sir Lancelot and Guinevere in *Le Morte D'Arthur* If ever they were to become one, they would have to surmount the mountain of odds in their way. They were on opposite sides of the war, both loyal to families embroiled in a blood feud. But one thing he had learned was that fate turns, and the unexpected often becomes reality. If he truly wanted her as his wife, and he did, he would have to be patient and wait for the day their paths crossed again. He was sure that would happen, for he planned to do everything in his power to make it so.

Adelia stood in frustration, watching as Richard whispered sweet words of comfort to the frightened Anne. With his voice so low, many of his words were unclear however much she strained to hear. Conversations had always come through easier than visions but something about this moment was so guarded, she could only watch their silent emotions. Anne's grieved face seemed to soften at the sound of Richard's soothing voice, his hands on the arms of her dress, smoothing out the wrinkled fabric that had been stuffed in a traveling trunk, with no time to be brushed and laid out on the long journey back to England.

Richard helped her onto the waiting horse, the color of gray ashes, its back barely dipping under her light weight. He would escort her to Coventry, to be kept in the charge of his brother George and Anne's sister Isabel. No doubt he had negotiated this arrangement with Edward, as a means of ensuring Anne was not treated as a traitor to the crown because of her alignment with the Lancastrians.

Edward had trusted his young brother's judgment and agreed, knowing that Anne had been a pawn. It wouldn't be long before Richard found that placing Anne under the control of George was a grave mistake. In the coming months, she would be treated poorly by her brother-in-law as he schemed to take control of her half of the Neville inheritance. As Richard sought permission from Edward to marry her, he would find himself resisted by George. Initially, George only agreed to give his blessing if he could keep Anne's inheritance, going so far as to hide her away. Richard would search for her, finding her dressed as a kitchen maid in London. Through the cover of darkness, he would whisk her away from his brother's clutches to St. Martin's Sanctuary.

In the end, he would marry his precious Anne, salvaging her claim to her inheritance and exalting her to the role of Duchess of Gloucester. She would be his loving and devoted wife for about twelve years, bearing him just one child, a son named Edward. When Richard became king in 1483, Anne would walk beside him in a joint coronation, a rare thing in those days. She would die a few months after her son, and just shy of her twenty-ninth birthday, leaving behind a husband who would say, "My heart is as heavy as a man's could be."

They rode off into the distance, a procession of gray knights accompanying them, their banners flapping in the wind. The images became faint particles and Adelia turned to look back at Daniel, standing patient at the base of the hill. Cassandra sat on the hood of the car, sunning her long legs, not interested in the least at what had taken her cousin across the field.

"He loved her so much," Adelia said to herself. "She was his queen long before a crown was placed on her head. He loved her for so long that he could never have remarried after her death. Wherever she was, his heart followed."

Daniel made his way up the slope to her side. "What was here?" he asked, surveying the pile of rocks and overgrown vines.

"Do you remember how it was said that after the battle of Tewkesbury, when the House of York had beaten back the Lancastrians and the prince was killed, Anne Neville and Queen Margaret were found in a poor religious house? I believe this is the spot. I saw Richard and Anne. This is where she was found, then brought by Richard to Coventry."

His eyes widened. "You saw them together?"

"Yes!" She flapped her hands with excitement. "Right here in the flesh. It's as if Richard wants me to know that he loved her. That even in his life full of such upheaval, his love for her was constant. A safe haven for a ship lost in the churning of the sea. I don't know why but he wants me to know. He is insistent. Over and over, it plays out in my mind." She took a breath. "I know you think it's implausible"

He arched one eyebrow. "I am skeptical, it's true, and I do what skeptics do. I think there are plenty of reasons to believe that Richard never put himself in a situation where Anne could not be played to his advantage. Yet, even I cannot say that he didn't love a woman with whom he spent the greater part of his life. He was only a man. I think it's implausible that he would have done what he did for her without caring about her wellbeing."

"Do you think Richard wants me to know that he really loved Anne?" She gave him an expectant look. "Maybe they had a love so deep that time cannot erase their bond? I can feel it so clearly—it is so strong."

"Maybe he wants to dispel the rumors that have swirled around him for years, like the vicious gossip that he tried to poison his wife to marry his own niece in order to keep his crown secure. Maybe he just wants to show you what real love looks like. Perhaps his message is more personal than you realize."

Adelia tongued the inside of her bottom lip, uncomfortable with Daniel's words. They hit a little too close to home. She felt a strong bond to Richard but it was impossible to believe it was reciprocal, that he was trying to speak to her about his life, or her own for that matter. Her gift, to the best of her knowledge, allowed her to see the past, not to engage in it. Richard was just existing in his own day, a man of his own time, unaware of her presence. The energy that brought forth the whispers had its own ambitions. Whether it was to see what needed to be seen, or show some depth that could never be conveyed in the archives of history, the energy chose what came through. She had learned how to connect in such a way that she could manipulate the visions. What meanings were to be derived were always subject to her own interpretations. Nothing was ever explained. Closure was never given.

"I have held us up on our journey to Devon," she said, casting one last glance at the remnants of the church. "We should be going. I can do the rest of my thinking in the car."

Daniel nodded once, not giving her any argument, and they made their way back to Cassandra, who smiled as they approached, sliding off the sun-drenched hood and taking her place on the backseat again.

As Daniel pulled onto the road, Adelia could not help but look back to the clearing where Richard had stood. Writing her research had proven difficult so far, and it was not going to get any easier. She was less than a month into the summer and had already learned so much about Richard as the man, long before he'd set sights on being king. In reality, most of what she learned came through her gifts as a keeper of the whispers, a descendant of the Babington line. Not one shred of that could be included in any submitted research. The academic circles would laugh her right back to Boston. Just as Daniel had done when they revealed the truth about Amy Robsart Dudley, she would have to chronicle two stories: write about Richard in a way that pleased the judgmental scholars, and keep the real story to herself.

Chapter Nineteen

C oldridge, Devon, was just about as remote a village as a recluse could desire. As no main roads passed through, it was only accessible by a succession of winding back roads that snaked through the countryside. The church of St. Matthew sat high up on a hill, its clock face overlooking the village a few miles away. Coldridge was a remarkable preservation of the past, with thatched cottages and cob-stone buildings bordered by low garden walls of mortared rock. Like many others, the village was so picturesque, it could have sprung from the pages of a storybook.

Daniel drove along its narrow streets, his expression confirming that finding parking was something of a chore. The town boasted only one inn, as overnight guests to the tiny speck on the map were somewhat rare. Most visitors to the area would have chosen to stay about twenty miles away in the cathedral city of Exeter. Coldridge hosted a population of less than five hundred people, while Exeter's was near one hundred thousand. Cassandra would, no doubt, have preferred the city feel of Exeter, her need for entertainment far greater than Daniel and Adelia's. Neither of them had to say a word, agreeing that the isolation of Coldridge was just perfect.

She had to smile as Daniel cursed to himself as he searched for a parking spot in the cluttered town square. Cassandra wasn't bothered. Even as they bumped along the uneven street, she slept, sprawled across the backseat. Adelia gazed out the window, examining each of the businesses dotting the main street, the left side lined with a bakery, butcher shop, tailor, and the village hall. Off to her right, a small family-owned restaurant was situated near the old inn. No surprise that, even in a village so small, there was at least one notable pub. She imagined it to be a gathering place at the end of a long work day. All the buildings looked as though they had been lovingly preserved, passed down from generation to generation, like a box of priceless family heirlooms.

A few buildings were tucked away off the main street, making it impossible to discern what they were. All in all, Coldridge's downtown was rather uneventful, but it was the kind of quaint little village a writer could hide themselves away in for a while and emerge with something that might rival the inventory of Ross's library back at the old manor house.

On their second circuit of the village, Daniel let out a low triumphant whoop when he managed to find a suitable spot for the car. When Adelia stood on the sidewalk and stretched herself out, she realized she was in love with every element of the village.

After pulling out their luggage, they trudged along the narrow sidewalk to the inn, a modest old stone building with chipped yellow paint on the door. Daniel, ever the planner, had called ahead, booking the three rooms for four nights. Coldridge was not the tourist attraction that many of the towns in Devon were, so getting rooms in the only inn proved no issue.

He checked them in with ease, and handed off the room keys, much to Adelia's delight. Their drive from Tewkesbury had not been a long one, but the whispers, and analyzing them, had taken it out of her, and even though it was only early afternoon, she found herself in need of rest before venturing out.

She slung her heavy bag onto a small upholstered chair in the room, then flung herself across the bed's soft cotton coverlet. Slumber came easy, as did dreams, as vivid as the visions back at the old abbey. There on a hill, high above trees and rolling fields, she stood, staring at a bright light in the sky. It was so intense that, even as she lay in sleep, it stung her eyes. The sun shone like a magnificent ball of fire, melting itself into two then three orbs, hanging like a trio of golden plates, casting their brilliant light upon every living being below.

Then, without warning, the orbs melted back into a single circle. With slow and steady grace, its silhouette became cloaked in darkness until the entire day gave way to night. Her breath became labored as her blood pulsed through her with increasing speed. The splendor of summer was gone, its brilliance blacked out by an imposing, rain-soaked winter that felt as though it might rage on for years.

Still lost in the incoherence of her dream, she felt a twinge along her legs and looked down to her feet. There, against the shadowy grass, a long stem reached up out of the ground, supporting the most beautiful white rose she had ever seen. It was in full bloom, attached to nothing but the single stem. As she bent to touch the white cloud of petals, the stem gave way and released from the ground without so much as a pull. Beholding the delicate masterpiece in her hand, she frowned as a red liquid seeped from between its alabaster petals. Its flow quickened, covering her hand, and just as she dropped the stem, she jolted awake.

Bolting upright, she blinked at the pale sunlight streaming through the window's heavy plaid drapes. It was still daylight. She glanced at the clock, surprised that she'd slept no more than an hour, though her body felt as though she had been asleep for days. Her breath came shallow as she tried to relax. Someone laughed outside the door. Cassandra. No mistaking her. Then a man laughed. Daniel. Their voices faded as they moved down the hall, chatting away. A sharp pang of an emotion she had a rare occasion to feel circled her heart, hitting her deep. While she and Daniel may no longer be an item, was she willing to let him go entirely? The heartfelt sound of his laughter had provoked it, and she realized that she hadn't heard him laugh so genuinely in quite a long time.

As she slipped from the bed to gather herself, she couldn't help but wonder if Daniel had somehow fallen for Cassandra's effortless charms. Up until now, he seemed disinterested in her, hardly noticing her existence. Perhaps he has grown weary of my indecision. Maybe he has finally opened his eyes to see that the world is full of other women, most of whom are not so hell bent on holding him at a distance. She always thought the day would come when he would tire of being her puppet of sorts; she had seen the signs creeping in but never took the time to heed them.

She grabbed up her things and left the room. As she walked down the hallway, the faint sound of conversation filtered up the stairs. Daniel's voice, jovial and light. She took a moment to clear her thoughts. He was a grown man, old enough to make his own decisions, but Cassandra could beguile a man without even trying. In reality, she probably had no interest in him, but if he had the notion to take an interest in her, he would be pulled in before he knew what happened. She mustered up a smile as she entered the inn's front parlor.

"Sorry I took so long," she said, sliding into the empty chair between Cassandra and Daniel.

"No bother," he responded, not appearing to pick up on her over-friendly demeanor.

Cassandra slouched back in her chair, oblivious to Adelia's side-eyed glance, well accustomed, it seemed, to that expression being thrown in her direction.

"I was planning on making a quick trip to Exeter this afternoon," Daniel said. "I need some things and Cassandra has a list. Do you want to ride along with us?"

"Actually, I was hoping to visit Saint Matthew's this afternoon." She retained her smile. "Would it be too much trouble for you to drop off Cassandra and I at the church before you go? We could spend an hour or so there and be done by the time you come back."

Cassandra made a little face at the prospect of going to a boring old church rather than the bustling city of Exeter. Even though her preference was clear, Adelia did not relent.

"I was hoping to go with you," Daniel said. "I would like to see the building myself. Besides, I wouldn't want you to be waiting on me if I get held up. The church is out in the country and you will not be able to just walk back. Why don't we go tomorrow?"

"We can go tomorrow too," she said. "I will be glad to visit it more than once, but I would really like to go today, if you don't mind?"

Of course he minded—his expression made it clear. As with all the places they had visited so far, she would have preferred to visit on her own. Even in the company of Daniel and Cassandra, she always made a point to wander off by herself. Things came through so much clearer when she could be alone with her thoughts. However, the prospect of Cassandra and Daniel traveling into Exeter together was not the most desirable option, and so she took the best recourse she could to prevent that from happening.

Seeing her steely resolve, Daniel gave a tight shrug to indicate that she had won. This time she refrained from smiling, even as she caught sight of Cassandra's pout.

Daniel got up and fumbled in his pocket before pulling out the car keys. "Let's grab a late lunch first, then I will drop you two off."

After a quick bite to eat, they headed off. The drive out to the old church wasn't long, but it would have been difficult to reach on foot. Its proximity to the village reminded her a bit of Whytham Church back in Oxford, where she had worked to solve the mystery of Amy Robsart Dudley's death. Not far by car but a bit of a haul on foot. She hoped this venture would bring the whispers to her, as it had back then.

The narrow road twisted and curved along a stretch surrounded by small farms and the occasional house set down long gravel lanes, and while the scenery was serene in daylight, she could picture it being dark and eerie come nightfall.

St. Matthew's was located in the remote countryside, high upon a ridge, its tower visible for miles. It had once been a private chapel, situated on the lands of Coldridge Manor. The manor, church, and its surrounding grounds were once owned by Thomas Grey, son to Elizabeth Woodville. After the Wars of the Roses, the Greys continued to be power players in England, even trying to put a granddaughter of Thomas on the throne. Jane Grey lasted only nine days as queen, becoming just another member of the lineage to meet an unfortunate fate on the executioner's block. The insatiable desire for power was fused into this family's bloodline—so much so, it always dominated over risk factors. Time and time again, they would test the wheel of fate.

Daniel pulled into a small stone driveway just off the main road and brought the car to a stop in a makeshift car park.

"I will be back as soon as I can," he said as Cassandra and Adelia climbed out of the car. "If the church closes up before I get back, just wait here."

"We will be right here waiting for you," Adelia assured, waving him on. "I promise we won't leave this spot."

He gave her a distrusting look, no doubt already picturing her becoming impatient and trekking down the road before he could return. As his car disappeared over the hill and out of sight, she gave him a wrinkled-nose face in rebellion. She couldn't dispute that he only insisted she stay put because he knew her so well, but his bossy tone could still be irritating.

The Devon winds felt cool on her skin—surprising for the end of June. Here, on top of the grassy hill, there was little to break the sharp blasts, sending her thick locks whipping about.

Cassandra opened the gate and stepped into the churchyard, commenting on the old weather-beaten tombstones, though the grass around them was well kept. The relentless ravages of time had worn most of the carvings from their surface, and only now and then a name or date was visible. Centuries of exposure to the unpredictable climate had given them a patina that reminded Adelia of the stories of old haunted graveyards she had heard as a child.

The church building was no less foreboding in its appearance—a mass of gray monochromatic stone with a matching slate roof. It was plain in structure, in stark contrast to some of the more elaborate chapels she had seen during her time in England. Its sharp-squared edges were only softened by the gothic arched windows of leaded glass dotting its façade. A small priest's door was inset into one of the side walls, with unruly ivy vines covering its lower portion. The building held a simplistic beauty, with golden wisps of sunlight streaming onto its stony skin. She couldn't help but imagine how haunting it would look at nightfall, its dark figure looming in the twilight.

After a brief examination of the grounds, they padded their way along the uneven cobblestone walkway to the church's entrance. The day was warm and dry but, despite the lack of rain for the past few days, the soft mosses bordering the stones underfoot were slippery. Adelia could not help being nervous about going inside. Its quiet ambiance had her nerves on alert, and even in the deafening silence, the energy around her felt loud. It was hard to distinguish if that was down to excitement or fear, or something in between. With its weight, she had to make a conscious effort to propel herself forward.

Cassandra seemed to sense it too. She had grown far quieter, glancing behind more than once, as if she might have heard something.

"Just the wind," she muttered, her relief obvious.

Adelia stopped at the old weathered door, smiled back at Cassandra, then reached for the heavy iron latch. The metal was warm to the touch, and it surprised her that the door opened with a creaking ease. Coming from America, where things were diligently locked up tight, buildings in England had an unfamiliar accessibility. So much of its history was considered owned by the people that it was never difficult to gain entry to just about anywhere.

She stepped into a narrow entryway that resembled an old gatehouse, on a miniature scale. Again, she found herself struck by the eerie calm. Cassandra meandered through the doorway, thumping against its latch, disturbing whatever peacefulness existed. Adelia shot her a look of reproach, only to have her cousin return it with a sheepish grin and her typical shoulder shrug.

They came to a second door, similar to the first, and she opened it with the same ease. At last, she could behold the church of St. Matthew.

The entire place was empty, at least of the living. Even in the light of day, the chapel looked dim, with the ancient oak rafters adding to the gloomy effect. Old country churches never failed to amaze her. While they were nothing compared to the chapels in the royal palaces, they held a beauty that was all their own. Something that demanded appreciation, even if only for their simplicity. She opened up her purse and deposited a few coins in the donation box, the plink as they fell resonating into the nave.

Cassandra moved to the back of the church, while Adelia found herself drawn to the front. The nave was much smaller than expected, separated from the chancel by an ornately carved rood screen. If she had to guess, the screen was fifteenth century, maybe older. She made a mental note to look that up in the book Paul had given her. As she walked in further, she traced her hands along the wooden pews, their carved ends depicting unique biblical scenes and medieval symbolism. Bright-red leather-bound hymnals were placed along the back of each row.

She examined the screen separating the chancel from the nave. Its flawless construction was of oak, and she focused on the intricacy of its patterns, trying to imagine how many skilled men would have labored for months or even years to accomplish such a feat. Screens like this required the highest quality of materials to complete, and perfection on this scale could only come from a perfect tree. Though Devon itself was peppered with ancient trees, the strong coastal winds were far too brutal for them to grow to full maturity without damage and imperfections, so the lumber would have been imported from elsewhere.

The old chancel, which was plain, held only a simple altar and space for the choir. An area to her left was partitioned off by another carved wooden screen, far simpler than the one she had just examined. It formed a type of side room, sectioned off by a locked door, with "Evans' Chantry" etched above it. She peered through the door's carved spindles, taking note of an old prayer bench, no doubt used by the vicar. As the afternoon sun burned through the clouds, brightening the space, she was struck by the colorful image of a stained-glass window high along the far wall. Butterflies fluttered through her tummy as she realized it was the window from Paul's book, though it looked different in its full-colored radiance. So much more detail sprung to life. The fair locks of a young would-be king, a golden crown resting on his head. Though the window was littered with symbols, she was too far away to make out much detail. She needed to find a way to get closer.

As she scanned the space, she spotted something extraordinary, and unexpected: a stone crypt, tucked into a cove in the wall, with a carved effigy of a man on top, his hands folded in prayer, his head turned, gazing at the bright rays of sun shining through the window. He was weathered by time, yet the prominence of such a figure in the church told her he must have been a man of great importance.

In that moment, as she stood there transfixed by the contents of the Evans' Chantry, a gust of cold wind moved right through her, sending tendrils of her hair dancing across her forehead like the sway of wild flowers in a summer field. She looked around, knowing the church's thick stone walls were sealed too tight for a heavy draft, and shuddered at the icy prickles tiptoeing up her arms. Then a warmth spread through her like black coffee on a lazy winter's day. It started in her toes, inching its way up her legs, until it came to rest in her flushed cheeks. She stiffened at a slight buzz in her ears that morphed into distant voices, drawing closer, and from every direction.

Way too many—thousands—so she closed her eyes to zero in as they echoed off the walls. As she did, something happened that she'd never experienced before: a stream of energy flowed into her, connecting, then pulling her forward to the old wooden screen. When she opened her eyes, she balked at the sight of a foggy ribbon of white dust leading straight from her heart to the stone crypt, its force commanding her to look at the worn effigy. The whispers filling her head had never felt so powerful, yet she could not make out one single word, only feeling the relentless force between herself and the crypt.

She flinched when a spark shot up from the form, like a blacksmith's hammer on hot iron, revealing a shimmering silver glow. The glittering heat dipped and peaked in a slow steady rhythm, like a needle stitching its way through fabric. As it spread across the figure's chest, she recognized the familiar sight of chainmail. Perhaps this man had been a soldier. Maybe for Edward IV's army in one of the numerous battles of his tumultuous reign. Did he know Richard?

"Might I help you?" a man called.

His voice reverberated off the high rafters, shattering the silence and almost making her jump. The energy force released her, sending her stumbling back, and she stood there, staring at the effigy, now devoid of the radiance it had harbored only seconds ago.

She placed a steadying hand across her thumping heart, then turned to face the man, silver haired, clad in a vicar's attire.

"Hello," she said, trying to sound cheerful as she caught her breath. "I am just...admiring the woodwork of these screens. They are absolutely beautiful."

"They are definitely a source of pride here at Saint Matthew's," he replied, his smile beaming.

"I am struck by the craftsmanship of the pew ends too," she added, walking back through the screen entrance to admire the carvings, all too aware of the sudden need to distance herself from the crypt. As she asked about the church's history, the friendly country vicar seemed happy to oblige. He spoke about its general history, his pride obvious as he shared that it still held services each Sunday. It was also frequented by visitors eager to see its beautiful rood screen and arched beamed ceiling.

"And what of that crypt in the chantry?" she asked, raising her hand in its direction. "It seems unique. He must have been a man of great importance to have his own tomb right here in the church.

"That tomb belongs to John Evans. He was Lord of Coldridge Manor and deer parker before his death in the early fifteen hundreds. Over here, you will see another window with a figure that is believed to be him."

She examined the smaller work of glass, depicting an older man, solemnly staring down at her. It wasn't in Paul's book, or maybe she just hadn't seen it. She turned back to face the vicar. "He was a patron to the church, I assume?"

"Most likely," he said, his smile pleasant. "Did you happen to see this ornate pulpit over here?"

His intention was clear: to draw her away from the wooden partition. She had to acquiesce. The pulpit was indeed beautiful, and under normal circumstances she would have wanted to spend time scrutinizing it, but her interest now lay elsewhere.

"It really is marvelous." She brushed her hand over its façade but couldn't take her focus off the locked room that held John Evans and the stained-glass window. "What about this window? Do you know much about it?" She nodded to the magnificent depiction of the fair-haired king.

"It is a rare find indeed. You would be hard pressed to find anything similar in all the country. I have heard of one or two more but have never seen them with my own eyes." His admiration for it was evident.

"It is wonderful, and so complex." She bit back her impatience, unable to peel her gaze from the colored glass.

"Well," he continued, "you see, it is said that it pays homage to Edward V. Are you familiar with him?"

She almost chuckled. "Yes. Son of Elizabeth Woodville and Edward the IV. Most commonly known as one of the princes in the tower, I believe."

"Well, what makes it unique is that Edward V was never actually crowned, you see. He was declared illegitimate by his uncle, Richard III, who took the throne in his stead."

"Ah, yes. I believe these lands were owned by his half-brother, Thomas Grey. I suppose it is not unreasonable to think that his family may have wanted to privately honor his memory. They surely would not have spoken up, but I doubt his mother and brother ever truly believed he was illegitimate."

"That is probably fair to say," he agreed. "We really don't have much information about when or why the window was constructed. As you can see, there is a portion of the top crown missing. Some speculate that the piece came from another window entirely, but I suspect it is most likely from damage at one time."

"There are no records of when it was installed?" She asked the question more to herself, than to the vicar.

"Nothing definitive, but I suspect it was late-fifteenth century, early sixteenth at most."

It made sense. If Prince Edward never made it out of the tower alive, this was a fitting tribute his family may have given to his memory. As custom commanded, there were probably many paid to pray for his eternal soul. Perhaps John Evans had been among those individuals.

St. Matthew's was rife with symbolism, none of which seemed to fit any of the narratives she had already prescribed in her mind. She could almost hear Daniel's censure now: "Look at things objectively. Don't allow yourself to only see what you want to see. Stick to the facts."

But nothing in this place made logical sense. There were dozens of signs, all with meaning, but they didn't fit here, in some small country church in the remote stretches of Devon. Unable to puzzle out any of it, she pressed on, hoping the vicar's vast knowledge of his prized parish could help. She let him rattle on some more before commenting further.

"There is so much Yorkish symbolism here. I suppose being the lands of Thomas Grey, it makes some sense."

Something stirred in his once-bright and friendly eyes, and his expression darkened. She wondered what she had said to warrant this change. His lips thinned and his brows furrowed. Is he analyzing me?

"Are you here on holiday?" he asked, his voice deeper.

"Not exactly—" She cut herself off, caught by a sweep of sheepishness.

"Not exactly?" he echoed.

His demeanor had morphed, though it was subtle, but she couldn't shake the notion that he'd just smelled a rat. She wasn't sure admitting her true purpose would help the situation, but she couldn't think of what else to say. Being a college professor, conducting research for her doctorate wasn't exactly a capital offense. Besides, she was a dreadful liar. She went with honesty. What other choice did she have?

Clasping her hands together, she gave her best attempt at Cassandra's coy coolness. "I am here from Leeds. I work at a university there, and have been studying the life of King Richard III. I came across a picture of this window in a book, and I have been curious why an image of Edward V would be here in Devon. I thought I might come here to find out more about its history."

At the mere mention of her intentions, his eyes darkened even more. He straightened and cleared his throat. "I don't think you will find anything about Richard in here, madam."

"No," she agreed, not missing the chill in his words. He had become more businesslike, no longer the convivial tour guide. Her willingness to show her cards had backfired.

"I don't think this is an area Richard would have frequented during his life. I thought perhaps the church's connection to Edward V might reveal something. Now I am equally curious about John Evans. Are visitors permitted in the Evans' Chantry? I would love to get a closer look, if I may?"

"That area is strictly off limits," he said, his tone clipped. He coughed into his hand, his shoulders softening, as if he knew he had gone too far. "Well, we don't know much about him, outside of what I have told you. Records were not so good in those days."

"I am actually surprised by that," Cassandra chimed in, moving from the back of the church to where they stood. "Documentation in the fifteenth and sixteenth century was usually quite good. Especially within the churches."

Adelia almost laughed out loud at the vicar's startled jump, his gold wedding band clanking against the metal cross hanging around his neck as he clasped his hand to his chest.

"I am sorry, my dear," he said, through a ragged breath. "I did not see you back there."

As he focused on her, taking in the angelic proportions before him, his jaw moved up and down, as though he wanted to speak but couldn't get it out. Adelia almost couldn't hold her laughter in. The man was paralyzed, as if gripped by the same force she had felt earlier. As Cassandra smiled, flashing teeth whiter than the cliffs of Dover, his shoulders shuddered and he began babbling an incoherent stream of words. Well, at least it was an attempt at words. For crying out loud, the woman just compromised a man of God. That poor soul is going to suffer penance for weeks to come.

In that moment, her mirth turned to anger, knowing that her attempts to inspect the chantry had been thwarted. As with every other man in the world, or so it seemed, the pious vicar was no match for Cassandra and her Greek goddess-like attributes. All attempts at having a coherent conversation were now futile.

In utter frustration, she thanked the man for his time and made for the door, seeing no use in staying any longer. With Cassandra's presence serving as nothing but a distraction, she would be hard pressed to get any more information out of him.

Outside, she passed through the rows of weathered tombstones, pacing out her anger. Cassandra didn't follow, and she found herself more than grateful to have space to breathe.

For the thousandth time since the summer started, she wished she'd never agreed to let her cousin into her life. She was barely any closer to finishing her research than a month ago. Whenever she stood on the cusp of progress, Cassandra blundered in and derailed all hope. The woman was simply along for the ride, and her presence had become cumbersome, her contributions minimal, always overshadowed by her constant habit of interrupting.

She let out a low growl in an effort to release the building tension, then rolled her eyes at the sound of the door squeaking behind her. No, the girl had gone too far. Nobody could be so stupid not to see the damage they were doing. She stared out to the valley below as Cassandra approached. Even when her name was called, she refused to respond, knowing well that her words, if she could muster them, would be less than kind.

"What did I do?" Cassandra asked.

Adelia spun around to face her. "You don't have to do anything. Girls like you can just be. You're distracting enough to men by just being present."

"What is that supposed to mean?" Cassandra said through gritted teeth.

"Exactly what I just said. You just waltz through life without a care. Some of us don't have that luxury, Cousin. Some of us have to scrape and claw to earn what we desire."

"Why are you being such a bitch?"

"I'm not being a bitch. My life is a shambles right now and I need you to take the brunt of it at the moment. Okay?"

"Not okay!" Cassandra snapped. "I am not here to be your emotional punching bag."

"Emotional...?" Adelia groaned, then flipped her a dismissive wave. "You wouldn't understand."

"Really?" Cassandra jammed her fists onto her hips and leaned forward. "You have the world by the ass, but it's still not enough." Her fury erupted in a way Adelia had not expected. "You have a guy who would walk through fire for you. Who stays loyal even when you treat him like dirt. You have a great career, with even greater things on the horizon." She inhaled through her nose as she straightened. "No, I definitely would not understand what that is like at all. You are absolutely correct."

"Stop acting like your life is the one in disarray here. You don't know the first thing about struggle."

Cassandra's mouth hung open for a moment before she pursed it, her nose wrinkling. "You are always grumbling about how everyone expects so much of you. Try it from this angle, Adelia. How about when people don't expect anything out of you, be-cause all they think you have to offer is a dazzling smile? No one bothers to have a real conversation with you because all you are is some showpiece. No one expects great things from me. I don't have people falling all over themselves to help me get anywhere, other than to open a bloody door or carry my bag." She sucked in a deep breath, biting her trembling lip as she steadied herself. "I didn't come to work with you to be a distraction. I came to prove that I have self-worth."

Adelia stood in silence, realizing she was the one with her mouth open. Since the day Cassandra had come into her life, she had done nothing but pass unfair judgment on her. Her cousin had every right to say such things. She was beautiful, and many women would never be able to relate to that. Deep down, it saddened her that Cassandra had spent her life feeling like there was no one who really believed in her.

Low expectations were something she could not relate to. She had spent most of her life trying to live up to the great expectations laid before her. While she would never be able to fully understand what life was like for Cassandra, she could do a better job of trying. For starters, she could stop feeding into the narrative society had already assigned to her cousin—start treating her as an equal, and stop holding some deep-rooted jealousy for the poor girl. It was time to grow up, to start seeing herself as a champion for other women instead of their competition. She thought back to all the women who had done the same for her. Like Ms. Charles had said back at the university: "Success doesn't come in isolation."

"Please forgive me, Cassandra," she said, speaking from the heart. "I have never taken the time to put myself in your place. That wasn't fair, and I know it." She took one step forward. "Let's start again. I really do need you."

Cassandra gave a half-hearted smile. "I really do want to be here."

Adelia reached out and gave her hand a light squeeze—a wordless attempt at an apology. However, Cassandra would not let her off the hook so easily. Before she knew it, she was being pulled into an almost smothering embrace, her stiff arms hanging like over-starched shirt sleeves. It seemed her cousin had forgotten her dislike for hugging.

The initial moment of abhorrent awkwardness passed, and she found herself relenting, giving her a gentle pat on the back—an effort to return the sentiment, and to help put an end to the hug.

They started the descent down the hill back to the car park to wait for Daniel's return.

"For the record, I don't like to be told off," Adelia said, smirking.

Cassandra arched her eyebrows. "For the record, I *liked* telling you off. At least one of us got a win today."

Adelia laughed. "Now who is being the bitch?"

"Well, at least we got another lead to follow." She nodded with confidence. "That was a win too.

Adelia glanced at her. "No, we didn't. Aside from finding out about John Evans, which, by the way, left me with more questions, we got nothing."

"You got nothing." Cassandra threw her a beaming smile. "He slipped me a scrap of paper before I left." She glanced behind before unfolding it. "He said I should find Mister Mortimer at this address."

Adelia snatched it out of her cousin's hand and scanned the scrawled writing. "Did he say why we should find this...Mister Mortimer?"

"No, but I felt him seize up the second you mentioned Richard III and the prince. He definitely knew more, but didn't want to say."

"Yes, he acted odd when I asked to get closer to the window too. I picked up on that right away." She pondered it for a moment. "I think this address is in the village. We could go there in the morning."

"Sounds good."

"By the way, I can't help but wonder what he was thinking when he stood there staring at you like a lovesick boy in grade school. Did you happen to pick up any brain activity there, or did it just cease completely?"

"Oh, I picked it up, alright." She wrinkled her nose. "Actually, for a vicar, and a married man at that, he should be ashamed of himself. It was so foul, I can't even repeat it on church grounds."

Adelia grimaced at the thought of the debauched vicar's inner musings. Cassandra rarely held back on anything in her brain, so the girl's reluctance to share convinced her that she really did not want to hear it. No, they needed to get to the car park to meet a man who had nothing but respect for women.

Chapter Twenty

After asking the innkeeper for directions to the address, it turned out it was a bookshop just down the street. Adelia's only thought was making it there the moment it opened. She had left Daniel a message at the inn's front desk, explaining that she and Cassandra had a few things to pick up at the local general store. At first, she was hesitant to bring her cousin along, in no mood for another of her unwanted disruptions, but the prospect of going alone heightened her anxiety, so she was relieved in the end to be accompanied by her younger relation, and considering the girl had endured the leering vicar to get the address in the first place, she could hardly deny her.

They turned down a narrow alley lined with trash cans.

"The innkeeper gave me the directions," she said, looking down at the hand-drawn map. "It doesn't seem right, though."

"Why on earth would someone open a shop in a dark damp alleyway?" Cassandra scrunched her face in disgust as she dodged a murky puddle—remnants of the morning's rain. "I can't imagine you would get much foot traffic down here."

"I know," Adelia agreed. "It is a little odd." She stopped after a few more steps down the shadowy lane. "I think we must be in the wrong place. Let's go back to the main road and ask someone for directions. I must have read this wrong."

"What's that?" Cassandra pointed ahead.

Adelia caught sight of a small wooden sign projecting from above a side door. She took a couple of steps to her left to get a better view. The storefront consisted of old wooden casement windows with rectangular leaded panes that looked like they hadn't been washed in months. She feared the old shop might have closed up but, on closer scrutiny, a hint of soft light was visible behind the foggy glass. The words on the paint-chipped sign were so faded, she had to move right up and squint to make them out.

"Sunne in Splendour Bookshop. This has to be it."

"Really?" Cassandra wrinkled up her nose, leaving no doubt that she was far from excited about the find. She glanced around, as though a band of thugs was about to jump out of somewhere.

"Sunne in Splendour," Adelia repeated. "Yet another Yorkist reference. How very strange to see these here in Coldridge."

From as far back as she could recall, she'd loved dusty old bookshops. Never had she entered one where she hadn't been able to find a treasure of some kind. Something about the scent of old paper and ink brought her back to the days of her youth with her father, and there was nothing so compelling about a shop, as its owners. They were always a trove of knowledge, ready to impart it to anyone who would listen. Her heart raced as she turned the old rusty door handle. A sharp clack of the overhead bell resounded, alerting the shopkeeper to an intrusion.

As they entered, the familiar smell came rushing at them like a coastal storm. Shelves lined the tiny store from floor to ceiling, each brimming with volume after volume of assorted books. They were so full, someone had begun double layers on several of the shelves. A rack of old newspapers sat in the corner, piled so high it had spilled onto the floor. Toward the back of the shop, a desk had boxes of books covering just about every square inch. A tidy person by nature, Adelia found herself a little anxious at the chaotic clutter surrounding her.

From behind the wall of boxes on the desk, a tall thin figure of a man emerged. His gaunt face made him look as though he had spent many hours preferring reading one more chapter over partaking in a proper meal. He was so lean, he looked almost skeletal. His deep-set eyes made her feel as though he was staring right through her, causing the hairs on her neck to prickle. He was clothed in simple attire, and his silver hair looked in dire need of a cut. By and large, he was a curiosity to behold.

"Good morning," he said, giving each of them an assessing glare.

Adelia almost bristled, struck by his cold demeanor, getting the sense that this bookshop was located here for a reason—not meant to be found by just anyone.

"We are looking for Mister Mortimer," she said, all too aware that her voice was shaky.

He looked at her for a long moment. "For what business?"

"We can always return later, if he isn't here," Cassandra said. No sooner had the words crossed her lips than she was halfway to the door, ready to escape.

"I am Mister Mortimer. What is it you want?"

His tone was so brash, Adelia doubted he made a great number of sales with such an approach. She scrutinized him, thinking that he reminded her of a living corpse. Friendly guy. Remember to ask him over for dinner sometime.

Vibrations through the old floor told her Cassandra was creeping up behind her, and for once she was grateful for her presence. This was the first time since her cousin had come into her life where she willingly welcomed any distraction she might put forth.

"The vicar at the old Saint Matthew's church suggested we come here. I had some questions about the window there. He thought you might know more about its history."

He brushed a stray strand of wiry gray hair from his face. "I don't know much. He was mistaken."

It was a small village. A place with lifelong residents. People knew each other well in these places, and she found it hard to believe the vicar would have steered her here without purpose. She needed to try another approach. The shopkeeper wasn't keen on giving up anything, which told her she was onto something.

"The name of your bookshop is...unique," she said, starting with something that might soften his guard.

"This shop was passed down to me through my father. His father owned it before him. I never changed the name." His voice was hollow, devoid of all feeling.

"It's just that Sunne of Splendour is a Yorkist term." She gave him a moment to take that in. "Somewhat unexpected all the way across the country in Coldridge, Devon."

Something sparked in his eyes. Maybe recognition. She had struck a chord. In what way, though, she couldn't be sure. With Cassandra still hovering behind her like a frightened child, it was up to her to crack this man's icy façade.

The shopkeeper blinked, as if turning a page in his head. "What brought you here to Devon, Miss...?"

"Oh, I do apologize. My name is Adelia Grey. This is my cousin Cassandra." She flicked a nod behind. "We are doing some research on Richard III."

He raised an eyebrow at the mention of the reviled king. "Deep topic." His mouth twitched at one corner. A hint of a smile? "There is plenty about him you can easily find in a book. I am not sure I have any to speak of here, though."

"Yes," Adelia agreed, "there is plenty out there about his life."

"You say your name is Grey?" He pulled on a large pair of dark-framed glasses to study her. "Who is your father, if I might ask?"

"John Grey, son of Marjorie Babington and Colonel Charles Grey."

He nodded, his expression indicating that none of the names rang a bell.

"Back to Richard." She opened the brown leather satchel draped over her shoulder and pulled out the book Paul had given her. "I am doing a different kind of research, though. You see, Mister

Mortimer, I don't think the history books got it correct. I think there is more to this story."

Grasping hold of the scrap of paper that marked the page, she found the image of the window, then stepped forward to let him see it. He glanced down at it, then looked away with indifference but she knew he was uncomfortable with her presence. The man was as flat in personality as one could imagine, but a good liar he was not.

"This window. It is one of the few of Edward V in—"

"Who told you it was Edward V?"

She stared at him as if he had just sprouted a unicorn horn. "This book. The vicar. The window itself says Edward V."

"No," he snapped, his voice ringing with arrogance. "They are all wrong."

"But the vicar said—"

"He was wrong about me, and he was wrong about the window. He is a country vicar, looking to tout some rare treasure in his obscure little church. It brings the tourists in, and they drop a few pounds in the donation box. I suppose he forgot to mention that there are just as many theories that it is Edward the Confessor."

"No, he did not mention t-that," she stammered in surprise.

"That is far more likely an explanation." His face was as stoic as a mortician with melancholy.

"But the window says—"

"Did that Rhodes' scholar of a vicar tell you that the window may well be bits and pieces from others?"

Indeed, he had, but she was feeling far too put-off to say. The insufferable man wouldn't even let her finish a sentence. Thus far, the entire encounter had been a setback, but she wasn't finished yet.

"I don't see how I can help you, Miss Grey. I don't have any hidden relics of a long dead king here. Nothing that will lead you to whatever it is you seek. You won't find his bedside journal among these paper towers."

"Funny you should mention towers, Mister Mortimer, because I believe Richard never killed his nephews in the Tower of London. I don't believe he was the sinister man fiction portrayed him as."

"Somehow, you think Coldridge holds the answer?" His smirk oozed condescension.

"I know Elizabeth Woodville's son held vast lands here. There was a definite Yorkist connection to this place. Even your bookstore name tells me so. There is a story here. I just have to find it." She traced a fingertip across the image. "Just who was John Evans?"

At the mere mention of the name, Mortimer's dark eyes flashed but he blinked it away as if it never happened. No quick enough, though. She had hit on something of significance, and now she found herself almost obsessed with uncovering the secret he was doing his utmost to hide. An unspoken battle waged between them: she, desperate to uncover the truth; him, determined to keep it hidden.

"He was a citizen of Coldridge, Miss Grey. A deer parker for Coldridge Manor. Died in fifteen-eleven. I don't know much more than that."

"When did he come to Coldridge?" she asked, deciding to push a little further.

"Just why is it that you want to know? This seems an obscure topic for a girl of your age to even care about. What could John Evans possibly have to do with Richard III?"

"I am twenty-four years old, Mister Mortimer."

"My apologies. Congratulations on your advanced age. Still, that doesn't answer my question."

"According to the vicar, John Evans also became Lord of Coldridge Manor. That is a high position for someone of common birth. What was John's affiliation with Thomas Grey before he came here?"

"There are a great many people who think as you do. You are not the first to come snooping around here asking questions. Just what is it you think you will find?"

"I honestly don't know. Perhaps nothing. But I think that window holds the key."

"You think a window is going to help you solve the mystery of whether Richard III was a good guy? My, if only Shakespeare had thought of that. Richard III and the Window of Destiny. Great name for a play."

Adelia blinked, opened her mouth, then snapped it closed again. She had been disrespected before, even insulted, but Mortimer had a way of making her feel like an illiterate back-alley trollop.

"I'm undeterred," she said, her voice shaky. "I am going to find out about Richard. And if John Evans has a story, well, I shall know his as well."

"Good for you." His lips quirked—he had bested her and he knew it. "If John Evans had a story to tell, he would have told it himself before he died. He was a simple country man with a simple country life, who did his duty as a soldier, so let the man rest in peace. He deserves that much." Without another word, he turned his back on both women and disappeared into the back of the shop.

As they made their way out to the main street, Adelia couldn't get over the man's cold evasiveness. Even Cassandra, who cast a spell over every man she gazed upon, had no effect on him. He was forged in some impenetrable steel, impervious to her attempts to weaken his resolve, which told her there must be something worth finding at St. Matthew's.

"This is so damn frustrating. I don't know why we even wasted our time coming here. It is just dead end after dead end."

"We have been here a little more than a day," Cassandra said, giving her a side-eye look. "Give it some time. It is not like good old Mister Mortimer is going to open up and bare his soul to two strangers."

Adelia growled inside. "Can't you go back there and woo him with your looks or something?"

"T-that is rude," Cassandra stammered, her cheeks flushed. "You can't parade me around like I am some whore brought here to entice men, l-like some truth serum. No, I cannot, nor will I, flirt with that old corpse back there, so you can get your mystery solved."

Adelia almost slapped herself. "I'm sorry, that was out of line. I am just so freaking tired of not being able to sort this out. I can't solve any secrets without the whispers, and it is not like I can stay here for months until my visions give me the answers. I have got to get back into that church."

Cassandra huffed. "Stop relying on the gift to tell you everything. It can lead you to knowledge but it can't make you interpret it correctly. You have to understand human nature. What is Richard trying to tell you over and over? That he has a heart, that he loves, that he fears. He wants you to see that everything isn't black and white. That everything he did wasn't strictly business. He was not just some power-hungry villain—he was just a man. The gift can tell you a great many things, Adelia, but some of this you have to figure out for yourself. Think like a human and you will find the answers."

"You don't even use your gifts," Adelia snapped back. "How exactly do you know what the whispers intend to do when they come?"

"That is where you are wrong. I do use my sight, when I absolutely need to, and only then. My life is not defined by this gift. Neither is yours. Or it shouldn't be. You had a life before you knew you even had this power. Perhaps your life is different with the sight, but you had a life just the same before it."

"Oh, my life is better now. I used to see things and think I was half-mad, like some lunatic who hears voices all the time. Now that I know, it has at least given me some confidence in myself."

Cassandra straightened. "Well, I don't want my gift to define me, to make me think that I am less than capable of living if I can't use it to my advantage. There is so much the whispers do not tell you for a reason. You have to maintain some sense of self-reliance. My aunt taught me that you can easily lose sight of yourself if you allow them to take over. Adelia, you cannot forget that you are intelligent without help. That you are insightful without the voices. You are a woman with a gift, not just a keeper of the whispers. Lean on your own understanding of the world from time to time."

Adelia stood in astonishment at the wisdom Cassandra had just imparted. It made absolute sense, and for once she could not bring herself to scoff at her cousin's words. Every feeling, every vision, every word that came to her had come with a purpose. Richard's story wanted to be told, not as a history but as a story about true humanity. The whispers had shown her how to get to the answers, not told her. It would have to be up to her to wade through all the fragmented information to put the final puzzle pieces in place.

This was the moment of truth, the moment of choice. She had spent so much time being frustrated, not understanding why her visions had left her no closure, no real concrete answers. They had come in merciless snippets, evading every attempt at comprehension. She had waited, her patience running thin, sure that everything would fall into place when the whispers revealed what she needed to know. Cassandra knew all along that would never happen, and it would be down to herself to make sense of it all. This was what her cousin had been brought into her life to do, bringing her the final pieces of wisdom to feel whole, at last. She was capable of solving one of the greatest mysteries, and with her own mind.

She had always been hell bent on proving herself to others, but, in truth, she never fully believed in herself. Her visions had given her some false sense of confidence, like Dumbo with the magic feather. Outwardly, she came across as self-determined and unstoppable. Inwardly, she had used her gift to help her, so much she no longer saw herself as capable without it. Her grandmother had warned her a few years back that she could lose sight of herself in the story of others. How right Marjorie had been.

Mortimer was not a setback. He was presenting her with the opportunity to do this on her own. She took a deep breath as the fire of determination burned inside her—the same sensation she'd felt after being rejected by Oxford years ago. Her heart ignited, and that only made her want to work harder. Right then and there, she knew she would not leave Coldridge without answers. The whispers could help guide her, or not, but either way, she would discover the truth about the secrets hidden away in St. Matthew's Church.

Chapter Twenty-One

I t was Cassandra who led the way through the front door of the inn. She only made it in a step or two before coming to an abrupt halt, which sent a distracted Adelia crashing into her back. Her growl of frustration was cut by the sight of Daniel sitting in a comfy armchair in the small lobby. His brows furrowed as he took in their shocked expressions. Then his gaze locked in on their empty hands.

"I take it your shopping trip was unsuccessful," he said, his tone as dry as desert sand.

She knew the game was up. He may believe she wouldn't buy a single thing on such an excursion, but not Cassandra. An impossible thing to even consider. And it didn't help that the girl stood there like a world class idiot, fumbling with the folds of her skirt, like an adolescent preparing to get grounded.

A shaky giggle escaped from her. "I thought for sure they would have had a Harrods there."

Adelia's ears burned. Surely her cousin, of all people, could have mustered something a touch more convincing than that.

Daniel's glare drilled into her as she searched for something logical to say, but she had never been good at lying. To make matters worse, Cassandra made some farce of an excuse to retreat to her room, and before anyone could object, she was gone. So much for loyalty. That's the last time I'll help her dodge leery tour guides.

If irritation could take human form, it would now be named Daniel. His exasperated gaze never left her face, though her own focus volleyed about the room, admiring the chairs, noting the cobweb hanging from the corner molding, and wondering how many planks made up the floor?

"Have a seat," he said, though it came as more of a command than a suggestion.

She hesitated, then more or less shuffled to the empty chair beside him. Unable to settle under his intense scrutiny, she took a long time straightening the fabric of her skirt, even rearranging the hem more than necessary. Under normal circumstances, she would have stood up to an impending scolding, but she supposed she was deserving of this one.

"I came on this trip to help you," he said. "If you want to do things on your own, fine, but there is no need to lie."

"We didn't—"

"You didn't even bother to move the car."

"Oh." Doing so hadn't crossed her mind. The village was small enough to cover by foot, but now didn't seem the ideal time to offer up that little detail. She pinched her hem again. "Sorry, Daniel."

His shoulders softened. "Look, I can just as easily find a pub to keep myself occupied. I told you before, if I am in your way, tell me."

"You are not in the way." She looked at him, focusing on his clean shaven chin, still unable to meet his gaze. "Cassandra got a small lead yesterday. I didn't even want to bring her along, but since the vicar gave the address to her—"

"What address?" He leaned closer.

She glanced around, glad to see they were alone. As she went on to recount the experience in the church, and the encounter with Mister Mortimer, Daniel remained silent. The more she spoke of Mortimer, the more her agitation grew.

"He said the window was Edward the Confessor, which is absolute pish posh if you ask me. Clearly it says Edward V."

Daniel tilted his head, arching a brow. "That theory has been put about by many academics of high esteem."

"Wait, you knew this?" She stared back at him in disbelief. "Why didn't you say something before?"

"Would you have listened? You are letting your heart lead this one, and far too much if you ask me. I thought it best for you to hit that wall on your own. I'll be damned if I was going to put that stumbling block before you and suffer your wrath."

"Suffer my wrath?" She glanced around again, aware that her raised voice may have carried. A man was now behind the reception desk, his prolonged stare sending a shiver through her. She leaned closer to Daniel to ensure privacy. "You make it sound like I am so obsessed, I cannot see the truth."

He shot her a questioning look, and she curled her lip. I am emotionally invested, not obsessed. I am not obsessed, am I?

"Are you planning on going to Saint Matthew's with me today, or should I go by myself?" he asked, his tone curt.

"Yes. I mean, we can go together." She could hardly blurt it out fast enough. She needed to get back to that chantry again. "Give me a few minutes to freshen up, and I will check in on Cassandra."

"I will meet you back here in half an hour," he said. "We can grab a bite of lunch before we go."

She got up and turned to make her way toward the stairway. Almost by accident, she glanced back at the man occupying the front desk. His gaze was still locked on her. What is with that guy? Has he been watching me this whole time? She hastened her steps, taking the stairs two at a time.

They had been in such a rush to head out that morning, Adelia hadn't given herself much care in terms of appearance. She made a quick attempt at making herself look presentable, then headed to Cassandra's room. It came as no surprise that her cousin was chomping at the bit to hear how the situation with Daniel had unfolded. She gave her an abridged report, assuring her that he hadn't stayed mad for too long. To be honest, she wasn't sure how true that was—his frustration with her had to be reaching its peak. She was slowly pushing the man too far—his kindness close to its limits. Her level of selfishness had even begun to annoy her. She was officially becoming an undeniable ass, and that was not on her desired list of life accomplishments.

After failing to persuade Cassandra to come with them to the church, she made a quick departure, her head filled with questions—so many left unanswered. Her visit to Coldridge had plunged her deeper into confusion. If there was a secret hidden away in St. Matthew's, what was it? How was Mister Mortimer, the lanky old wisp, the key? Or was he? Most of all, why had she been called to this place? A flurry of possibilities danced in her mind, not one of which made logical sense. All she knew was getting back to that church had become her priority, and her thoughts wouldn't be stilled until she did.

Chapter Twenty-Two

W hen she made her way back down to the lobby, she was relieved to see that the man at the desk was gone. She looked up the stairs, fidgeting with the dangling charm on her bracelet, hoping Daniel wouldn't be long. Her head was too busy to endure being leered at by that clerk, or anyone for that matter.

Maybe Daniel was right. He was as logical as her father at these things. John Grey's voice echoed over and over in her head: "One can make something out of anything, if one is so inclined."

There was a real chance she was doing just that, making something out of nothing. Maybe it was just a church, its past no more secretive than any other. Mortimer might just be your everyday misogynist, taking pleasure in coming across as all enigmatic because he knew she was on a quest. Maybe, just maybe, she wanted more than anything to make some great discovery and was willing to manufacture one to fulfill her desire. These were all strong possibilities, but none satisfied her. She still could not discount the way she'd felt at the chantry—that strong magnetic pull radiating through her like an electric charge. Having lived with her gift for over four years, she didn't need a vision, a voice, or even a grand revelation to know it existed. Ever present, it called to her in the most unsuspecting of places. The whispers did not beckon her when there was nothing to be revealed, and were quite insistent on the stories they wanted told. She may have traveled across half the country, having no clear answer yet, but that did not mean there wasn't a purpose. It just wasn't clear yet.

More than anything, she wanted to lay out all the pieces of the puzzle for Daniel, in a place where she could speak freely, so he might share his own take on the matter. When he came down the stairs, after what felt like an age, she smiled at the sight of his pressed shirt tucked into the waist of his trousers. His hair was combed back and his glasses glinted from a fresh polish. He grinned his boyish grin as he took her by the arm, which she was glad to see after his bit of a rant earlier. She much preferred the smiling Daniel.

They stepped out onto the street and walked the few doors down to a small café for some much-needed nourishment before heading off.

"Cassandra was not up for the trip this afternoon?" he asked before taking his seat at a table by the window.

"She doesn't want to go back." She let out a heavy sigh of relief. "Apparently, the thought of being visually pawed at by the vicar isn't too appealing. Besides, she wants to do some shopping here in the village. Actual shopping, this time. As if she needs any more stuff to drag back to Middleham."

They placed their order and the waitress returned with a teapot and two cups. Daniel flipped both their cups over and poured a stream of hot brew.

"I'm anxious to go back to Saint Matthew's," she said, swiping her hand across her section of the table before moving her cup closer. "I want to take another look at the Evans' Chantry. I may need your help keeping the vicar distracted, though. He didn't seem keen on letting me near it the other day."

"Me, serve as a distraction?" He smiled. "I will do my best, but it sounded like Cassandra did a fine job the last time you were there. Maybe she should be the one doing the distracting."

"I tried to talk her into it but she was insistent on staying back."

"Then it shall just be you and I," he said, failing to hide his enthusiasm. "Let's enjoy our lunch and we will be on our way."

When the sandwiches arrived, they both ate in haste. Excitement filled Adelia, so much she wasn't inclined to finish her tea. Seeing her clear impatience, Daniel all but gulped the rest of his down.

Outside, he walked alongside her the short distance down the sidewalk to the car park. Movement off to the side caught her attention—a figure rounding the corner along the lonely street—and she shifted over to prevent a collision, meeting the dark hollow gaze of Mister Mortimer. For a moment they stared at each other, not uttering a word, then the shopkeeper heaved a gruff snort and continued past them.

Daniel shot her a look of confusion.

She leaned in. "The infamous Mister Mortimer."

He looked back at the disappearing figure. "Goodness, that man is frightening." He frowned. "He looks like some kind of stalking butler in a horror film."

She couldn't hold back a chuckle, though she shivered inside, still affected by Mortimer's icy gaze. In all her life, she had never known herself to be disliked by someone. As a rule, she always managed to be on pleasant terms with just about everyone she knew. The bookseller's clear loathing left her with a frigid chill she wasn't sure how to shake. Had she done something worth his disdain, she might have understood. The fact that she could not pinpoint why he detested her only fueled her confusion.

As she slid into the passenger seat of the car, she tried her best to wipe all thoughts of the encounter from her mind. Mortimer was inconsequential right now. The only thing that mattered was that she and Daniel got back to St. Matthew's and, with any luck, she might be able to shed some fragment of light on John Evans' connection with the figure in the mirror.

As they traveled along the isolated winding road, she shared some of her apprehension about the visions she'd had at Ludlow, Tewkesbury, and Coldridge. Daniel listened without interruption as she recalled the experiences. He was always good at putting things into perspective.

"Who do you want to be?" he asked, keeping his focus on the road.

She looked at him, confused by the question, not understanding how that had anything to do with Richard's life, the tomb of John Evans, or anything else for that matter.

"All I know is that I am not who I was yesterday, and I have no idea who I will be tomorrow." She realized straight away how cryptic it sounded.

"Is it so hard to believe that your Richard felt any different?" He raised an eyebrow without looking at her.

"I-I suppose not," she stammered, unsure where he was leading her.

"Think of it this way. Richard was raised with all the aspirations that were prescribed to men at the time. He knew what he was expected to be, but that doesn't mean he didn't have his own ideas. It's nineteen sixty-one, with a great many social norms, but in one hundred years, people will look back at the sentiments of today and judge those norms. Realistically, you and I don't have to agree with any of society's ideas, though we still live and function every day. History can't tell you what was in Richard's head. Whether he loved the life fortune's wheel endowed upon him, or whether he wanted something different. Maybe that is what the whispers led you towards. Who knows? Which is why I think you will have to decipher some of this on your own."

That had her sitting up. "Have you been talking to Cassandra? That sounds exactly like something she said yesterday."

"No," he answered. "But I can't disagree with her thinking. I believe you are looking for historical facts from your visions. Time, dates, events that are black and white. You want something logical and indisputable. I think what is coming through to you is grayer, because it is supposed to be sentimental. You are looking for a mindset, not facts this time. The mindset will lead you to the facts."

She sat quiet, pursing her lips as she peered out the window, so lost in thought she didn't notice them approaching the old church on the hill until the car came to a halt.

As she walked up the cobblestone pathway, she felt more secure knowing Daniel trailed behind. On her first visit, she had been way too impatient, but now, with him accompanying her, she was sure they would accomplish so much more.

She opened the outer door with ease, as though she had been to St. Matthew's a dozen times before. Once through the second door, she moved up the aisle, stopping to let Daniel size up the nave. It was always entertaining to watch him take in a new place. His face filled with a boyish wonder, like a child entering an amusement park for the first time. Sharing these experiences with him brought joy to her. She would have these days for the rest of her life, if only she could commit to him once and for all. That is all he ever asked of her. However, the finality of that decision still filled her with hesitancy.

As they stood there in silence, she sensed someone approaching from behind. She turned to see the vicar, his face scrawled with a nervous tension on recognizing her. Daniel saw it, too, and moved in to do his job as the distracter.

Hand extended, he greeted the man with an effusive smile. "Good morning, sir, we are visiting the area and I missed the chance to come out and see this splendid little church yesterday."

"Pleased to have you," the vicar replied, his skeptical gaze flicking from Daniel to Adelia.

"I'm doing some research on medieval architecture and Adelia suggested that this would be a great spot to visit." He gave her a quick nod. "I was in Exeter yesterday, so I wanted to stop by before we left the village. Do you know much about the church's history?"

"Well..."—the vicar straightened, chest out— "you won't find Saint Matthew's is nearly as impressive as the cathedrals in Exeter, but it holds a certain charm just the same. I have been here many years, and know a fair amount."

"I'm most intrigued with these exquisite carvings on the pew ends. These figures with long curling tongues. What do you make of the symbolism?"

The second he had garnered the vicar's full attention, Adelia took her chance and slipped away up the aisle, looking as though she had no particular destination in mind, pausing here and there to study some intricate tilework or oak carving. Step by step, she made her way to the front of the nave.

She was no more than ten feet from the rood screen that led to the chantry when her legs became heavy, as though she were wading through deep waters. Fatigue overcame her, and she feared she might collapse. She grasped the back of a pew and slid over to sit down, but she still couldn't throw off the overwhelming sense that all her energy was being drained. Her legs were numb, and she reached down to knead what felt like rubbery stems.

When she looked down at her hands, her vision turned to a liquid blur, almost as if she were peering through teary eyes. Tiny particles, like beads of water, floated up into the space in front of her. What began as just a few beads, multiplied until a vibrant stream of iridescence flowed from her body to the empty space ahead.

She felt his presence before seeing him. A deep trouble filled his soul—warring emotions that allowed him no peace. The shimmering figure came into focus, his brown hair framing strained features, his pained eyes conveying a sorrowful past. He was a newcomer, humble in disposition, and insignificant to the people of Coldridge. His clothing intrigued her, clad as he was in the weathered attire of a peasant when she'd expected something...more. His appearance, much like his soul, was somewhere between.

It has to be John Evans. The image in the window lacked a real likeness to the young Edward V, and there were no contemporary paintings of him, yet this man bore no resemblance. His muddy brown hair didn't match the historical accounts of the would-be-king's golden locks, and he was far older. An intense sensation swelled in her chest, telling her this was, indeed, John Evans.

He sat in a beautifully carved oak pew, his head bent in prayer, and she felt a weight of guilt at sharing this private moment with him. Though nearly five hundred years in the future, she still considered this intrusion on his personal reflection invasive. He felt protected here—something he had not experienced in many months.

She studied him as she would a long-lost manuscript, reading every etch of worry upon his face. Yet deep within his internal strife lay a shred of hope.

In his silent prayer, he yielded no further clues, evaporating into thin air, though leaving the image blazing on in her mind.

She was unsure how much time had passed when Daniel slid in beside her. A glance behind determined that the vicar wasn't nearby. He had somehow managed to garner sufficient trust from the man that he felt comfortable enough to go back to his work, leaving the two of them alone.

"John Evans was here," she whispered. "I came here for the window. It was all about Edward V, but now I can't seem to see anything but this Evans man. In him, I feel such pain. Maybe that is why he comes to me, overshadowing everything else."

"Maybe he was a soldier," Daniel suggested. "The Wars of the Roses were a bloody and turbulent time. Between the houses of York and Lancaster, there was barely a family who didn't experience great loss. Death and destruction were not exclusive to nobility either. Families of every social class had their part in the thirty years of war. It's a sad fact that regular civilians suffered far more tragedy than the ruling classes. Their lives were completely expendable, their loyalty expected. It was not a choice."

"If he was a soldier, maybe he was still grappling with the emotional scars of battle. Sometimes I think England holds too much horror in its past for me." Even with the vicar gone, she kept her voice low. "The emotional connections I feel here are too strong for me to bear at times."

She could not let go of the immense sadness she had felt in John Evans. Was he at peace with his life? Were his choices within that life what brought him this pain? Did the whispers draw her to him, because of her own discontent? The strongest energies were those with whom she shared a connection, and his soul had called to her like a child lost in the night. She could relate to this feeling, and for the first time, she wondered if he could hear the ache in her heart as well as she could his.

"There is something about John Evans. Maybe he was a soldier, his raw emotion borne of deep trauma. Whether he has a story that needs to be told, or he simply wants to come through to someone who understands, I can't be sure. All I know is that he calls me."

"If the whispers want you to follow, then you must go with it. Let his story be told. His soul is seeking out a voice, and you are the vessel."

"This is going to sound so unfeeling." She wrung her hands as if she couldn't bring herself to finish.

"Try me," Daniel said, a hint of a smirk curling the corner of his mouth.

By now, she supposed, he was used to that side of her. It was the side he saw most of the time these days.

"It's not that I don't want to hear his story. If he holds some heavy burden that needs to be released, of course I would want to help. I want to do that for all the people who come through to me. But…"—she looked up at the rafters—"I just don't have the time.

I am here for Richard's story, and I don't have time to decipher the emotional turmoil of a deer parker from Coldridge who died centuries ago."

"I don't think you have much choice in the matter," Daniel said, giving her a knowing look. "I think, if John Evans wants to dominate your thoughts, he will."

"Then what is it Mortimer knows? I know he is hiding something. Is it about John Evans or about Richard? I can't decide."

Daniel made no effort to hide his eye roll as a heavy sigh escaped his lips. He looked exhausted with this endless need she had to connect dots that were not there.

"From what I've heard, you are a fool if you think that old goat is going to give you anything. I honestly don't think he knows a thing. He just enjoys the game of making you believe he holds some secret. What else does he have to do with his time?"

"Probably nothing," she conceded. "He seems to be quite content in his solitude, shielded from the world behind stacks of untouched books. I still can't seem to shake the feeling, though. I believe the vicar knows something he isn't keen on sharing. Now that I think of it, his leading me to Mortimer may have been him shifting responsibility to another. Mortimer is like the guard at the gate to the great palace. Whatever lies behind it, can only be acquired through him and his blessing."

"Mortimer strikes me more as a troll on a bridge to nowhere. A leprechaun guarding a pot of coal." His shoulders shook as he released a hearty laugh. "He is a waste of time, Adelia. Nothing more."

She looked at him. "Do you think this place has any connection to Richard? Tell me honestly, Daniel."

"Honestly? No." He shrugged one shoulder. "I'm sorry but I see no historical evidence that Richard ever came here. Thomas Grey was his brother's stepson, and part of the Woodville faction. Richard and the Woodville's were certainly at odds, but I don't see any real reason for him to be connected to Devon after he became king."

"What about Edward V, and the window?"

"Honestly? It is just a window." He gave her a stone-faced look, then softened it with a gentle smile. "I know you don't want to hear this but those boys died in the Tower of London. If it was for Edward V, and I still have my doubts, I think that window was placed here to honor what should have been. Nothing more. Thomas Grey provided the funding and John Evans oversaw the project. It is just a window, Adelia. This is not some cryptic message. There are others that exist in the country. True, it is a rare find—it's just not the only one. And you still don't know for sure if the Edward the Confessor theory holds weight."

"You think I'm making too much of this," she said, defeated. "I just don't understand why John Evans comes through so strongly to me."

"Well, as you said, he has a story he wants to tell." He rubbed her shoulder, the contact light but supportive. "You hear many voices. See many visions. They don't all have to be connected to Richard. You want this to be about him, but you just have to accept that it has nothing to do with him."

"You're right," she said with a grimace. "I can't find Richard in a place he has never visited. This is about John Evans now and whatever he wants me to find."

Chapter Twenty-Three

It was her third day in Coldridge and Adelia felt as if she were no further on in her quest than the day she had arrived. She sat at the dressing table in her room, staring back at her empty expression, looking as excited about life as dear old Mister Mortimer. Just thinking of his name sent her pulse racing. What a beast of a man. An arrogant scoundrel. His smugness still burned in her mind, and the more she thought about him, the more she seethed. Somehow, she felt comfort in placing the entire failure of this trip square on his coat-hanger shoulders.

Blaming him had no real credibility but it soothed her wounded ego just the same. It wasn't his fault the window had nothing to do with the lost boy kings. It wasn't his fault John Evans kept interfering. It wasn't his fault she had failed to uncover some far-fetched conspiracy she so desired. The simple truth was the man had become her scapegoat, because she would have to blame herself otherwise.

With little more to be found in Coldridge, Daniel wanted to travel to Exeter to visit an old friend from school. Having seen all there was around here, Cassandra offered to tag along, suggesting she might catch a movie she had been dying to see. Adelia's jealous bone had subsided—it was ridiculous anyway—and she was happy to bid them farewell. While she used the excuse of wanting to spend the day poring over her notes from the previous sites, the truth was she had no other intention than to brood and sulk away the day.

Her self-induced isolation was going well until her stomach decided it had other plans. It was almost one o'clock, and she'd barely managed to choke down a cup of tea and some toast at breakfast. That wasn't going to sustain her until her companions returned.

With reluctance, she picked up her handbag and left the room. She could grab a quick sandwich from the café and return. A pity-fest of this magnitude required nourishment.

As she descended the stairs, she avoided looking over at the front desk. Keeping her focus forward, she headed for the exit.

"Miss Grey."

She almost jumped, and was tempted to keep going, being so close to the front door. The man's clipped tone was unfamiliar, though she had a suspicion who it belonged to.

When she turned, it was to face the steely-eyed desk clerk. His gaze was so intense, she felt like a recalcitrant child as she made her slow approach. She could have sworn he did not blink as he watched her.

"Y-yes?" she said, mortified by her stammering squeak of a voice.

"A letter has arrived for you." He turned to the back counter and retrieved a small ivory-colored envelope, which he then held out to her.

"A letter? For me?" She stared down at the untidy script scratched on the front, legible enough to see it was her name. Still not taking it, she looked up at him in confusion. Aside from Paul, and her traveling companions, no one else knew she was here.

It was clear the desk clerk had neither the time nor patience for her to sort this out while his hand hovered in front of her. With a polite nod, she took the envelope from him, relieving him of his unwanted obligation.

She waited until she was out on the sidewalk to open it, drawing out a thin sheet of folded white paper. There were no words, only a crudely drawn picture of a white boar over the words 'Loyaulte me lie.' Her face and neck went cold. It was Richard III's livery badge.

Crumpling the paper, she set off down the street. Daniel was quite accomplished at drawing, and Cassandra had the most beautiful handwriting she had ever seen, so this wasn't the work of either of them. She knew who was responsible. Well...she hoped she did, otherwise she was about to make a gigantic ass of herself. At that moment, she lacked the good sense to care.

She had forgotten about her hunger when she reached the bookshop door. The little bell clanged as she barged in, its sound still reverberating as she almost skidded to a halt.

Mortimer stood smack dab in the middle of the shop. She hadn't been expecting that. No, in her hasty stomp down the alleyway, she had envisioned his dark solemn gaze rising up from behind his makeshift barricade. Damn it all to hell, she hadn't even worked out what she was going to say.

Thankfully, her labored breath gave her extra seconds to collect her thoughts.

"You sent this to me," she barked.

His face didn't move. Not one muscle dared twitch. She had never found another man's composure so irritating. He was a vile creature to the highest degree.

She held up the crumpled ball of a letter. "This is Richard's badge. His motto. Loyaulte me lie. Why did you send it to me? You have been following me too. Yesterday on the street. The desk clerk at the inn." She sucked in a shaky breath. "Just last night, I saw a dark figure standing out on the sidewalk peering up at my window. This is all you."

"My, what a wild imagination you have," he said, his cheek dimpling as he smirked.

"This is not imagination, Mister Mortimer. You underestimate my abilities to get to the truth."

He glared at her. "This truth you toss around, what is it?"

"Everything, and maybe nothing. The truth about Richard. The truth about John Evans. Either one will do. All I know is that there is something you are hiding, and this game of wits is making me want it all the more."

"Are we in a game of wits? Have your wits helped you in any way thus far?"

Her spine stiffened as she clenched the letter in her fist. *He truly sees me as an idiot.*

He nodded once, basking at having the upper hand, his thin lips pursing for a second. "What if you find out this great truth? What if it's more than you ever imagined in your wildest dreams? Then what? What if there is absolutely nothing more than an old stone crypt of a man who lived a simple life in the country? Then what?" He flicked a look around the interior. "We like our simple lives here. We don't want a bunch of college eggheads beating down our door with questions, creating a controversy where one doesn't exist."

"If John Evans had a story to tell, doesn't it deserve to be told?"

He closed his eyes for a moment and sighed. "Let me ask you again. Just what do you plan to do with that story, if you discover...something?"

"I...happen to be one of those people who is content with simply knowing. I am not looking to expose some long-hidden secret. Something has called me here to Devon. Something that defies my understanding completely."

"Content with simply knowing, huh?" His expression dripped with skepticism. "If there was a story, I imagine you would be gone in a cloud of dust, to the papers, ready to bask in your brief notoriety. Would you open your own Richard III fun park?"

She glared at him. *Richard III fun park? Yes, I would install the Duke of Buckingham roller coaster where the riders dodged the axe* blade. There would be boar-shaped tea cakes, and they would sell figurines with Shakespeare's depiction of his hunched back and withered arm. Capital idea there.

The horrible man wanted to push her over the edge, but she wouldn't give him the satisfaction, even if she was teetering on the precipice.

"I solved an Elizabethan cold case once, Mister Mortimer. The death of Amy Robsart Dudley. One that would have every historian across the globe salivating to know the facts. It would curl your toes if you knew what really happened."

"And yet, Miss Grey, I stand here with my toes nice and straight. Why didn't you wow the world with your findings?"

"Some truths aren't meant to be shared," she said, squaring her shoulders. "Some things are best left alone. I solved that case for Amy, not for the likes of the world. I care about people's stories, not notoriety."

He tilted his head ever so slightly, and she could tell her words had struck a chord.

"I never said there was, but *if* there is a story, it is yours to find, not mine to share. People around here are not the trusting type."

"I have gathered that much already."

"If there is a story, it lies in that church, not in an outdated old bookshop."

In that one statement, he had given her nothing and everything. She eyed him under furrowed brows, unsure what to make of this curiosity of a man.

"I leave the day after tomorrow. I would appreciate it if you and your disciples would quit following me around the rest of that time. Your lurking will not deter me, not by a long shot." With that, she made her silent retreat, knowing well her request would not be honored.

By the time she got back to the street, her stomach was no longer in the mood for lunch. She still clutched the letter, and realized it was her head that was ravenous now, desperate to get to the bottom of whatever this all meant. This morning, she had accepted there was nothing to be found here—her quest little more than a meteoric waste of time. Now she wasn't so sure.

She decided to stop by the café after all. Even if she wasn't famished, she would do murder for a cup of tea. She needed time to sort out the past half-hour of her life. Most of all, she needed to devise a way to get back to St. Matthew's. To get out there alone, it would take more scheming to shake off Daniel and Cassandra. As good as she was at so many other things, she knew now that she was becoming quite the accomplished schemer too.

Chapter Twenty-Four

After dinner with Daniel and Cassandra, Adelia retreated back up to her room. Once again, she found herself stretched out on her bed, retracing every one of her notes in her little black notebook. She had just two nights left—not nearly enough time to make head or tail of this mess.

A light tap on the door interrupted her thoughts. She let out a heavy sigh as she left her perch and crossed the floor. Cassandra stood there, giving her an expectant look, though she hadn't said a word. She motioned her in and crossed back to her warm spot on the bed. Her cousin joined her on the mattress, perched on the edge.

"Aren't you tired of being cooped up in here? You have been in this room almost all day."

"Not all day." She tucked a dark lock behind her ear, straightening up a wayward stack of papers with her free hand. "I went out this afternoon for a bit."

Cassandra gave her a curious look, but she didn't bother to elaborate. What would she say? Tell her she'd returned to the bookshop, to take her second lashing from Mortimer? That she left with what she thought was something but, in reality, was nothing at all? No, she had nothing to tell.

As Cassandra blathered on with a long and unwanted synopsis of the movie she had seen earlier, Adelia continued with her paper shuffle.

Her concentration was broken at the sight of a long slender finger with a brightly painted red nail tapping the corner of a page. Cassandra pointed to the pencil sketch of the white boar resting atop the words "Loyaulte me lie." It was a careless doodle, done in a moment of boredom, though its quality outmatched the bookseller's attempt.

"Mortimer's ring."

Adelia furrowed her brow at the mention of his name.

"The gold ring. The one he wore on his pinky." Cassandra stared at her as if she couldn't believe she had no idea what she was talking about. "That day at the bookshop, he brushed his hair out of his eye. It was on his finger."

"This? This picture?" Her face went ice cold. How did I manage to miss that? "Mortimer had this symbol on his ring?"

Cassandra nodded, slinking back on the corner of the bed, as if afraid she had provoked her cousin's anger by not telling her about it before.

"Cassandra, you darling girl." She could barely hold back her delight. "You just gave me the break I needed."

Her eyes widened. "I did?"

She nodded, unable to contain an enormous smile. Cassandra beamed at the notion that she had pleased her cousin. Her eagle eye for detail when it came to fashion and jewelry had paid off. After that, it wasn't difficult to pull her into the scheme she'd devised to keep Daniel distracted while she returned to St. Matthew's tomorrow. Within a few minutes, they had it all worked out. It was good to see Cassandra reveling in her accomplishment. After all, she was supposed to be her cousin's assistant and, at last, she had the opportunity to prove her worth. She all but danced to the door as she said goodnight.

A few minutes later, Adelia had managed to regain her focus over her notes when another rap at the door had her groaning. She peeled herself off the bed, fully expecting Cassandra but finding Daniel instead when she opened the door. They stood there looking at each other, and she all but laughed at the sight of him clad in his pale-blue pajamas, his long green robe cinched at his waist.

"I hope you aren't trotting around the halls in that," she said, backing up to let him into the room before closing the door behind her.

"Lord, no. I reserve all this seductiveness for you."

"Then you had better come back as a heavily muscled Scottish highlander in a Clan Campbell kilt." She laughed.

He gave her a look of bewilderment. Over the last four years, they had shared everything, but, apparently, she had held back on something quite so specific. Mortimer wasn't wrong about her vivid imagination.

She returned to her spot on the bed. Daniel lingered for a moment.

"Have you given any thought to it being Edward the Confessor."

"I gave it some thought, then promptly ignored it." She pulled her knees to her chest and rested her chin on top of one. It wasn't the answer he wanted to hear but it was the truth nonetheless.

"You think I have lost my mind," she declared as she leaned her head back to stare up at the ceiling. "I am not thinking as I should. I am leading with my heart and tossing all good sense out the window along the way."

He moved closer, until his legs brushed the side of the bed. She looked at him, taking him in for a long moment. He fumbled with the belt of his robe. It took her back to the days when they had just met, that summer he was doing research at Hampton Court. They were both vastly inexperienced relationship-wise—strangers to love and all of the complicated thoughts that came with it. After four years together, they should be well past all that. Somehow, they had freefallen back to those days of second guessing each other, not knowing what was enough, too little, or too much. She had plunged them back to this space, and damn it all to hell if she didn't feel guilty for it.

"I think you are passionate about this case," he said as he lowered himself to the mattress. The safe distance he kept gave her another solid punch to the gut. "I think you care about a man's life so deeply that, if he deserves justice, you will stop at nothing to give him it. I only wish I were that man. The one you would lavish such loyalty on."

"I am loyal to you," she said, focusing on the coverlet's swirl pattern. "I am just struggling with myself. I have been so fixated on work, and this project, and I haven't been fair to anyone, really. We have just two nights left before heading back to Middleham. Things will get back to normal soon."

"Last I recall, our normal didn't include me."

He smarted at his own words, drawing in a breath of such restraint, she wondered if she had finally broken him. She was thankful they had one more day because, deep down, she was sure when they returned home, he would take his leave of her for good.

"I have things to work through, I know, but I am getting there—"

The mattress dipped as he moved closer.

She looked up as he reached to take her face in his hands. His warmth spread through her, and for a moment she thought he would lean in to kiss her. He didn't, only softened her core with his gaze locked on hers. It wasn't the pale glow of the lamplight that gave his eyes a glossy sheen, it was the heartless woman he held at arm's length.

"I think I shall love you until the day I take my last breath. Even then, that won't be the end of it. Then, I will love you through the whispers. You can never be free of me."

Her cheeks rested against his palms, the steadiness of his hold conveying an honesty that moved her. She wanted to tell him how hollow her life felt without him—how this void had gnawed at her every waking moment, leaving her with nights just as troubled. Right then, she wanted to confess every single time she had branded herself a capital idiot for tossing away the only person who would ever know the deepest recesses of her soul. She wanted to tell him how she was sorry for all the pain she had caused him, and push herself deeper into him until they shared the same breath. But she didn't say or do any of those things. It wasn't that she lacked the courage—she didn't—it was because they were not alone.

Just behind Daniel stood a man, his piercing eyes drawing the breath out of her. It was none other than John Evans. He stood there only seconds before disappearing into a cloud of dust.

The confident brush of Daniel's thumb across her cheek slowed, his hands trembling. He leaned forward, pressing his lips to her forehead, then slunk back from the edge of the bed in silence, and within a few torturous seconds was out the door.

Its latch shutting sent a tearing jolt through her heart. Daniel was gone, and she never got the chance to explain.

She let her body slide down from the headboard, not even bothering to clear the mass of papers from the coverlet. When she rolled onto her side, she drew the pillow up to her cheek, letting it catch each of her hot tears as they fell.

Chapter Twenty-Five

T he next day, Daniel and Cassandra took off to Exeter again, where he planned to go on an excursion with his old school friend, and she intended to reacquaint herself with civilized society. Adelia had way too much on her mind to even consider going, and it seemed that Daniel was only too happy to leave her to herself; she hadn't joined them for breakfast. Their absence would allow her to pass the day focusing on her plan for that evening. She took time to update her findings, enjoyed a light lunch, then spent a pleasant couple of hours exploring the nooks and crannies of the village and its surroundings.

Early that evening, the three of them ventured to one of Coldridge's two restaurants for dinner, a spot recommended by the innkeeper. It was a tiny place, family owned, with several small tables, and faded paper menus that should have been replaced ages ago. The locals seemed to like it, which is why they chose it over the other.

The silence between them hung heavy. This was the first time she and Daniel had been together since last night. After they placed their order, she found herself fidgeting with the napkin under her silverware, unable to shake an endless gnawing in her gut. She wanted to return to St. Matthew's—on her own—but knew she couldn't say it without offending Daniel further. He had traveled across the country with her on this venture and, at almost every turn, she'd disregarded his help, shaking him off whenever the chance presented itself. The rift this caused between them seemed irreversible, with their relationship probably beyond repair. With that in mind, one more white lie didn't feel all that bad.

The mood was strained—beyond uncomfortable. When the waitress returned with their food, Adelia was more than relieved with the break in tension, even if it was temporary. As they ate in silence, she tried to ignore Daniel's side-eye glances.

She finished her last few bites, every bit aware of Cassandra's flitting looks, waiting for her cue. It felt like they were playing a poker game, each one trying to calculate the next player's move. She pushed her plate out of the way and pulled her purse from the back of the chair, setting it on the empty spot. Then she riffled through it, heaving a long sigh.

"I must have left my notebook in the car yesterday. I really need it to update my findings. I'll go grab it, once we have paid." She flicked a look at Cassandra, then at Daniel. "Mind if I have the car keys?"

He responded with that skeptical look she'd grown used to over the last while.

"I shall fetch it for you."

He gave her a half-hearted smile, but she saw the hurt that still lingered in his eyes. At that moment, she was ready to abandon the ruse altogether.

"Would you mind checking the backseat for my Vogue?" Cassandra asked, with a perfectly timed interruption. "Daniel can walk me back to the inn, and I will come get it from you later."

"Of course I will," Adelia said. "The car's just up the road, so I won't be long. You two head back to the inn so you can get started packing up for tomorrow." She turned her attention back to Daniel. "I can give you back the keys in the morning."

She struggled to maintain a cool demeanor, hoping her cheeks wouldn't flame up. Lying did not come easy, and she doubted she would last a full minute in an interrogation room with even the most mediocre of detectives from Scotland Yard. She could already feel beads of perspiration form along her hairline.

Daniel opened his mouth, as if to say something, but the waitress returned and began clearing the plates, thanking him when he helped her stack them. Adelia was sure he knew something was amiss but she seized the moment and made her way to the counter, where she set about paying the bill. Just as she was finishing, Cassandra stepped to her side, car keys in hand. They flashed each other a knowing look before Daniel joined them.

"Thank you," she mouthed.

Back out on the street, Daniel turned to the two women. "Let's plan on leaving after breakfast. There is no sense in starting out such a long drive on an empty stomach."

Clutching the cold metal of the keys in her palm, Adelia gave a fast nod. Cassandra turned on her heel and headed in the direction of the inn, telling Adelia she would see her in a bit. Daniel hesitated, looking from one to the other, before falling into step behind the younger woman. He may have looked back at Adelia as he walked but she didn't see him, far too busy making a beeline for the car.

She slipped into the driver's seat and sat there staring at the silver keys. It was true she hadn't driven much since coming to England, because it was rare that she needed to. In Oxford, she lived within walking distance of most anything she required, and in Middleham, Paul had always been happy to oblige if she needed a lift anywhere. She had driven in Boston when she lived there—not often but enough to have weathered heavy traffic a time or two. If she wanted to return to St. Matthew's alone, she had to drive.

When she turned the key in the ignition, she gave a little jump when the engine fired up. With eyes wide, she shifted into first gear, but not without a considerable amount of grinding, and eased out of the parking spot. Her hands trembled as she inched down the narrow street, heading for the road that would take her to St. Matthew's.

While her guilt over lying to Daniel grew, it did not stop her. In a sad way, she had become rather good at ignoring such feelings. Anyway, there was no turning back now, with the urge to return to the church stronger than ever. What she'd felt through John Evans had been so powerful, but his appearance in her room had left more questions to be answered. *I know I'm close to bringing* these clues together but I need another look—another chance—a little more time.

Her knuckles whitened as she gripped the steering wheel, winding her way out to the countryside, her state of near panic reminding her why she preferred not to drive in England. It didn't help that she had to travel on the opposite side of the road than she was used to. Had her need to return not been so great, she would never have attempted something this foolish. But right now, her desire outweighed her fear.

As she rounded a bend, the church stood silhouetted in the distance, the sun casting a mystical pink glow around it, like a cotton-candy haze. So caught up in the sight, she failed to see a small stone wall that bordered the road, and let out a shriek as the corner of the chrome bumper skid across it, shooting up sparks. She hit the brakes, the tires skidding on the loose gravel in a puff of white dust. Her heart raced as she looked around, and she released a sigh of relief that hers was the only car on the road.

She hesitated, wondering if she should get out and survey the damage. How she would explain this to Daniel was beyond her comprehension. Dinner had run late and there was probably no more than two hours before the sun sank behind the hill. If she didn't keep going, it would be pitch dark out here on the desolate road before she returned home. Trembling all over, she continued on, shifted gears as she eased further up the road. The damage was done now; it was a predicament she could handle later.

After pulling the car into the parking area, she sat for a minute just staring out at the beautiful view below—a quilt of fields. Her legs still trembled from the mishap down the road, and she took several deep breaths to steady her fluttering heart. She fully expected the church to be locked up for the night, and that wouldn't be the worst thing. Walking the grounds might be enough.

She exited the car and eased the door shut, as though afraid of disturbing the silence beneath the gentle birdsong. The evening was calm, with not a hint of a breeze floating on the heavy summer air. As dusk began to settle across the land, the church took on an unearthly look of mystery. She found herself blinking several times, just to be sure she was looking at it in the present day and not some image of the past that had invaded her mind.

Before moving to the next stage, she walked around to the bumper to check for damage, wincing at the scrapes across the chrome surface. It could have been much worse but it would still fire Daniel's ire. Nothing to be done about it now—she would have to face his wrath when the time came.

As she walked, she kept her steps soft, tiptoeing so her heels wouldn't sink into the tiny pea gravel as she approached the wooden gate of the fence surrounding the ancient churchyard. She jolted at the high-pitched squeal of rusty hinges when she pushed it open. If anyone saw her now, they might think she was up to no good, but she'd come this far so had to go on. She passed the fragile limestone markers of the graveyard with reverence. This place had a hard-earned peace, one that may not have been afforded to its residents in life. To disturb that sanctity felt disrespectful.

Still somewhat uneasy, she continued on but stopped dead when she caught sight of a dim flicker through a window. Was it inside, or a reflection on the glass? She squinted to better make it out, and bit on her bottom lip when it grew. For a second, she was unsure if she might be intruding on some sort of evening service, yet there was no sign of any other person here, and hers was the only car. No voices, either. Just the low hum of nature.

She rocked back on her heels when a pale stream of light burst through the windows, illuminating the cobblestone path. It was only when she looked up that she realized she had hunkered down. And lucky she had, because someone inside had switched on a light. She weighed her options. I can leave whoever is in the chapel to their work and return to town, hopefully keeping Daniel's car from any further damage on the drive back. Yet, a familiar pull refused to allow her to move in any direction but forward—the same sensation she had experienced at Ludlow Castle. Without hesitation, she gave in to its will and stepped along the path, as if drawn by an invisible hand.

When she reached the wooden door, she placed her hand upon the iron latch, and it gave way with almost no effort. She eased the massive door open, again with no discernible effort, and passed through the entryway, stopping at the second door, unsure of how her arrival at this late hour might be perceived. After a moment's hesitation, she gripped the latch, and the door opened with even more ease than the first.

As she stepped onto the stone floor, she squinted against an intense light that took her eyes a few seconds to adjust to. With the door closed behind her, she stood at the back of the nave, questioning how on earth she should be so bold as to have wandered into a place that was supposed to be closed for the night. If she faced harsh words from the vicar for her intrusion, she could not be offended. She was the invader after all.

She scanned the rows of pews, and almost gasped on seeing the thin frame of a man seated near the front. Even from behind, she recognized the gaunt figure. Mortimer. She let out a breath, not of relief but of sheer angst. Prepared to be scolded by the kind old vicar, she felt sure Mister Mortimer would not be so forgiving of her uninvited trespass. Then he turned his head to look at her.

Much to her surprise, he said nothing, and no discernable expression crossed his sallow features. He just turned back to face front, giving no indication that she was present. For a moment, she questioned whether he had seen her. She felt like one of the many ghosts who inhabited this place, invisible to anyone else but herself.

She considered turning and darting out, but the ever-present force that brought her in had formed an impenetrable wall behind her, blocking any conceivable means of escape. Doing the only thing possible –the only thing her rubbery limbs would allow—she moved forward, gripping the cool wood of the pew backs to steady herself.

A few rows behind Mortimer, she came to a sudden stop, and not of her own accord, her legs as firm as gelatin as she lowered herself onto the bench. They sat in silence for a few minutes. She couldn't tell if he was praying, or dealing with his rage at her presence.

"There is blood in this Chapel Royal," he muttered, his words so low it took her a second or two to fully comprehend them.

She glanced around her. "I...thought the term Chapel Royal was reserved for those housed within a royal palace." She failed to bite back her sense of accomplishment at correcting this arrogant man.

"What is a palace, really, but a home? A chapel can be anywhere we talk to God."

He turned but not enough to face her—more seeing her from the corner of his eye. Given their past interactions, she could only assume this was yet another attempt to slight her, as though looking her straight in the eye might give her some advantage—some modicum of respect she wasn't yet entitled to.

"I guess I don't understand your reference to blood being here. Was someone killed in this church?" She sat up. "Was it John Evans? What blood are you talking about, Mister Mortimer?" She sighed with frustration. He enjoyed his riddles, but she wasn't about to allow him to think she could be lured into another of his dead ends. Daniel was probably right that everything was just a game to this man.

"Your years of having your nose in a book have made you too literal," he said, almost spitting the words.

She jolted at his brash voice echoing off the walls. While she'd assumed her presence would anger him, she may have underestimated just how much?

"You yourself said if he had a story, it is best to let it be. What does it matter, anyway? I just want him to leave me alone—" She broke off, meeting his assessing gaze, knowing she had said too much.

"There is nothing at Saint Matthew's that is given to you. It was never meant to be easily deciphered. The story was only meant to make sense to those it mattered to most. If you are one of those people, then it will come to you. Think, Miss Grey. Use your head and think."

"I came here to find out about Richard. To prove that, for whatever good or bad he did in his life, deep down he wasn't a bad person. I wanted to put his soul to rest. Not for the notoriety, or to further my career. It matters little what I find. The critics will spend the next few centuries disputing it anyway."

"You're not wrong about that," he said with a wry grin.

She couldn't help but respond with a little chuckle. "Now that I am here, I can only see John Evans. It's not that I don't think he wasn't important, just because he wasn't of the upper classes, but, save you and I, he seems inconsequential to anyone else. He may have been lying in that crypt for four hundred and fifty years, but his soul is not at rest. Don't ask me how I know but he wants me to decipher this secret he took to the grave. It was his to share with the world. It's not my place. If I am worthy, he will lead me to the answers, and maybe then he can finally have his rest."

He remained stock still for a long moment, then blinked and straightened. "If you can decipher it, then you are worthy."

She had no idea why she was inclined to share the depth of her feelings with this man, but it felt right. The heaviness she'd experienced since coming to Coldridge had lifted, and now it was like she could breathe for the first time in days.

"Okay, then." She took a deep breath, got up, and walked down the aisle. The mystery of John Evans was strong, and she had to remind herself that this wasn't about Richard anymore. She had wanted to pry whatever Mortimer knew out of his bony frame, word by word, but now she looked to herself. This was between her and John Evans.

She walked into the rood screen's entryway and passed the altar on her way to the Evans' Chantry, the pull strengthening with each step. When she got to the locked wooden screen, she closed her eyes and soaked up the magnetism radiating from his crypt. She repeated his name in her mind, over and over, until the rainbow shimmer of light from his tomb hit her square in the chest. A flurry of emotions—feeling and thoughts—invaded her mind, like a phalanx of marching soldiers. However, they were not her own emotions. No, they belonged to someone else—someone she could only hope was the real John Evans. As she leaned against the door, it gave way and swung wide. The old rusted chain and padlock had been removed. She recalled her first visit, when the vicar had been adamant that the area was off limits to visitors.

Just to be sure, she looked at Mortimer, her question silent but clear. He responded with a simple nod, as if giving her the answer she sought. She could almost picture him like a guard at a castle gateway, clothed in his lord's livery, banner unfurled and waving in the wind.

She stepped into the chantry and moved closer to the crypt. And while the stream of colored light between her body and it lessened, the gravitational pull became stronger. Without doubt, a connection existed between her and John Evans, but its meaning remained unclear.

"Let me start from the beginning," she whispered, as distant, frail voices filled her ears. "John Evans came here to live a simple life. I get the sense he wanted self-fulfillment, just not the kind everyone wanted him to have."

"Just how do you know this?" Mortimer asked.

She looked back to see him standing outside the rood screen, his deep-creased brows shadowing his eyes.

"You prefer not to reveal your secrets, Mister Mortimer. Nor do I." She exercised every bit of defiance she could muster. He didn't seem the slightest bit moved, turning his already sideways glare a little more, as if to remind her of her insignificance. They were back to that again.

"He came here as a young man, and lived on the lands of the Marquess of Dorset, son of Elizabeth of Woodville from her first marriage. Yet, almost immediately, he is titled as Lord of Coldridge Manor. Odd?"

"Why so?" Mortimer asked, picking at his fingernails.

She wasn't sure if he was skeptical of her assumptions or encouraging her to think deeper. Either way, she liked the challenge.

"To be titled Lord of the Manor implies he was a man of some importance. He wasn't of the aristocracy, but he wouldn't be living in complete poverty either. Perhaps he was accustomed to living in a certain manner. Perhaps he did something that deserved patronage as a token of appreciation. I believe he was a soldier, but what deed he performed that might make him worthy of such high esteem, I have yet to determine."

"Either could be true. I wouldn't spend too much time dwelling on it, though."

She looked over the effigy before turning back to Mortimer. "Throughout his time here, he served as both deer parker and Lord of the Manor, which gave him sufficient funds to bestow on Saint Matthew's Church, as it also sat on Coldridge lands. In addition to adding the chantry, he likely commissioned the window of Edward V. I think he believed that Edward was the rightful heir to the throne. I think he left the clues to his beliefs in plain sight, even if he dared not speak it publicly."

As Mortimer attempted a rare smile, she could have sworn she heard a faint creak in his cheeks.

"Henry Tudor was on the throne by that time," he said. "To pay such homage would have caused a stir. John Evans kept his 'gift' hidden away, to ensure it was only seen by those he felt were loyal to his own belief."

She paced around, her mind now ablaze after the bookseller's response. When she got to the window, she stopped short. "This clearly says the name of Edward V, even though he was never crowned the true king. The crown gives it away, hovering above the prince's head. Lined in ermine, it could only be worn by royalty."

"Could be Edward the Confessor," Mortimer offered.

"It's not Edward the Confessor," she snapped, eager to put that whole thing to rest. "I have studied medieval art and windows like this extensively. There are only a few depictions of Edward V, and this image is exactly as he is described. Even if a few panes aren't from the original, it is mostly intact."

She stared at it for a long moment. Keep thinking, Adelia. John wanted the window to honor the young prince, yet in a way that did not attract attention. Why was John Evans so dedicated to Edward V, a royal prince in his teens?

"The Woodvilles," she said. "They were well known to be a self-serving lot. Hmm, I have a theory that I just can't shake."

"Do go on." The arrogance in his voice grated on her nerves. He was such a beastly man. Save good old Gerald, her co-worker back in her performance days at Hampton Court, she couldn't recall loathing any man quite so much.

"What if Thomas Grey wanted this window commissioned but he didn't want to evoke the ire of Richard or Henry Tudor? What if he used John Evans as a scapegoat in case things went wrong? Giving him the money to commission it." She tapped her bottom lip with her forefinger. "That would explain why John's status after he came here was elevated so rapidly."

She turned to see Mortimer had tilted his head as he regarded her, looking as if it was a theory he hadn't considered. That amused her. Not so brilliant now, are you, Mister Bookseller?

"What about this window over here?" he said, motioning off to his right. "What do you make of this?"

She couldn't tell if his question was meant to distract her or lead her to more clues. As she approached the small side window, she saw that two panes contained images. One held the white rose of York, while the other contained the symbol of Edward IV: The Sunne in Splendour.

"Those are just as compelling." She gripped her bottom lip between her teeth as she studied the visuals. "There may have been more to this window at one time but it is hard to say. Yet, to have two heraldic symbols of the House of York in Devon cements my impression of there being a strong Yorkist connection here. John Evans must have found meaning in them too. Throughout his life, he remained loyal to the Yorkists—he just wasn't willing to make it public. As you say, the Tudor king played a big role in that, but I still sense there was something more. That connection makes my theory about John Evans hold some weight."

Mortimer almost groaned as he released a heavy sigh, shaking his head. "The truth is, there is no surviving record of John Evans before he came here to Coldridge. How Thomas Grey even knew him is unknown." He snorted as he leaned against the door frame. "The mystery will always remain, I am afraid."

His delivery was hesitant—too hesitant—and Adelia could feel his indecision almost as clearly as if it were her own. The man was experienced at dodging the facts, and gave nothing up without a fight. Yet she felt his resolve weakening. She wasn't so different from him, always keeping her true identity in the shadows. They were both "keepers," in their own right, guarding secrets from a world that would do nothing good with the knowledge.

She capitalized on this tiny shred of fragility in his will and moved back to the chantry, unfettered by his attempted distraction. "What I struggle with is the fact that John Evans' name is misspelled on his crypt. That seems a highly disrespectful thing for a stonemason to do without at least attempting to fix it."

That thought stuck with her, and she sat for a moment in quiet observation.

"EVAS," she said, enunciating each letter, her voice filling the space.

She looked up at the window, then back at the crypt. Why is his name misspelled? Again, she read the letters aloud to herself: "E-V-A-S." She stared through a slow exhalation, allowing her mind to do its thing, without force, searching as deep as necessary. Let it happen, Adelia. Let it happen. She snapped straight when something sparked in her brain. I have it. Oh my goodness.

Chapter Twenty-Six

S he could not deny that the pieces had been there all along, but damn it to hell, how had she missed them? This was a misstep she would be questioning herself on for weeks.

"It's Latin. EV is Edward V. AS is 'in asylum.' In exile." She looked at Mortimer, whose eyes had widened, his lips parting as if he wanted to respond but couldn't form the words.

Her mouth had gone dry, and she wet her lips with the tip of her tongue. Right now, her heart was thundering. Was Edward never killed in the tower, as had been speculated? Could he have been brought here to Devon, in hiding? If this were true, there was no way Richard III would not have known. Had he taken the blame for killing his nephew, when all along he'd hidden him here for his safety? Did he allow people to assume his nephew was dead to save him from the inevitability of Henry VII coming to take the throne?

She shot to her feet and stared at the image in the window, far too caught up in her own thoughts to consider Mortimer's temporary state of paralysis. The light wasn't great but she took her time, scrutinizing every detail. When she came to the crown, she stopped dead. The ermine lining.

"Those black spots are not ermine. They depict an animal, though. A deer. A stag, to be precise." She counted each one, coming to forty-one. Why forty-one exactly? Why that number? She moved back over to the figure on the crypt, studying the stone face, its features peppered by the ravages of time.

"Edward V would have been forty-one when John Evans died." Her mouth hung open for a moment. She looked at Mortimer, swallowing a dry tightness in her throat. "J-John Evans died when he was forty-one." She shot her gaze back to the window. "The stags! He was a deer parker."

She could hardly contain her excitement. "John Evans is Edward V. He was sent here by his uncle, Richard III. He was never killed in the tower. He lived out the rest of his life in Coldridge Manor. That explains everything. The window, the crypt. Everything."

"I believe most of the country would think your discovery a bit far-fetched," Mortimer said, taking his seat in the old pew. "You are not the first to make such an outlandish claim." A look of total satisfaction blazed across his face. Despite his balking at her conclusion, it was clear that he looked relieved. Who could know how long he'd kept the secret only to himself.

"That's okay," she said, her confidence high. "That is perfectly okay. Being a keeper of secrets has kind of become my calling."

"Is that right?" The corner of his mouth quirked up a bit. "That might be one of the few things we have in common."

"For all of my life, I have wondered why Elizabeth Woodville never said a word about the disappearance of her two sons. That was so out of character for her. She was such an ambitious woman." She said this as though speaking to one of her oldest friends. "Why she didn't take the opportunity to defile Richard's name when she had the chance always eluded me. Then, right after they were last seen, she came out of the sanctuary with her remaining children. That always struck me as a strange thing for a woman who feared for her family's lives. She must have known she had nothing to fear."

"So, you are implying she thought good old Uncle Richard was trustworthy?" Mortimer gave a lighthearted chuckle.

Adelia could not help but grin. The atmosphere had lightened now the weight of Mortimer's secret had lifted, leaving behind an ordinary man. And what a difference that made. The harsh creases in his face had softened, and his once-dark, lifeless eyes had changed to true hazel, with tiny specks of emerald green. Indeed, the intimidating "stalking butler," as Daniel had so lovingly referred to him, was now the kind old neighbor who helps you find your lost dog.

"She had to have thought he was," she answered, "or she would not have come to court to live with him after. She even brought her daughters. The woman knew where her sons were all along. It makes perfect sense to me now. Despite all the rumors that Richard killed his nephews, he never so much as uttered a word about them, nor did he try to defend himself against the accusations. That was out of character for him to remain quiet at such an atrocious accusation. And that's one of the reasons this story has remained alive all these years."

In silence, he raised his head and stared at her, his bright twinkling eyes assessing every element of her character, or that's how it felt to her. And that's when she realized that, for the first time in her life, she had a sensation that was far more than intuition. She found herself looking into Mortimer's thoughts as if they were her own. It was Cassandra who possessed this ability, never herself. Now, even if only for a moment, she could read the entire world, both the living and the dead. Mortimer was on the cusp of showing her something remarkable, yet he still harbored the question of whether or not she could be trusted.

She sat back and took him in. He had held onto the secret of the prince for so long. Protecting this church and the secret it contained had been a sacred duty for generations, handed on each time to the chosen one. Mortimer did not want to see it end with him, nor confirm her discovery only to have her exploit it for her own gain. He could end this by dismissing her conclusion as a common conspiracy theory—one of many nearly five hundred years had conjured up. Richard III had been sensationalized time and again, even becoming a subject of William Shakespeare himself.

At this point she understood they would move no further unless she was willing to reveal something of her own. Something that bore equal weight to what he had carried with him all his life.

"When I was a child, I began to hear voices. Tiny whispers all around me in the silence. For a long time, I blocked them out, but as I got older, I found that task harder and harder. Then, just a few years ago, I came to England to stay with my grandma. As luck would have it, I was to spend the summer at Hampton Court Palace. I have always loved history, so you can imagine how much I looked forward to actually living in such a place. I hadn't been there long before I became convinced that I was on the verge of some mental apoplexy. I could no longer just hear the voices, I could feel every single emotion as my own. Then I began to have visions, as clear as images across a cinema screen. It was then I learned of a gift—the Babington gift—one that has crossed generations through the female line of my family. I can hear the past. I can feel the past, and I can see it too. That is how I knew about John Evans, Mister Mortimer. Even before I knew he was the prince, I could feel his angst, his indecision about following his duty or his desires. Just like you, Mister Mortimer, I have a heavy burden. I am a keeper of a secret that will bring me nothing but despair if revealed to the wrong people."

Mortimer looked at her with wild wonder, as though he had spent a thousand years searching an ancient forest for a unicorn, and found it at last. His pew creaked and groaned as he pushed himself to his feet. He raised a long slender finger, indicating she should wait as he moved past her to the chantry.

She stepped back to the front pew, dropped onto its hard surface, and waited. Furniture shuffled, then stone scraped upon itself as he knocked about for several minutes. What is the man up to? Always full of mystery.

Her anxiety was peaking when he emerged through the rood screen with a tiny metal box in hand. This time he surprised her by seating himself at the end of her pew. The box was covered in dust, which he swept across the surface with his long bony hand, sending the particles drifting to the floor. If he opened it, there could be no turning back—the secret in all its entirety would be revealed.

As if in slow motion, he slid open a metal bolt from the front of the box. A tiny puff of dust floated into the air as he raised its lid, its hinges creaking. Inside, a square of fine red velvet had been folded to conceal the treasure beneath. With meticulous dexterity, he grasped each corner of the cloth and folded them back, revealing the ivory tarnish of velum. He rubbed the fingertips of each hand off their respective thumb, then lifted a letter from the box, as though holding the most fragile item created.

Adelia held her breath as he eased forward and placed it into her open hand. Then, with silent pause, he looked her in the eye and nodded, the action almost imperceptible. She understood his simple gesture. He was trusting her with the reason for his entire existence.

She turned the object over and squinted at the intricate wax stamp sealing the parchment. Her scalp prickled when she realized it was a king's seal—the seal of King Richard III himself. She looked up at Mortimer, tears welling as she released a wide smile she couldn't hold in. Then she went about unfolding it with calculated determination, treating it with the reverence it deserved.

Right away, she recognized the handwriting as Richard's—there could be no mistaking the gentle curves and dips of his pen. Astonishing. She had seen many documents written by him, but most had been copies. To hold such a treasure was unimaginable.

"It's dated fourteen eight-five," she said, somewhat breathless. "Not long before Richard was killed at Bosworth by Henry Tudor." Mortimer remained silent, just watching her. She read the letter, mouthing each word to herself. "It's a missive to Thomas Grey, Marquess of Dorset. Richard is letting him know that one of his most trusted men, James Terrell, will be bringing John Evans into his keeping here at Coldridge Manor. He trusts that the Marquess will show great generosity to the man placed in his care." She turned it over, then back before looking up at Mortimer. "That is all it contains."

Again, Mortimer remained silent, and still.

She almost flinched at a strange pulsating under her fingertips. Richard himself had held this sheet of velum. Somehow, she could smell the wet ink, before it had been powdered dry. The scrawl of his pen scraping against the fine grain of the velum reverberated through her head, and in her mind's eye, the pale flicker of a lighted taper danced upon its surface as he penned the missive. With acute focus, she saw the writing desk, undoubtedly deep in the Tower of London. And there was Richard, as though she was standing right in front of him. How much he had aged, both in time and experience. He was king now, far from the lovesick seventeen-year-old in Tewkesbury. By this stage he had lost both his wife and his son to illness, and war with Henry Tudor loomed on the horizon.

Though her vision was fixed on Richard, she was still conscious of Mortimer's presence.

"There comes a point in every cause," she said, "where our paths diverge. Where the loyalty that binds us must face our inherent need for self-preservation. Despite Richard's efforts to overcome those obstacles, they had become greater—unceasing. The battle had not lost its purpose, and that purpose had evolved. When he arrived at this crossroads, it was here that he had to abandon his quest, the only one he had ever known, in favor of preservation. He did not come to this conclusion with ease. It kept him awake many nights. Over and over, he rolled the memories through his head. The sacrifice, the oaths, had never been forgotten. The loyalty to his father. The love of his brothers. Yet the world around him was different now, much smaller than it had once been. There was no one to lead him in this peril. His father was gone, as were his brothers. He was alone, fighting a long-standing war that had somehow dwindled in its meaning."

"All of this comes from the letter?" Mortimer asked, near mesmerized by her words.

"It is difficult to explain, but I can feel Richard's thoughts. I can feel his sense of loyalty to his father's war for the throne torn by his need to preserve the family line."

"Is there more?" Mortimer's tone was almost demanding. He shifted forward. "There must be more." Something in his excitement reminded her of her father whenever he watched her work through some historical unknown. It was a touch endearing, seeing that loathsome façade he had brandished cease to exist.

She closed her eyes, clinging with every fiber of her being to the image of the solemn-faced Richard. His heart still ached for the wife and child he had lost, his soul like a void of perpetual blackness. Everything around him felt hollow and meaningless. Not even his crown meant anything anymore. Richard was lost, even to himself.

The air around them almost crackled when she looked at Mortimer. "Richard moved the young princes from the tower in the summer of fourteen eighty-three. The precise location is too fuzzy to make out. All I know is that he did so to protect them. There were so many plots in existence: to restore them to power, even though they had been declared illegitimate and ineligible for the throne—plots to murder them by those who wanted to see Richard securely fixed on the throne, and by Henry Tudor's supporters to ease his path to usurping the throne from Richard. He knew he had to move them again, this time separately. They had to go to locations that would remain secret, even if he met his end against Henry Tudor."

Mortimer nodded once, more to himself than her. "I do not know where the boys were housed before Prince Edward arrived here as John Evans. If ever any of my ancestors did know, it has been lost to time."

"I understand," she said. "Richard looked upon his protection of his nephews the same way a knight would protect his lord. He knew that all those who achieve true greatness must have proved they could walk through fire. Admiration and respect are attributes that must be earned. There was no other way to die than with the same honor his lineage expected. His entire life had been lived with a sole purpose, and he would breathe his last breath for the cause, the one placed upon his fragile shoulders as a child kneeling by the altar. Even at his last stand, with his options running as thin as a cerecloth, he would fight to preserve the legacy that had been his greatest burden. He could sense that his own death was drawing near. The House of York would indeed live on, not in his blood but the blood of his kinsmen. There would not be a Plantagenet on the throne, but the blood of the house would survive. Indeed, Richard III, the last son of the Duke of York, would fulfill the destiny of his lineage."

"And so, John Evans arrived here in Devon," Mortimer said. "His uncle was slain on the battlefield not long after. For over twenty-five years, the prince assumed the identity of another man. He changed his appearance, and shed all indications of his high-born status. He became a simple country man, living an even simpler life. Until today, I assumed it was out of necessity, rather than choice. I guess it's good to know that he wanted to live this way. It explains why he never came forward to stake his claim to the throne."

"Edward V never came forward because he had no aspirations to take the throne," Adelia explained. "He was happy here at Coldridge, having grown up with the impending pressure of always knowing he would be king someday. In truth, he had scarcely been able to play as a child. Training was a constant in his life, with little time for fun. When the boys were declared illegitimate, I don't think they or their mother knew for certain that Edward IV had not been married in secret before Elizabeth. His own brother George made mention of it in the past. As illegitimate, they would have no actual right to the throne. There is no evidence Prince Edward ever disputed the claim. Whether he believed it to be true or not, he was still relieved not to be forced onto the throne."

"That is not so hard to believe," Mortimer said, looking off into the gloom. "If I had a choice not to be guardian of this secret, I likely would not. You, yourself, might not wish to have your gifts if given the choice. Choice was rarely an option in Edward's time. To be able to control his own destiny was a rare thing."

Adelia remained silent as she stared at the letter still laid out in her hands. The images of Richard had faded and she became aware of the presence of John Evans hovering in the nave. This was a place that meant so much to him in his life—the only location on earth he could bare his soul as his own true self. In St. Matthew's, he came to peace with the choice he'd made in abandoning the crown.

It was well documented that the prince was thought of as an intelligent boy, wise beyond his years. Edward was studious enough to have fully learned and understood the history of his family, even years before the fractures between the houses of Lancaster and York. He would have known there was no more dangerous a job than being King of England, facing constant threats to his life and sovereignty. When given the choice to pick a life of glory and danger in equal measure, he did not want that for himself.

His mother, Elizabeth Woodville, would have understood that once Henry Tudor arrived on England's shores, he would try to take the throne for the House of Lancaster. Ultimately, he would have tried to invade the country even if Edward had been crowned. As fate would have it, he ended up facing Richard III at Bosworth, and won.

Elizabeth, who was always power hungry, was still by rights a good mother to her children. Given that she had already negotiated a betrothal between her daughter and Henry Tudor, she knew she had secured a path to the throne for her family. Keeping her son's whereabouts a secret was the best move she could make to ensure their survival. If their existence was revealed, they may have been killed and her daughter's marriage destroyed. If Edward did not want to be king, anyway, she may have just kept the secret to allow her son to live the rest of his life in peace.

"What of the second son, Richard Duke of York?" Mortimer asked, his brows raised. "What do you think happened to him?"

"Slow down, Mister Mortimer. I haven't even fully processed the fact that John Evans was Prince Edward." She looked around them. "Well, Prince Richard didn't come here, that's for sure. Sending them both here was way too risky. It would have given the secret away too easily. If I had to guess, he might have been sent to France. That was a common practice among the Plantagenets when their lives were in danger. Besides, neither of the boys were raised together, and were probably not close as brothers. Throughout Henry Tudor's reign, he was plagued by 'pretenders' claiming to be Richard Duke of York. He spent a great deal of money trying to track them down. Being that he had married the princes' sister, and she was the key to keeping his reign secure, finding either of them alive would have jeopardized his rule."

"You are right," Mortimer said. "Henry spent a great deal of resources trying to track down Perkin Warbeck, who claimed to be Richard Duke of York, and Lambert Simnel, who claimed to be Edward Duke of Warwick. I agree with you that Henry Tudor had to have real suspicions that the princes might have survived."

Adelia offered a knowing smile. "Henry had no real idea whether or not Richard III killed his nephews in the tower, even though he worked to spread the rumor to his advantage. In fact, I think he suspected Elizabeth Woodville knew their whereabouts all along. After being implicated in some of the pretenders' plots, she was mysteriously retired from public life and isolated at Bermondsey Abbey." With real tenderness, she handed the letter back to its keeper. "That really should be in a museum, you know."

His face lit up with a mischievous smile. "Miss Grey, I think you and I both know that is never going to happen."

"Tell me, Mister Mortimer, just how does your family figure in the whole Coldridge thing? Why are you the keepers of John Evans' secret?"

He took a quick look around them before regaining eye contact. "Well, you see, Miss Grey, what most people do not know is that John Evans did marry and have a child. His child, a daughter, became the first keeper of the secret here at Saint Matthew's. Eventually, she went on to marry a Mortimer, and since then our family line has passed the duty from one generation to the next."

"That is fascinating," she said. "I'm sure keeping this secret has been a heavy burden on you. Tell me, why did you decide to share it with me?"

"Like you, being the keeper of secrets has come at a great cost to me." He took a deep breath and smiled, as if the weight of the world had been lifted at last. "I guess it is nice to know that I am no longer entirely alone. You see, Miss Grey, this world was not filled with people so we should spend our days in solitude. I am not the trusting kind. Never have been. Yet I find myself compelled to tell you the truth. My gut tells me that it will not be misplaced in your care."

"I find myself saddened knowing Richard never had someone he could trust with his secret. He never tried to clear his name. I wonder if he ever imagined that he would be painted as such a vile character for centuries to come."

"I suppose it didn't matter. His detractors would say what they wanted, and he knew that well." He gave her a look of certainty, his eyebrows arched. "He sacrificed his legacy to protect those he loved. I think we all would do the same. Well, many of us anyway. Richard went to his death knowing what kind of man he was. He had made peace with his own soul and that was enough for him."

"It's enough for me too," she said. "All along, there have been people who knew he was an innocent man, even if the rest of the world thought otherwise. Perhaps we can never publicly clear his name, but it is cleared just the same."

"Don't you wonder how you factor into the equation yourself?"

"Me? What do you mean?" She leaned back. "I just came here on a hunch. I had no earthly idea I would discover something so profound."

"Oh, but I don't think your presence here is by coincidence at all, Miss Grey. I believe whatever power you possess has brought you here on purpose." He tapped the letter with one fingertip. "You are not here by chance."

"I can't deny I felt a strong connection to John Evans, but that is probably because he wanted his story told." She shook her head. "No. I am just the vessel."

"Do you recall the first day I met you? That day you and your cousin visited the bookshop?"

"How could I forget?" She laughed. "You were not exactly the friendliest person I had ever met."

"I asked you who your father was, but his name did not ring a bell. It was your grandfather's name that struck me, though, and I did a little digging after you left." Adelia looked at him in surprise. "Your grandfather was awarded his accommodations at Hampton Court Palace for two reasons: his impeccable military career, and his aristocratic lineage. As I traced the family line back, it was no surprise when I came upon the name of Thomas Grey, Marquess of Dorset." He looked about the nave again. "There is the blood of three in this Chapel Royal at this very moment."

She stared at him as his words swirled within her head. "You really think I was called here for this reason?"

"I believe so," he said. "It was the same thing that must have inspired you to come here tonight."

She mulled that over. He was right—she had been compelled to come this evening, more so than any other day since their arrival.

She had been so desperate to get out here, she had lied to Daniel, and used Cassandra in her scheme.

"Oh, crap—Daniel," she blurted out. "I am so sorry, Mister Mortimer, but I have to get back to the village." As she jumped up, she didn't bother to explain that she had deceived the once-upon-a-time love of her life to come here. Afterall, she had just managed to convince that man she was trustworthy.

Chapter Twenty-Seven

Agreeing to seek out Mortimer before she left the village, she sidled past him, grabbed up her handbag from where she had left it a few rows back, and almost sprinted to the exit. On her way to the car, she stopped dead at the sudden realization that it was by far one of the most beautiful nights she had seen in a long time. Out here, along the desolate country road, there were no lights from the village to diffuse the tapestry of stars that blanketed the sky.

As she fumbled to find the keys in her purse, she flinched on seeing the dark outline of a person leaning against the car's hood. Without meaning to, she let out a muffled squeak, the stars swirling as she stumbled sideways. When she landed on the unyielding gravel, she wondered for a moment if she had been struck by the mystery figure, but the only source of pain came from her hip.

Then a familiar hand reached out from the darkness, and she knew her fall had been self-inflicted. Nothing more than clumsiness borne of haste.

"Goddammit, Daniel, you scared me!" she said, brushing herself down.

"Adelia, you *are* in a church yard."

"No, no, I am outside the gate, so technically I'm not." She almost growled at him. "*You* scared me!"

His shoulders went up. "You stole my car, I was worried."

She huffed like a petulant child, which didn't please her. "Technically, you gave me the keys. I just wasn't truthful about their use. Either way, it was not actually stolen."

"Em...no. I don't think you're doing any favors for yourself." He laughed. "Rather, I think you are making a muck of things right now. If you are done, can we please head back to the village? It's pitch black out here, and I will be lucky to be able to see the road. I don't want to wreck the car, for Christ's sake."

She held her finger up and looked him square in the eye, though the gloom cut visual clarity. "Let's be mindful that we are here in a churchyard when I say that I may have already wrecked the car...a little."

"A little? You wrecked the car a little? What the hell does that even mean, Adelia?"

"I..." She balled her hands into nervous fists. "I am pretty sure I clipped a stone wall on one of the curves on my way out. Just a little scrape. There were some sparks, though. Definitely some sparks."

Thankfully, it was far too dark to see his expression, though she imagined it to be a gaping glare.

"All I want to know is did he do the right thing?" he asked, his hands placed on his hips like an angry father.

She stared at him. "Who?"

"Richard, of course. Did he do the right thing?"

"Ah, right. Yes, he did." How much could she reveal? "In the end, he did what was just."

"Good! Now, please get in the car."

She got in, preparing herself for the silent drive back to the inn. That wouldn't be so bad, considering all she had to think about.

Just as she suspected, it was a quiet drive home, the tension too heavy for her to dare utter a word. Daniel had never been one to resort to anger so fast, and she knew she had pushed him too far, just like she'd done a dozen times or more in the last few weeks.

Her mind kept traveling back to St. Matthew's, to the letter, and to Richard as he scribbled those words in the darkness of his chamber. To have the answers at last was bittersweet. Just as she and Daniel had once found the truth about what happened to Amy Robsart Dudley back in Oxford, this truth was something she could never share. She wasn't even sure it was something she could tell Daniel, though she suspected he knew, and eventually she would. As an experienced history professor, he loved hard facts and was far better at thinking abstractly than her. He probably had a hunch all along about what she would find. If so, he'd kept it to himself, allowing her to be the one to make the discovery on her own.

To know that Richard was not half the villain he'd been painted filled her with real satisfaction. In his later years, while he had become somewhat callous and cold, he'd still held on to his humanity. There was never a time when he didn't know the great cost that comes with failure. Yet he always forged ahead, carrying that little boy within him, eyes wide with dreams of Excalibur, and coveting the bravery of knights in distant realms, with a sense of honor and duty that no battle, no matter how brutal and bloody, could shatter.

Richard was far more a hero than the cruel distortion of history afforded. He put his love for others above his own ambitions. This resonated in her heart. Here, in the icy silence, she sat beside the man she loved more than any dream, more than any goal. As the car wound down the narrow roads of Devon, it came to her that she must have the same courage with Daniel as with Mortimer earlier. I must tell him the truth about my feelings. He deserves closure. Not only because I damaged his car, but because I am bound by the same duty and honor as the men and women in my family. It is my responsibility to remain loyal to my most trusted circle. Loyalty binds me.

Daniel pulled the car into a car park just down from the inn, and cut the engine.

Adelia took a steadying breath, blinking welling tears away. "I had forgotten what I said to you."

"I'm sorry?" He looked at her with tired eyes. She didn't doubt that he was ready to jump headfirst into his bed and sleep for a week.

"That day on the street in Oxford? You said that for as long as you lived, you would never forget that was the best day of your life." She shifted to face him, placing her hands flat on her lap to prevent them trembling. "I knew that day that I loved you, Daniel. I knew then that there was nothing in the world I would not do to be with only you. Somehow, I let my ambitions get in the way, and I forgot how to be in love with you."

"Just like Richard III," he said. "Just like how he almost let his ambitions cloud who he really wanted to be. But he did what was right in the end."

"Let's not talk of history, Daniel. We always talk about history. I am talking about here and now. You and I. I forgot how much I love you, and for that I am truly sorry. I cut you out of my life trying to find myself, all the while not understanding that you bring out the best version of me. The only one I like, to tell you the truth. I walked out on you because of what I wanted. But it turns out, this isn't what I wanted after all. And now I can never get us back." She sucked in a shaky breath, her shoulders rising. "I can never come back home."

"You can always come back home. There will never be a day that I don't want to be with you."

"It's not that easy," she said, shaking her head, having no idea where to start on all the reasons why.

"It is just that easy." He touched the back of her hand. "Home is wherever we are together. If you can't come home to Oxford, then I will come home to Middleham. You left America to be with me—you don't think I would move across England to be with you?"

This time the heat of his touch pooled in her heart, filling that long-held void only he could. There was no one else for her. If she never advanced in her career beyond where she was today, she would be perfectly okay. If she lost his love, she would not—the choice was plain as day. Nothing else mattered anymore but him.

"I could never ask you to give up your life in Oxford. That would not be fair."

He sat up so he was looking down at her. "I will turn in my resignation letter when we get back and sleep like a baby tonight. I love you that damn much. I won't ever be home until my address is yours. Until my last name is yours." He held her shoulders, his arms straight. "Let me come home to you this time, woman."

Her mouth fell open for a moment. "Did you just call me 'woman'? You know I don't like that." He sounded like a caveman dragging her back to his lair by the hair, and that was a bit off-putting.

"Please stop talking." He pulled her to him and kissed her—a fiery, passionate kiss to rival the thousand he had given her before—the type Rhett Butler gave to Scarlet O'Hara—one meant to sweep her off her feet and teach her a damn good lesson at the same time. It worked brilliantly. That kiss made her melt like a hailstorm in July. To be scolded that well, she might have done it all over again. She let herself fade into him, their energies merging like waves on a beach.

Chapter Twenty-Eight

Daniel made good on his promise and Adelia made good on hers. She married him on a crisp autumn day on the sprawling lawn of Middleham Manor, with both their families in attendance, and the fall leaves clinging to the tree limbs like drops of boiling copper in an alchemist's pot. The wedding was modest, thrown together in haste, but no less beautiful.

When the time came to throw the bouquet, she flung it into the air with a carefree laugh, turning just in time to see Cassandra dodge it like an awkward schoolboy forced into a grade school cricket match. It landed on the ground with the sharp thud of a pigeon that had flown into a plate-glass window, and every bachelor released an audible groan, devastated that a love match with the long-legged angel was not in the cards today.

Ross gave Adelia his prized copy of the *Discoveree of Witchcraft*, telling her there were a few recipes she might need to survive a marriage. This came with an odd little wink.

"I wish I had this book before I married Laura," he grumbled. "Might have saved myself a thousand years of misery. Treacherous witch." He shot his wife a look of malice and sulked away.

Adelia rocked back on her heel as she took them in, moving like oil and water about the room. A part of her could not help but wonder what life was like when affection existed between them. Given their deep-seeded passion for despising each other, she could only imagine they must have been furiously passionate as lovers. Life has a way of numbing us over time, dulling the sharp edges of the worst parts, and allowing us to lose sight of the best of times. Would she and Daniel ever be so careless as to let their love fade like Laura and Ross had?

She hadn't pondered the notion for thirty seconds before shaking her head and gazing over at her husband, cheerfully conversing with the guests. Richard and Anne's love had survived every war, both internal and external. That was a love to emulate. The same love she shared with Daniel.

Later, as the wedding guests filed out, she'd gotten the chance to talk to Cassandra. She pulled her cousin into a warm embrace, holding tight to her for maybe longer than expected. At summer's end, Cassandra had returned to school in London. Though it was only October, it felt as though they had not seen each other in ages. Having her there for the wedding meant so much, and she couldn't let her leave not knowing how much their friendship had changed her life.

"Cassandra,"—she pulled back to make direct eye contact—"you taught me so much this summer. So much about myself I needed to know. I know that's why you were brought into my life, and I am eternally grateful. I just wish I could say that my coming into your life was a blessing too."

Her cousin flicked her blonde waves back with a confident flick of her head. "Adelia, I know that I never really got the chance to tell you how much you did for me, but I want to do it now. You taught me so much in return."

"I doubt I did," Adelia said with a laugh. "All I did for you was drag you halfway across the country to dusty old castles and gloomy churchyards."

Cassandra's eyes widened. "It was so much more than that. You taught me about Shakespeare. You taught me that Richard was a man, not a villain. But above all, you taught me that I don't have to deny my gift to be accomplished. You taught me to be confident in myself, what I want, and to let nothing stand in my way of the great things ahead. Before you, I never thought I had a chance of being taken seriously. Before you, I didn't even try to find knowledge. I just assumed I should follow in the path that was paved for me. You taught me that the hard way is the only way to prove my worth. That I can mess things up along the way and make it right again."

"What a terrible message I sent you," Adelia said, laughing out loud.

It was just the two of them now, the last of the keepers of the Babington secret. They shared the bond of the whispers, but now it was so much more. No amount of time or distance could ever break the friendship between them.

As a wedding present, Daniel had spent every last penny on buying Middleham Manor from Ross and Laura. When Adelia had protested the idea, he'd held up a finger and smiled. "We have always done things on your terms. Let me take the risk just this once."

He had big plans for their new adventure together running the bed & breakfast. As much as he loved the idea of owning such a relic of time, he was firm in reassuring her that he would never get used to the unrelenting sound of the wind howling across the fields surrounding Middleham.

"It's the wind. Nothing more," she'd insisted, rolling her eyes as they stood out in front of the massive house, their faces illuminated by the silvery full moon and the brilliance of the stars that hung above.

"Well, that's a turn of events," he said, throwing his hands up in defeat. "You are taking the side of science, and I insist it's something otherworldly. Who would have ever thought?"

She made a half turn, sweeping her arm out. "Not everything is some dark foreboding omen cloaked in mystery. Some things are easy to explain."

"Forgive me, Wife, but our entire relationship was founded on dark omens cloaked in mystery. Why on earth should they stop now?"

"Touché," she said, slipping her arm into the crook of his and pointing to the front door. "Let's go in, Darling. I am far too tired to carry on this conversation out here."

Arm in arm, they walked across the threshold of this ancient time capsule they called home, with gentle whispers of its past echoing off the walls. They were so absorbed in one another, they failed to notice the big black hound lurking deep in the shadows of the night.

About the Author

As a child, Tasha Sheipline wanted to be a ballerina, marry a doctor, and have a pony. Since none of these dreams came to fruition, she became a teacher instead. Teaching others has proved an empowering endeavor.

An avid reader, Tasha has a long held belief that you can never have too many books. Her favorite authors include Alison Weir, William Shakespeare, Edgar Allan Poe and Jane Austin. She is certainly not opposed to sprinkling in a good Tessa Dare romance novel when time allows.

She began writing as a creative outlet, and it soon blossomed into a real passion. A lover of history, Tasha has a specific fondness for the medieval through early modern eras. She loves to infuse characters and events from these areas into her writing.

Her favorite pastimes include traveling, watching historical documentaries, and adding to her growing collection of antique books. Tasha lives in a small town in Ohio with her husband, children and two corgi's.

The Whisper Series

Dark Palace
Blood in the Chapel Royal
Yorkshire Rose